CHEERS TO . . .

MALICE DOMESTIC 1

"Pull up your coziest armchair, brew yourself a pot of Earl Grey, and settle in to enjoy as these sleuths, both amateur and professional, solve crimes of murder and mayhem."

—*Prime Suspects*

MALICE DOMESTIC 2

"The second very solid volume in the series of mystery short stories offers ample evidence that a skillful writer can deliver a worthwhile read in pared-down prose."

—*Publishers Weekly*

MALICE DOMESTIC 3

"A perfectly delicious new feast."

—*Mystery News*

Elizabeth Peters Presents *Malice Domestic 1*
Mary Higgins Clark Presents *Malice Domestic 2*
Nancy Pickard Presents *Malice Domestic 3*
Carolyn G. Hart Presents *Malice Domestic 4*
Phyllis A. Whitney Presents *Malice Domestic 5*
Anne Perry Presents *Malice Domestic 6*

Published by POCKET BOOKS

ANNE PERRY

presents

MALICE DOMESTIC 6

An Anthology of Original Traditional Mystery Stories

POCKET BOOKS

New York London Toronto Sydney Tokyo Singapore

This book contains works of fiction. Names, characters, places and incidents are products of the authors' imaginations or are used fictitiously. Any resemblance to actual events or locales or persons, living or dead, is entirely coincidental.

An *Original* Publication of POCKET BOOKS

POCKET BOOKS, a division of Simon & Schuster Inc.
1230 Avenue of the Americas, New York, NY 10020

ISBN: 0-671-89633-4

First Pocket Books printing April 1997

10 9 8 7 6 5 4 3 2 1

Cover art by John Zielinski

Printed in the U.S.A.

Copyright Notices

Contents

A Dance with Life, Death . . . and Laughter

Anne Perry

Where do we get the name "cozy" for our particular type of crime stories? It suggests to the mind something warm and comfortable, such as tea and buttered crumpets by the fire on a lazy winter afternoon. Rain beats at the window and you curl up with a good book, and possibly one or two affectionate cats to accompany you, with a stretch and a sleepy purr.

Not at all! That is the wrong end of the stick entirely. That is how to *enjoy* such stories, or at least it is one way. Of course there are numerous others. You can be entertained, alleviate boredom, dispel loneliness with good, varied and colorful company. You may, by chance, be informed on almost any subject under the sun, ancient or modern, indigenous or exotic, pedestrian or arcane. You may be lifted for a while out of any of your own pains or difficulties from which you would like a little respite.

The stories that fall into the "malice domestic" category are hilariously funny at times, and why should laughter and tragedy not walk hand in hand, or terror and farce not dance with each other for a while? They can in life! And our tales are drawn from life—all the material of human good and evil, "domestic matters" in the broadest sense . . . human relationships.

Is it really more "comfortable," or "real," to be killed by a deranged serial murderer or an armed robber—people who are strangers to you, looming out of the night—than in the well-lit order of your daily life, by someone you know, someone you never suspected of such a thought, let alone act? Surely it is the ultimate terror to think that behind the smiling, familiar face of some friend or relative there is a hatred or a fear so violent it can end only in your death? Or is there a corroding jealousy, a hunger or a greed that will no longer be denied?

It is the slow peeling away of secrets, layer by layer, in a well-written "malice domestic" that fascinates us. We do not care a great deal about forensic evidence, although we like to be accurate. We deduce from character, and the understanding of human nature, needs, and reactions.

Few people have known serial killers, or even professional criminals, but we have all seen families where all manner of passions simmer beneath the calm surface of a mealtime conversation. We know neighbors who hate each other. We have seen bad marriages, sibling rivalry. Our homes are often the places where we reveal ourselves most clearly. The loves and hates can be subtle, the tyrannies and rebellions, the torn loyalties and the betrayals run long and deep. We unravel them delicately, using intelligence, observation, and intuition.

The "home" may be anywhere: in a teeming city, on a windswept moor, in a smiling village. The whole panorama of history is open to you in terms of time; past, present, future. Your "detectives" may be of any age or occupation, or lack of it, or of either sex. All that is necessary is the relationship between people, and that is universal. There have always been the motives, and the belief that violence can bring a desired result. It began with Cain and has been intertwined throughout history and legend, in great dramas and little ones. Kingdoms have come and gone on "malice domestic." And think of the Caesars, from Julius to Nero, or of Macbeth or Hamlet, to name only a few. Ordinary lives that we shall never know have been changed forever.

At least within the pages of a book you can begin with chaos and tension, injustice and uncertainty, and by the end reach understanding and some approximation of justice, legal or poetic. You can attain an order. And you can laugh and cry on the way, and be thoroughly diverted for a while.

So return to your crumpets by the fire, or your lilo in the sun, or your airport lounge, or wherever, and for a space of time enjoy yourself with a little transatlantic malice of the domestic type.

Anne Perry is the author of 25 acclaimed Victorian-era mystery novels, one series featuring Superintendent Thomas Pitt and his outspoken wife Charlotte, and the other the driven investigator William Monk and ex-Crimean nurse Hester Latterly. Two Monk books, *The Face of a Stranger* (1990), and *Defend and Betray* (1992), were nominated for the Agatha Award for Best Novel in their respective years. Perry was *Malice Domestic*'s Guest of Honor in 1993.

MALICE DOMESTIC 6

The Corbett Correspondence

"Agent No. 5 & Agent No. 6"

Merrivale Hall
Dunseaton
Reading, Berks.

November 1st, 1995

Dear Agent No. 6,

How refreshing to have a female operative in the Secret Service! You are an example to us all. That clapped-out Volkswagen is the perfect camouflage for you, though a trifle Third Reich for my own taste. However, it is the ideal complement to the Luger pistol you keep strapped to your right thigh.

Calamity! Delightful as it was to have you as my guest at Merrivale Hall last night, there has been an unforeseen consequence. A few hours after you left, Balzac, my butler, happened to try the door of the bedroom where you slept. It was locked from the inside! Balzac alerted me at once and I produced the master key, which I keep hidden in my wardrobe beneath a pile of discarded false mustaches. We gained entry to the bedroom to be met by a hideous sight.

Lying in the middle of the floor was a dead body. He (for the corpse was patently male) was an Oriental gentleman with a sinister cast of feature. His shoes were of such contrasting sizes—four and ten, respectively—that we can only assume he walked with a pronounced limp. There were no marks of violence upon him, but a steady trickle of blood was coming from his mouth, staining my Turkish carpet, a treasured gift from a grateful government in Ankara.

There was, alas, nothing in the man's pockets to suggest his identity. Grasped tightly in his left hand was the manuscript of an unpublished novel by someone called James Corbett. My butler and I agreed that we were gazing at a murder victim.

To preserve the good name of the Department, I wish to solve this crime rather than hand it over to those baffled buffoons at Scotland Yard. I am in urgent need of your help. Did anything strange happen in your bedroom last night? Is the murder connected in some way with Halloween? Was the room unoccupied when you departed this morning? And who is James Corbett?

Needless to say, I questioned my staff closely. They are four in number. Balzac is above suspicion, having been with me for twenty years, presented by a French administration indebted to me for services rendered. I would likewise exonerate Deeck, my valet, who, though American and thus subject to fits of grandiosity, is utterly trustworthy. About my cook, Dante, I am less sure. He can be temperamental.

Garbo, the maid, is another unknown quantity, having been recently bestowed upon me by a thankful Swedish parliament for my success in exposing the Stockholm Scandal.

I ask two special favors. Can you throw light on this mystery? And do you know a technique for removing bloodstains from a Turkish carpet?

Yours in desperation,
Agent No. 5

A safe house,
a secret place,
somewhere in England

November 2nd, 1995

Dear Five (let's be informal),

You don't surprise me one bit. Without disrespect to your hospitality, I had one hell of a night (or what was left of the night after you abandoned me in such haste after chancing upon my Luger). You call it the bedroom where I slept, but I had no sleep at all. Shortly I'll explain why.

First, I must tell you about James Corbett, the writer of the manuscript you found in the dead man's grasp. Corbett was a prolific author of mystery novels—he claimed seventy-three—written between 1929 and 1951. In those more trusting times many of his books were bought by the unwary, but by the nineteen-fifties he was ready for oblivion, his work turgid and unreadable to a public weaned on Fleming's James Bond. I tried reading Corbett myself, and I'm at a loss to understand how such drivel was ever published. How could anyone seriously devise a plot revealing the villain as an unknown twin? Corbett tops that: in *The Monster of Dagenham Hall,* twins are present from the beginning and he produces an unknown triplet. In another work, which I skimmed, a character produces a "single-chambered revolver." Elsewhere, someone is "galvanized into immobility." I could go on; Corbett did, for twenty-two years.

Here is the crunch. For some arcane reason, over the last couple of years dealers in used books have been deluged by requests for Corbett novels. Prices have gone crazy. I heard of one woman in California who said she would kill for a copy of *Death Comes to Fanshawe.* Another, in Bethesda, Maryland, is said to have her Corbett collection insured for a million dollars; it is kept, unread, in a bank vault. Madness on this scale is dangerous. It has thrown the book market into turmoil and is even threatening the stability of the money markets. Instead of hoarding Impressionist paintings or uncut diamonds, people are putting their fortunes into Corbetts. Inevitably, all this activity attracted the attention of the security services. Recently the CIA and MI5 called a secret meeting. I was given a mission to investigate.

I won't go into the tortuous trail that led me last weekend to your ancestral seat, except to state that I was acting on alarming information from an impeccable source. London had been advised that an unpublished manuscript by Corbett had been discovered in a Tibetan monastery. This script is said to be so unspeakably dire that in 1938 it was rejected by every publisher in London. Imagine the excitement! What mutilations of the language, what contortions of plotting, could sink below anything Corbett ever had in print? A novel worse than *Devil-Man from Mars?* The script will be coveted by all who are infected with this Corbett-mania. In auction it will fetch an unimaginable sum, maybe as large, I was told, as the entire British budget. It will destabilize the international money markets, and make the Wall Street crash look like a blip.

My mission is to seek and destroy. The Corbett manuscript *must* be shredded or incinerated. My name has been circulated as an expert capable of validating a genuine Corbett. The CIA calculated that this might persuade the possessors of the manuscript to make contact. Obviously they did.

My petal, I urge you, for the sake of us all, for the future prosperity of our children and our grandchildren—if that script is still in your possession—DO NOT READ ANY PART OF IT. DO NOT ALLOW YOUR SERVANTS TO READ IT. Destroy it at once.

For the record, here is what happened in the bedroom. Soon after you limply quit the room, I heard a tapping on the door. Thinking your vigor might have been restored, I blithely unlocked and discovered Balzac, your butler, who handed me a sealed message. I assumed it was from you, perhaps apologizing for what had happened (or failed to) between us. But the message was apparently in secret code. I devoted the rest of the night to trying to crack it, without success.

The rest is a blur. Sweetie, did you know that the bedroom you gave me has a secret passage behind the erotic tapestry? As dawn was breaking, I heard a sound from the general area of the Roman orgy and the whole thing moved. A secret door! Instinctively, I used my training in the martial arts and swung a stiletto heel towards the intruder's marriage gear. He fell at my feet. I didn't stop to examine the size of his shoes or the contents of his left hand. I rushed through the secret passage and came out at the railway station, where I boarded the first train. My Volkswagen must be still on your drive. Only today, with the aid of a Tibetan/English dictionary, have I translated the message. Roughly it runs:

> *Honored Lady,*
> *We shall shortly give you an opportunity to examine the first female private eye novel ever written,* Farewell, My Handsome, *by James Corbett. Your expert valuation is awaited with interest by the owners.*

Honeybunch, I am sorry about the inconvenience. What is one dead man between agents? But PLEASE heed my warning and destroy the Corbett. You can save the world from financial ruin. And the best I can suggest for your carpet is to stain it red.

I eagerly await your reassuring reply.

Devotedly,
Agent No. 6

Merrivale Hall
Dunseaton
Reading, Berks.

November 3rd, 1995

Dear Sexy Six,

Let me first put your mind at rest on one score. It was not lack of desire that made me leap out of your bed so unceremoniously. I despised myself for having to leave you at the very second when your Luger was about to go off with a bang. This was such uncharacteristic behavior on my part that I consulted a doctor next day.

Blood tests revealed the presence of a drug that inhibits performance and causes loss of nerve at the critical moment. It must have been administered to me in my soup. The drug is made from a poppylike flower that only grows in the vicinity of Florence, where it is used by the local maidenry to control the bambino rate. My temperamental cook, Dante, is a native of Florence. He made the soup.

On the other hand, it was Garbo, the maid, who served it to us, under the supervision of Balzac, the butler. All three had the opportunity to spike the master's soup. I incline towards Dante as the culprit. He has been surly towards me ever since I caught him standing outside the maid's window, serenading her with a mandolin. I happened to be with Garbo at the time, tucking her into bed with a concern for the bodily comfort of my female staff that has always made me a model employer. Dante was understandably vexed when I leaned naked over the balcony and asked him to play "O Sole Mio!"

Your warning about James Corbett came too late. A curiosity born of my Secret Service training made me read *Farewell, My Handsome.* It was excruciating. An Albanian telephone directory has more narrative drive. The novel features a female private eye called Miss Marbles who has the attributes of Sherlock Holmes, Dick Tracy and Boadicea rolled into one. A woman of advanced age, she keeps a derringer in her ear trumpet and a stiletto beneath her wig. Her walking stick is also a blowpipe and she fires poison darts—having first removed her dentures—with alarming accuracy. Needless to say, she is a mistress of disguise.

There is worse to come. Since the dead courier was of Oriental origin, I decided to read the book backwards and made AN AMAZING DISCOVERY. *Farewell, My Handsome* conceals a second novel called *Devil-Woman from Venus.* Instead of using twin characters, Corbett has outdone himself this time by writing twin novels, back to back! I thought at first I'd made the greatest literary discovery since the Rosetta Stone. Then I read *Devil-Woman* through. It beggars belief. Its protagonist is yet another female private eye, Dame Agatha Tea Cozy, who learns the state secrets of enemy powers by seducing their agents while wearing a rare perfume that makes her irresistible. The perfume can only be obtained from a demented, one-eyed French apothecary in Tours. A bizarre coincidence. Balzac, my butler, is a native of Tours.

I need your help more than ever, my Lugerbelle. Self-defense is not murder. You were right to kill the bearer of bad Corbett. Big questions remain. Your nocturnal visitor would have needed a key to open the subterranean door to the secret passage. Who gave it to him? Balzac has a key (and unfulfilled ambitions of being a novelist). Deeck, my valet, has one as well, though it has mysteriously gone astray. Dante's key turned up in my soup last night. And Garbo's key, alas, is in her bedroom door—she wants to be alone.

We found your Volkswagen on the drive, but we also found a bomb attached to its exhaust pipe. It was defused with great skill by Deeck, who, it transpires, was taught Bomb Disposal as part of his routine work as a civil servant in Washington, D.C. Do you see what this means? They wanted you to authenticate the Corbett manuscript and then blow you up for your pains! I couldn't bear to lose you, my angel. Thank God we frustrated their dastardly scheme.

Who is behind all this? If one Corbett novel could cause a financial earthquake, would not two bring an end to civilization as we know it? How can I tell if this double-barreled drivel really is authentic Corbett? When can you come to view it? I ask for two reasons. First, the fate of humanity may hang on your word. Second, I miss you dreadfully. (My doctor was highly complimentary about the love-bites you left upon my anatomy. He had never seen such fearful symmetry outside a tiger cage.)

The bloodstained carpet is no longer a problem. It and the dead body have both vanished, and there have been unconfirmed sightings of them heading across the Channel in the direction of Tibet.

By the way, I hid the Corbett manuscript in a lead container and buried it fifty feet under ground. When I dug down this morning, to make sure that it was still there, I met Deeck digging his way up. Am I wrong to trust my valet?

Come soon, my darling!

Excitedly,
Five

Still a safe house, I think,
a secret place,
somewhere in England

November 4th, 1995

My Poor Demented Five,

Didn't I implore you in the name of everything you hold dear NOT to read the Corbett manuscript? Your latest letter plunges me into despair, because it is obvious that Corbett has driven you out of your mind. You underestimated the power of his prose. I know of others who ended up as gibbering idiots after reading just a paragraph from one of his books, and I had hoped to preserve you, my genial host, my pajamaed playmate, from a similar fate.

Too late.

How can you expect me to believe this nonsense about reading the book backwards and discovering a second book? You say *Devil-Woman from Venus* beggars belief. I say that your story does. This is clearly the product of a demented mind. Dame Agatha Tea Cozy, indeed!

Can I believe any of the rest of your letter? Is it really worth my while agitating my gray cells to probe the mysteries of the master's soup, the key to the secret passage, the bomb beneath the Volkswagen, and the valet with the burrowing instinct? Are you trying to tell me in coded language that you fear Deeck is a mole? I am desperately concerned for more reasons than I can reveal at this stage. I will only state that a theory about your domestic staff is beginning to form in my brain.

Dear Five, for the sake of those few unfulfilled minutes we spent together, I am willing to give the benefit of the smidgen of doubt I still entertain as to your sanity. If you will dig up the Corbett manuscript and send it to me at once, then I shall see for myself if *Devil-Woman from Venus* is a figment of Corbett's imagination, or yours.

I remain your impatient, ever-loving,
Six

P.S. I rather care for Lugerbelle as a name.

Merrivale Hall
Dunseaton
Reading, Berks.

November 5th, 1995

My dear Lugerbelle,

How can you question my veracity? Have you forgotten that moment of truth we had in the blue bedroom at Merrivale Hall? Why do you doubt my sanity? I have been trained by the British Secret Service—the envy of lesser nations—and am therefore impervious to brain rot and to corruption by the written word. For the sake of what (almost) happened between us, you must believe me, my divine darling. You are the only woman who has seen me in my Union Jack pajamas without laughing. For that reason alone, I will never lie to you.

There is Malice Domestic in my household, and I need you to plumb its ugly depths. To convince you that I speak in earnest, I am enclosing a number of items.

(1) An article from the Tibetan Astronomy Journal about a UFO (Unidentified Flying Oriental) seen crossing the Himalayas on a bloodstained carpet.

(2) A report from an independent geologist proving that a fifty-foot hole was dug in my garden on the third day of this month. Soil samples attached.

(3) An infrared photograph of Deeck, my valet, burrowing into the main lawn last night. When questioned about his nocturnal recreation, he put it down to the fact that he was born prematurely when his mother became overagitated while watching the film of *Journey to the Center of the Earth.* "I can't help it," said Deeck. "I have to dig. It's in my blood."

(4) Fragments of the bomb found beneath your Volkswagen. Since it is November 5th, we detonated it as part of our Guy Fawkes Day bonfire celebrations.

(5) One of the poppylike flowers used to make a drug that can render a man impotent. The flower was found hidden beneath the chef's hat of Dante, my cook, but—and this was a shock to me—Balzac, the butler, was wearing it at the time. A French-Italian conspiracy?

(6) Garbo's membership card from an organization called Corbettaholics Anonymous. When people get the urge to read Corbett, they rush off to a therapy session and talk themselves out of it before committing suicide instead. Corbett in Swedish! Ye gods!

Every member of my staff is a prime suspect, and only you can pick out the real culprit or culprits. The future of the

English language hangs in the balance. Save it, my dove. I am sending you the manuscript of *Farewell, My Handsome* along with its Siamese twin, *Devil-Woman from Venus*. I am sure that they are genuine—they even bear Corbett's signature.

To ensure safe passage, the manuscript will come inside a reinforced steel strongbox, inside a picnic hamper, inside a coffin, inside a bulletproof hearse. The vehicle will be driven by Deeck, the Maryland Mole. The four suspects will deliver it to you in person, so that you can authenticate the document and nab the villain in one fell swoop.

If it is bona fide James Corbett, you must destroy it at once in the name of justice, freedom, linguistic integrity, and the spirit of international harmony. Unless, of course, its value is so immense that we can afford to retire from the Secret Service on the proceeds. In that event, my pumpkin, I would like to offer you my hand in marriage and my heart in perpetuity. Pronounce it a best-seller and I am your agent.

Yours with drooling passion,
Five

P.S. Where shall we spend our honeymoon?

A safer house,
more secret,
somewhere in England

November 9th, 1995

My Incorruptible One,

Before you read any of this, pour yourself a large scotch. Now knock it back. All of it. And pour yourself another.

Ready? You are going to be gob-smacked by what you read, but bear with me, dear heart.

The hearse arrived the day before yesterday with its precious contents intact and your four untrusty servants aboard. Believe it or not, they had an uneventful journey. I questioned them all in depth, and your sanity and integrity are not in doubt. Each of those bizarre incidents happened, no question. Now I shall explain.

First, has it ever occurred to you why you were appointed Agent Number Five? Think about it. For me, there is no difficulty. I am Agent Number Six because I was recruited shortly after they gave you your box of false mustaches and sent you back to Cambridge University to learn the spy trade. I was the next in line. Simple.

But have you ever speculated about Agents One, Two, Three, and Four? Have you never wondered why you were not introduced to them? Probably, being the upright fellow you are, you decided that, as this *was* the Secret Service, you had better not ask. I can now reveal that, until four days ago, they were all employed in your household. To you they are known as Balzac, Dante, Garbo, and Deeck. Number One, "Balzac," is the kind of spy known in the jargon of our trade as a sleeper, which is why he has been in your service as butler for twenty years. Number Two, "Dante," the temperamental cook, is in fact the world's foremost authority on passion-reducing drugs. His presence was necessary because Number Three, "Garbo," your maid, is the Mata Hari of the Service, the beautiful woman who extracts secrets by seduction; she has to be subdued at times. Number Four, your American valet "Deeck" with the burrowing tendency, is a CIA mole who recently defected to our side in order to devote himself to the study of the subversive writer James Corbett.

You must be asking why this formidable quartet infiltrated your domestic staff. It was on the instruction of "M," our spymaster. Their quest—and mine—was to probe your integrity and discover beyond all doubt whether you were reliable. The British Secret Service has had too many unfortunate episodes in the past with Cambridge men. Yes, my fearless Five, you were set up, put in the frame, and tested to the limit. I, too, joined in the deception, as did Harry Kirry, the well-known corpse impersonator. The Oriental gentleman in my bedroom was only Harry performing his turn. A pale face, a little stage blood, and the ability to stop breathing can produce wonderfully deathlike effects.

The bomb attached to my car was genuine, as you discovered, but it was put there to add credibility to the operation. I was hoping to get rid of that old beetle once and for all.

The Corbett manuscript was also a "plant." It was genuinely written by James Corbett, as "Deeck" will attest, but the claims I made as to its value were much exaggerated, simply to see if you could be tempted by the lure of money. You were not. You behaved impeccably, passing every test we set you. Even Garbo has sworn to me that nothing happened between you and her, naked as you were when Dante spotted you on the lady's balcony. In fact, Garbo erroneously believes you must be undersexed, for you are the first not to have succumbed to her charms. I didn't disillusion her. She has her professional pride.

All of this has been reported to "M."

What none of us anticipated is your discovery that the Corbett novel, read backwards, is *Devil-Woman from Venus.* Using the manuscript in the deception was my idea, and now I must tell you something in the strictest confidence. That manuscript has been lying in an attic in my house for years.

You see, in civilian life I am Constance Corbett, the granddaughter of the author. In Grandpa's lifetime the script was rejected by every publishing house in Britain, but none of them had the wit to read it backwards, as you did. What we have, my brilliant confederate, is a property that must be worth an enormous sum, notwithstanding its literary limitations. It is unique. It will be a sensation. That is why I shall not be destroying it. The final part of your penultimate paragraph said it all (though I liked the ultimate paragraph, too): its value is so immense that we can afford to retire from the Service. Grandpa's book is a surefire bestseller. You, braveheart, can remain an agent, but not of the secret kind. You are to be my LITERARY AGENT. You will find that the skills required are not dissimilar.

I accept your proposal of marriage, on one condition: that you do not ever call me "Con." So pack your Union Jack pajamas at once, and jump into the Volkswagen and hit the gas. I can hardly wait for our joint debriefing.

What a happy ending!

Your devoted Lugerbelle

Between 1929 and 1951, James Corbett published over 40 novels, including the immortal *Devil-Man from Mars, Death Is My Shadow, Her Private Murder, The Monster of Dagenham Hall, Agent No. 5, Murder While You Wait,* and *Vampire of the Skies.* The study of this British mystery "legend" became a *Malice Domestic* tradition when William F. Deeck, the world's leading Corbettologist, began writing a regular "Corbett Corner" feature in Malice's newsletter, *The Usual Suspects,* and in other mystery periodicals that illuminated Corbett's *bon mots.* It also led to such Malice panels as "'He Sat Up Like a Full-Blown Geranium': The Genius of James Corbett." In this story, two renowned Corbettologists pay a skewed tribute to this mystery author, "a master," says Deeck, "of the language. Unfortunately, no one knows *which* language it was."

Agent No. 5 and Agent No. 6 are, respectively, Edward Marston and Peter Lovesey. Now retired from the Secret Service, they have published nearly 40 books between them and are living happily ever after at the Corbett Institute for Demented Authors.

Like to Die

Catherine Aird

"The law," pronounced Superintendent Leeyes heavily, "is an ass."

"Sir?" Detective Inspector Sloan raised an inquiring eyebrow but didn't commit himself to the general proposition. However much he agreed privately with any sentiment of his superior officer's, he had always found it prudent to wait to hear first exactly what it was that had provoked the Superintendent into generalization. He wondered what it was going to be this time.

"A total ass," repeated the Superintendent, pushing about some papers on his desk in a fretful manner. "Doesn't the man know we've got better things to do?"

"Which man?" asked Sloan, very tentatively. In Leeyes' present mood, it might even have been better not to have put the question at all.

"The Coroner, of course," snarled Leeyes.

"Ah . . ." Now Sloan understood. Mr. Locombe-Stableford, Her Majesty's Coroner for the town of Berebury in the County of Calleshire, was an old sparring partner—not to say archenemy—of the Superintendent's. This was because he was one of the few people in the world whose authority exceeded his own.

"It isn't even as if he doesn't know that we've got more than enough other things on our plate," carried on the Superintendent in aggrieved tones. "Much more important ones than this potty little case . . ."

"What case might that be, sir?"

Leeyes ignored this. "There's that road traffic fatality over at Cullingoak, for instance, and . . ."

"Hit-and-run killers are very hard to find," put in Sloan by way of apology. "Everyone's working on that one flat-out."

"Just what I mean, Sloan," said Leeyes sturdily. "And I told him so."

"The Coroner, sir." Sloan came back to the matter at hand. "What exactly is it that he—er—wants us to do?" The detective inspector knew one thing about Mr. Locombe-Stableford and that was—like it or not—that his writ ran throughout the patch covered by "F" Division of the County Constabulary.

"The Coroner," said Leeyes flatly, "has decided, for reasons best known only to himself, to hold an inquest on a Mr. Thomas Lean, a wealthy, retired businessman. . . ."

Since this action was totally within that august official's prerogative, Sloan waited.

". . . who died yesterday in a nursing home." Leeyes tapped his desk and added meaningfully, "the Berebury Nursing Home."

"Ah," said Sloan. The Berebury Nursing Home was considered one of the best in the whole county. Only the well-connected and the well-off went there—Sloan silently amended the thought—well, the well-off, anyway. It was no use being well-connected unless you were also well-off if you wanted to be treated at the Berebury Nursing Home. He'd heard that the fees were monstrously steep.

"And they don't like it," said Leeyes.

"The Nursing Home, you mean, sir?"

"Naturally."

"Not good for business," agreed Sloan.

"The Matron's in a proper taking about there being a postmortem. Dr. Dabbe's doing it now."

"I can see that she might be," said Sloan, frowning at an elusive memory. "Isn't that where the Earl of Ornum's dotty old aunt is? Lady Alice . . ."

"Shouldn't be surprised," said Leeyes. "Now, this Thomas Lean hadn't been in there very long. He'd been pretty dicky for months, and just got too ill to be nursed at home. . . ."

"So why the inquest?" Sloan was beginning to see why the Superintendent thought the Coroner perverse, and making more work for the Consultant Pathologist to the Berebury District Hospital Trust into the bargain.

"Because his illness didn't kill him," came back Leeyes smartly, "that's why."

"I see, sir." Sloan reached for his notebook. That did sound more like work for the head of Berebury's tiny Criminal Investigation Department.

"It was food poisoning. Or so the patient's doctor says." The Superintendent sniffed. He didn't like giving medical opinion any more credence than was absolutely necessary.

"And what have the family got to say?" Their views, thought Sloan, might be just as relevant as those of the Matron.

"We don't know yet," said Leeyes. "They were away on holiday when Thomas Lean died. They're on their way home from France now."

Detective Inspector Sloan opened his notebook at a new page. "This old gentleman, sir—"

"He wasn't all that old," said Leeyes briskly. The Superintendent was getting towards retirement age himself and had turned against ageism. "He was just coming up to seventy-five, and that's not old these days."

"No, sir," agreed Sloan hastily. "No age at all."

Leeyes pulled one of the pieces of paper on his desk towards him. "That's right. Seventy-four and eleven months. His birthday . . . oh, his birthday would have been tomorrow."

The Matron of the Berebury Nursing Home seemed as upset about that as she was about everything else. "You see, gentlemen, we always try to celebrate the birthdays of all of our patients . . . poor dears. Nothing elaborate, naturally . . ."

"Naturally," agreed Detective Inspector Sloan.

"Not in *their* state of health," chimed in Detective Constable Crosby. Because they were so busy down at the police station, Sloan had taken the detective constable with him to the nursing home as being better than nobody. Now, he wasn't so sure that Crosby *was* better than nobody.

The Matron, who looked more than a little wan herself, waved a hand. "You know the sort of thing, a glass of sherry and a special cake and so forth—not that poor Mr. Lean would have been fit to join in anything approaching a celebration today."

"No?"

"And as it happened, none of us would have felt like eating. Not after yesterday." She shook her head sadly. "And this would have been his last birthday, you know. He wasn't going to get better."

Detective Constable Crosby looked interested.

"He'd come in here to die," explained the Matron. "He'd been going slowly downhill with cancer for a long time, but the chemotherapy was keeping him going—and the painkillers, of course. Then it got that the family couldn't manage any more."

"I see," said Sloan carefully. There were some homes, the police knew only too well, where the painkillers killed more than the pain, but this hadn't been what had alerted the Coroner about this death.

"And," she said, "they were certainly helping him to hold his own." She made a gesture of despair with her hands. "If it hadn't been for this terrible food poisoning, we might have had him with us yet for weeks—perhaps months. . . ."

It began to sound as if the Coroner was being pedantic to

a fault, and that the Superintendent was right after all. Mr. Locombe-Stableford had dug his toes in over a legal nicety: a verdict of misadventure, perhaps, rather than natural causes. "Tell me about yesterday," invited Sloan.

"Everyone was very, very ill." She shuddered at the memory. "But everyone—staff *and* patients."

"But especially Mr. Lean . . ."

"Well, no . . . well, not at first, anyway," she said, drawing her brows together. "That was the funny thing."

"Funny peculiar or funny ha-ha?" asked Crosby.

She stared at him and said repressively, "It was thought strange that he should appear to be less ill than everyone else and yet be the one to die."

Detective Inspector Sloan leaned forward. He would deal with Crosby later, but all policemen were professionally interested in things that were funny peculiar. "Go on . . ."

She winced. "I—we—that is, everyone else started off with some dizziness, and then abdominal pain. . . ."

"Quite so," said Sloan, making a note.

"And then there was nausea, followed by severe vomiting." The Matron obviously found reporting in the third person easier, and went on in a more detached way. "Several staff and patients collapsed and some of them then had diarrhea. . . ."

"But only Thomas Lean died," said Crosby insouciantly.

She inclined her head.

"How did you manage?" asked Sloan. Perhaps the Coroner wasn't just being difficult. . . .

"Dr. Browne was very good. He came at once and saw everyone and took away specimens and so forth."

Sloan nodded. He knew Dr. Angus Browne—a family doctor of the old school. Forthright but kind—and careful.

"And he sent for the Environmental Health people, or whatever it is they call themselves these days, too."

Very careful then, Dr. Browne had been. Which was interesting.

"Food poisoning, you see, being a notifiable condition . . ."

"And then?"

"I can't really tell you that,"—the Matron looked embarrassed and murmured apologetically—"because, you see, I was one of the casualties myself at the time."

"I see." Sloan turned over a page in his notebook. "So . . ."

"So we had to call in extra staff."

He looked up quizzically.

"Anyone," she amplified, "who hadn't eaten luncheon here on Thursday . . . night staff, people on standby, and some agency nurses."

"And then . . ."

"People started to recover later that night, and by the next morning everyone was all right again."

"Except Thomas Lean," said Crosby mordantly.

"We—that is, the substitute staff alerted by Lady Alice—sent for Dr. Browne again when they saw how poorly he had become."

"Lady Alice . . ."

"She," said the matron faintly, "was the only person in the whole establishment not taken ill, and spent her time wandering around seeing how people were."

"And she, I take it, was the only person not to have partaken of whatever it was caused the food poisoning?" deduced Sloan, since not even noblesse oblige protected one against tainted food.

"Casseroled beef," said the Matron with a certain melancholy. "Dr. Browne'll be here as soon as he's heard from the laboratory to explain to us exactly what was wrong with it. It was the only thing that everyone who was ill had eaten, and everyone who had eaten it was ill."

"But Mr. Lean had it, too," said Crosby.

"Oh, yes," said the Matron wearily, "Mr. Lean had the beef casserole."

"He had his chips, too," said Crosby, almost—but not quite—sotto voce.

The Matron, who still looked a trifle frayed at the edges, had too many other things on her mind to object to unseemly levity. "By the time Dr. Browne got back here, Mr. Lean was having trembling convulsions and he died very soon after that."

"We'll be talking to Dr. Browne," said Sloan, "as soon as he arrives."

"How long would the old boy have lasted otherwise?" inquired Crosby irrepressibly.

"Dr. Browne wasn't sure, and he didn't want to commit himself anyway. Not even when the family talked to him . . ."

"I was going to ask about them," went on Sloan smoothly.

"Mr. and Mrs. Alan Lean—he's the son—had the chance of a few days' holiday in France." She took a deep breath. "I said to go if they wanted to. It wasn't as if there was anything more that anyone could do for his father, and both Mr. and Mrs. Lean had been most attentive since Mr. Thomas Lean had been here."

Sloan made another note.

"We—that is, I—said they would have nothing to blame themselves for if he died while they were away. Obviously," the Matron expanded on what was clearly a well-worn theme, "it is—er—more satisfactory if the family can take their farewells here, but . . ." She paused for breath. Unwisely, as it turned out.

"All part of the service?" suggested Crosby into the conversational gap.

"But," she rallied, "I told them that if he were to die while they were away we could always cope—do what was necessary and . . ."

"And put things on ice," contributed Crosby helpfully.

"After all," she said firmly, "as Dr. Browne has been kind enough to say more than once, some of our patients—like Lady Alice, for instance—come here and forget to die."

"Except Thomas Lean," remarked Crosby inevitably.

"We'd like to see Lady Alice. . . ." said Sloan. What he would also like to do was to deal with Crosby. But not here and not now. Later, in the privacy of the police station.

Lady Alice might have forgotten to die: she hadn't

forgotten Thursday's excitements. It seemed that people vomiting all over the place had brought back the dear old days during the war when she had served in the Women's Royal Naval Service. Until stemmed, she was inclined to reminisce about the Bay of Biscay in winter in wartime.

"But you were all right," said Sloan, getting a word in edgeways. "Yesterday, I mean." She had probably, he decided, been all right in the Bay of Biscay on a troopship, too, submarines or no.

"Never have liked onions," she cackled. "They don't agree with me. So I don't eat 'em."

"Very sensible," said Sloan.

"They do me an omelette when there's onions about," said the old lady.

"And I understand you saw Mr. Thomas Lean . . ."

"He was like to die," said Lady Alice.

" 'Like to die'?" echoed Sloan.

"What they used to put first when they wrote their wills in the old days. They'd begin with 'Like to die,' and then you'd know they were making it on their deathbed." She looked at him and said sadly, "That's the worst of having ancestors . . . there's nothing new."

"But Thomas Lean ate some of the casserole?" said the detective inspector, struggling back to the point.

"As to that," responded Lady Alice, "I couldn't say."

"He was taken ill . . ."

"Oh, yes. But he hadn't been sick." She looked at Sloan suspiciously. "Did you say you were both policemen?"

"That's right, Your Ladyship."

"St. Michael-types in disguise . . ."

"Not really." It was Sloan's mother who was the churchgoer of the family: he didn't know the connection. "At least, I don't think so."

"He saved three people from wrongful execution," said Lady Alice. "We had a painting at home of him doing it. Never liked it. It went for death duties."

"I don't think that in this case there will be an execution."

"Pity." Lady Alice looked Crosby up and down. "Did you know that one of my ancestors, who was the Bishop of Calleford, used to hang people in the days when he had temporal powers as well as spiritual ones?"

Sloan thought it was safe to say that things weren't what they used to be, while Crosby hastened to tell her that he'd always gone to Sunday school when a lad.

"You were very lucky to have escaped the outbreak, Lady Alice," said Sloan, adding persuasively, "Tell me, did you notice anything out of the ordinary yesterday?"

"Only in the kitchen," she said. "I went down there for more water jugs. Dash of salt and plenty of cold water's what you need when—"

"What was out of the ordinary?" asked Sloan.

"They weren't shallots," she said.

"What weren't?"

"I may not like 'em," she said enigmatically, giving a high laugh, "but I know my alliaceous vegetables, all right."

"I'm sure," he said pacifically. "So?"

"They were daffodil bulbs, not onions. That dim girl who does the vegetables still had some on the sideboard. Saw 'em myself."

Dr. Angus Browne said the same thing, but more scientifically, twenty minutes later. "The lab found the alkaloids narcissine—otherwise known as lycorine—and galantamine and scillotoxin—that's one of the glycoside scillamines—in the vomit and in the remains of the casserole."

"And we found some bulbs of *narcissus pseudonarcissus* in the kitchen," said Detective Inspector Sloan, not to be outdone in the matter of a "little Latin and less Greek."

"Easily enough mistaken, I suppose," grunted the doctor, who was neither a gardener nor a cook.

"Animals seem to know the difference," said Crosby, adding brightly, "If they couldn't tell them apart, then they'd be dead, wouldn't they?"

"Just so." The doctor looked at the constable and said,

"Anyway, the lab people have sent a copy of their findings over to Dabbe at the mortuary."

"We've been onto the Environmental Health people, and they tell us they've taken the wholesale greengrocer's apart without finding anything wrong," said Sloan, "but we're going over there all the same."

"They say they haven't found anything but onions in their onion sacks so far," chimed in Crosby. "They come in those string-bag affairs, so you can see what you're getting."

"There's one thing that's bothering me, Doctor," said Sloan. "What I want to know is why, if everyone else who had that casserole was promptly sick, why wasn't the deceased sick as well?"

"Easy," the doctor said. "He was on a whole raft of powerful antiemetic tablets to stop him being sick. Vomiting is an established side effect of all his medication. He wasn't sick because he was on them, and because he wasn't sick he didn't get rid of the toxic substances, as everyone else did."

"It's a bit like a selective weed killer, isn't it?" offered Crosby cheerfully.

Sloan stared at Crosby, struck by a new thought. "I must say, Doctor, that I find all that very interesting. Very interesting indeed. But not as interesting as something my constable has just said. Crosby, let us now go the way of all flesh. . . ."

"Sir?" The constable looked quite alarmed.

"To the kitchen."

The vegetable cook, her color still not quite returned to normal, did her best to be helpful. Her job was to take what was needed from the cold store outside, weigh up what was needed for the day, and wash and prepare it, ready for the cook who came in later.

And if she had done anything wrong yesterday, she would like to know what it was, if they didn't mind, and they might like to know that they'd been asking her to come and work at The Red Lion Hotel if she ever felt like leaving the nursing home. Very friendly, they were, at the Red Lion. Not like some places she could mention.

"I'm sure they are," said Sloan pleasantly. "Now, will you just show us over the cold store again? There was something I forgot to look at before. The lock . . ."

"A warrant?" echoed Leeyes back at the police station. "Who for?"

"The son of the deceased," said Sloan. "On a charge of murder. Cleverest job I've come across in many a long day. Make everybody ill, but just kill the one person who won't be sick when he's poisoned. All the son had to do was substitute the daffodil bulbs for the shallots in the cold store—you can see where he worked on the lock—and go away. I thought it was strange that he and his wife went abroad for the old boy's birthday."

"What was so important about that? Couldn't it have waited?"

"Not if his father had written his pension funds in trust for him," said Sloan. "Thomas Lean would have had to die before he was seventy-five or take the pension himself. The son left it as late as he dared because his father was so ill anyway."

"I think," said the Superintendent loftily, "that I shall tell the Coroner that some new evidence came to light."

Born in Yorkshire and now residing in Kent, Catherine Aird continues her series of mysteries featuring Detective Inspector C.D. "Seedy" Sloan and Constable Crosby in this story of a dubious death in a nursing home. Aird is currently working on the biography of Josephine Tey.

Immortality

Jon L. Breen

It's funny how a combination of things will trigger a memory. George Burns died the other day, and I heard somebody laid a cigar (one for the road) on his star on Hollywood Boulevard. Then Ted Kaufman, an old pal of mine from the studios who has a pencil-thin mustache, took me to lunch at Musso & Frank's on that same street, and a panhandler stopped us outside asking for a handout. I was moving pretty well for a man of ninety-six, but glad to have my cane to keep me upright.

As Ted and I sat down in one of those high mahogany booths and studied the lists of old-fashioned dishes on the menu—crab louie, Welsh rarebit, chicken pot pie—I flashed back to another visit to Musso & Frank's, sixty-four years before, in another period when panhandlers were commonplace and cigars were fashionable, but one in which I had my own pencil-thin mustache. At that time, I sometimes carried a cane, too, not to help me get around but in the name of nighttime fashion.

"I don't think they've changed this menu since 1932," I said.

"Come on, Seb," said my pal Ted. "They've at least changed the prices in my *own* time."

"Still, it looks like the same menu to me. I used to eat my way through it and start again at the top. Can't eat that way anymore. I wish I could remember what I had the time Rosey Patterson and I came in here and plotted to get Victor Rasmussen into the movies. I'd order it again."

"I remember Rosey. Good agent."

"But you don't remember Rasmussen, right? We wanted to cement his immortality, but I guess we failed. Our plotting, I'm sorry to say, ended in murder."

"So tell me about it." Ted wanted to hear the story. That's why he's my pal.

The Americans of 1932 may not have been flush, for the most part, but they were still going to the movies, so the Hollywood studios were doing all right. A lot of people in the business knew Sebastian Grady—that's me—since I'd been employed in or on the fringes of the picture industry for a fair number of years. At the time, I was working in various and sundry unspecific but indispensable capacities for Classic Pictures. The name was a misnomer of cosmic proportions, but Usually Adequate and Sometimes Pretty Good Pictures wouldn't fit over the studio gate. I was thirty-two years old, same age as the century.

I just ran into Rosey Patterson by chance that day at Musso & Frank's. I was about to take a seat at the long counter when I spotted him at a table and went over to say hello. Soon I was sitting opposite him, exchanging show-biz scuttlebutt. He was in from New York on behalf of one of his Broadway clients, but it wasn't Victor Rasmussen, a great stage star who had shunned the flicks religiously for the usual snobbish legit-actor reasons.

"You know, your man Rasmussen is ruining his chance at immortality," I said kiddingly.

"Yeah, Seb, I know," Rosey said with mock weariness, though I knew he agreed with me. All my friends had heard me on talkies-as-actor-immortality, a hobbyhorse I mounted even in the days when most people (including, sadly, those who made them) considered motion pictures disposable product.

"He won't budge," Rosey said.

"His attitude's pure snobbery," I said.

"I don't know about that. Maybe it's more like self-preservation. Some stage actors looked pretty silly in the old silents, *and* the first couple of years of talkies, for that matter."

"Times have changed," I said. "We're almost as good at making talkies now as we were at making silents in twenty-eight. For a great performer like Rasmussen *not* to leave some definitive record would be a tragedy."

"Yeah, sure, a tragedy. But what can we do about it?"

"How is Victor's health these days?" I inquired.

"Terrific. In the pink. And he's over sixty now."

"Sixty, huh?" That was older than it is now; come to think of it, so was thirty-two.

Rosey added quickly, "But he's as strong and energetic as ever."

"In good shape for a guy who's been a Broadway star since 1890, huh?"

"No, in good shape for *anybody*. Actors are athletes, Seb."

"Uh-huh," I said musingly. "And does he have anything booked at the moment?"

"I think I have a new play lined up for him, but you know how tough it is to get financing nowadays."

"So he's been at liberty since *Stranger at the Door?*" That had been one of the big hits of the 1930 Broadway season, running eight months with Victor Rasmussen in the lead role of a crusading district attorney.

"He picks his parts carefully," the agent said. "He won't do just anything."

We may have sounded like we were waltzing around a deal, in the grand tradition of Hollywood lunches then and now. But I was in no position to make any deals, just to have bright ideas. As a publicist-cum-troubleshooter, I didn't wield a whole lot of influence with my employer when it came to casting the pictures, but I had connections with people who did.

"I guess you know that my studio acquired the movie rights to *Stranger at the Door?"* I said.

"So I heard."

"Manny Grumbach even put the playwrights, Van Ness and Claudia Hooper, under contract. They'll be coming out here to write some original screenplays. Manny has great hopes for them."

"That's terrific. They're nice kids. I like them. So who's slated to play the D.A. part?"

"Edgar Carpenter."

Rosey shook his head unbelievingly. "You mean your resident diamond-in-the-roughneck? No. Can't be."

"It doesn't fit like a glove, I admit, but this is an A picture and they need a star. Of the guys they have under contract, Eddie comes the closest."

Not many people remember Edgar Carpenter today, considering how big he was in the early thirties. Eddie wasn't much of an actor really, but he was a larger-than-life personality, a guy with a unique screen persona they usually wrote vehicles to fit.

"I can't see it," Rosey said. "Of course, it's tough for me to see anybody *but* Victor doing that part. Not that he'd be willing to do it on film."

"No, I thought not."

"What kind of a guy is Carpenter anyway? I never met him. He was off the stage and on to Hollywood before I got in the business."

"I like Eddie Carpenter," I said. "Everybody who works with him does. The thing about Eddie is that he doesn't have a great deal of talent, but he happened to be in the right place at the right time."

"You could say that about half the actors in Hollywood," Rosey said with a Broadway-bred cynicism.

"Yeah, but the difference is that Eddie *knows* how lucky he's been. He's grateful for his success. There's no big ego with him."

"So, if Victor Rasmussen were to be available to play that part, not that he is," Rosey said carefully, "there'd probably be no big objection from Carpenter."

"No, not from Carpenter. Do you really think Rasmussen might be available, Rosey?"

"Who knows, he may be to the point where I could convince him. Your immortality argument might be just the ploy to get through to him. Even if he never made another picture, people fifty and a hundred years from now would be able to see what a great actor he was. You know, I'm in the business of representing stage actors, not picture actors, but still . . . I'd give a lot to see Victor play that part on the screen."

"What would you give, Rosey? Your ten percent?"

He grinned. "Well, I hope I could collect that, too. So you think you could get Carpenter on our side?"

"Yeah," I said, "He told me he liked the play when he saw it in New York with Rasmussen in it, and he knows the part is outside his usual range. Also, the two of them are old friends."

"I think they worked on the stage together before the War." That, of course, being what we now call World War I.

"But I'm not sure how much good Eddie's support would do us. He's just like most of these highly paid contract stars. He doesn't have any real say about what he appears in, and as low a view as he has of his own abilities, he doesn't often venture an opinion. To keep the money coming, he just does what Manny Grumbach tells him." Grumbach was Classic Pictures' production chief.

"Any chance of changing Grumbach's opinion?"

I shook my head. "I doubt it. I've already tried. But if you really think you can soften Victor up, we may have an opportunity to go over Grumbach's head."

"Let's hear it."

"Well, you know the real decision-makers for the studios are stationed in New York."

Rosey said, "Of course," with a Manhattanite's acceptance of the natural order of things.

"Eddie's going back there next month on a personal appearance tour. Yours truly, as the studio's man-of-all-work, has been assigned to accompany him."

"He needs a nursemaid?"

"It's part of the package for a star. My job is to get him where he's supposed to be and keep him sober enough to do whatever he's supposed to do."

"Carpenter's a drunk?"

"Only occasionally, and he's usually a cooperative one. But he did get a little out of hand at a party for visiting exhibiters that Grumbach threw a couple of years ago. Nothing major, really. He was dancing with the wife of a theater-owner from Ohio and one of his over-fancy steps sent them into Manny's swimming pool. The lady didn't mind, but her husband took some calming down. Anyway, what I'm getting at is, the chairman of the board of Classic Pictures, Archer Poole—the one guy who can set Manny Grumbach quivering in his spats—has already invited Eddie to a dinner party at his Park Avenue apartment during his stay. If Eddie asked that a few other people be invited, I think his gracious host would oblige. If you work on Victor while I work on Eddie . . ."

That was how a typical good meal at Musso & Frank led to one of the greatest meals I ever ate—and we did eat well in those days, those of us who weren't on the breadlines. A few weeks later, Rosey and I were among the guests at the lavish Manhattan apartment of Mr. and Mrs. Archer Poole. I know you've heard the line, "Other than that, Mrs. Lincoln, how did you like the play?" Well, apart from the murder after dinner, I really enjoyed that party. Just the apartment itself, with French Impressionist paintings and Chinese vases and Persian rugs everywhere you turned, was worth the trip.

Archer Poole's dinner party, of course, was not a casual affair—or maybe to him it was. It was black tie, not white, so we could dispense with the tails, but I still had to put on one of those damned uncomfortable winged collars. Maybe that was as informal as the Pooles ever got.

There were ten of us in all. I knew most of them. I'd met our urbane host on one of his west-coast swings, and he seemed even more impressive and formidable on his own ground: small, prematurely gray, wiry but very commanding. Anybody who could wear evening clothes that well had an excuse to dress for dinner every night.

Our hostess, Myrna Dustin Poole, I had never met before, but she and Eddie Carpenter obviously knew each other—the polite coolness between them suggested they might have known each other really well. Of course, I had seen Mrs. Poole on the screen—she was, if anything, more beautiful and charming than she had been as a member of D.W. Griffith's stock company back in 1912. Like many of the leading actresses in that day of harsh, wrinkle-probing cameras, she'd only been a teenager at the time, so probably wasn't much past thirty-five. Today, I can appreciate attractive women into their nineties, but even then I realized that beauty increases with maturity. I spent her husband's lengthy lectures on the pre-1919 vintage wines we were enjoying just looking at her in her clinging white evening gown. The long, slim silhouette that was fashionable at the time flattered her, as did the impressive show of cleavage that had made a comeback after the end of the boyish flapper era. Her beauty was timeless. It wasn't just the cheekbones or the full lips—I think it was those penetrating green eyes more than anything.

Victor Rasmussen, whose booming voice and patrician features were even more impressive in person than on the stage, and Rosey Patterson, oddly reserved and diffident that night for a member of his profession, were accompanied by a pair of pretty young Broadway actresses who, untypically, made little impression on me. They were outshone by their hostess and seemed to be there for the sake of propriety, along with their decorative qualities—Victor and Rosey were both unmarried and probably gay, but I was never quite sure, which should tell you something about how much that time differed from now.

Eddie Carpenter and I, the visiting out-of-towners, attended stag, which shattered all dinner-party etiquette but did not seem to bother the Pooles, who, to my relief, didn't try to provide dates for us. Such was Eddie's on- and off-screen personality that he looked like a ranch foreman or a marine sergeant forced into black tie. Completing the group were a pair I'd met on one of my previous New York visits, Van and Claudia Hooper, the young husband-and-wife writing team who had achieved their first success with *Stranger at the Door.* They were slated to head out to Hollywood on the same train Eddie and I would take home. Claudia, taller than her husband or her host and awkwardly self-conscious, was one of those women whose lack of fashion sense makes them seem unattractive by choice. If she was over-awed by the company, the self-confident Van at least pretended to feel right at home, even if he laughed a little too loud and flashed his white teeth a little too often.

We sat at a long, formal dining table, contemplating china that looked too valuable to expose to food and enough knives and forks for a week of normal eating. The host at one end and the hostess at the other. The two old acting pals were seated across from each other at Mrs. Poole's end of the table, and we all were content to let them dominate the conversation.

Highlights of the oyster appetizer and the turtle soup course were Eddie and Victor's memories of a tour they'd been on in 1915.

"It was a terrible play," Victor pronounced.

"The hell it was," Eddie protested. "Any play that kept me in work for three months was a good play, damn it. We had some terrible *audiences,* though."

"Cincinnati was the worst," Victor said.

"Never, Denver was the worst."

In mock consternation, Victor said, "Can't you agree with me on something just *once?*"

"I agreed with you back in 1915, in Hartford, when you told me I was no actor and should take up another line of work. But by the time I came up with another idea for a career, I was making too much money to quit show business. Now things are different."

"How do you mean, Eddie?" Myrna Poole asked, in a melodious voice that had been wasted on the silent-picture screen.

"Now I've saved enough money that I *can* quit show business. Any time I want."

"You can, but I hope you won't," Archer Poole protested from the other end of the table. "It would be a terrible loss."

"To Classic Pictures, you mean?" Eddie said.

"To the world."

"Well, I may just not sign my next contract with the world when it comes up for renewal," Eddie said with a broad grin. "I may just retire to the life of a rancher or a yachtsman, the kind of guy one of those roughnecks I play in pictures would be if they had any dough."

The conversation then turned to the 1929 stock market crash and the resultant financial hard times, evidence of which was all around us in 1932, but the discussion mostly amounted to platitudes. It was a subject the wealthy and famous of the time approached with care. Putting up a front was important, and those who had lost on Wall Street through buying on margin—the most popular form of financial suicide in the late twenties—wanted either to conceal or downplay it.

Though they didn't reveal it that night, I knew a little bit about the fortunes of the people around the table. For one thing, I strongly suspected Eddie Carpenter was lying when he claimed he could quit pictures painlessly. Rumor said he'd taken a real bath in the crash, and with two ex-wives to support was living right up to his handsome salary. Archer Poole, on the other hand, had reputedly been among those to profit by the crash, buying up stocks when the market was at its lowest and entering the depressed thirties even richer than he'd been before.

Eddie's threat to quit was obviously a ploy in advancing Rasmussen's cause, and a more daring one than I'd expected from him.

As the filet of sole came first to the nostrils and then into view, Poole tried to keep the conversation light, but he seemed a little uneasy with the idea that Eddie, the star who kept the studio solvent, might not be kidding. He started to probe the wellsprings of Eddie's dissatisfaction. If he wasn't happy about something at Classic Pictures—his co-stars, his dressing room, the on-set kennels for his Scottish terriers—Archer would talk to Manny Grumbach and try to set things right.

"Nah, they treat me and the pups fine. Can't complain about that."

"Eddie was always easy to work with," Victor Rasmussen put in with a wink. "But you didn't have any dogs when we worked together."

"It's tough to take pets on the road," Eddie said. "Look, Archer, if I decide to quit, don't put the blame on Manny or anybody else out there. They're the best. They've been swell to me, and it won't be because of them if I retire. It'll be because I'm ready."

"Actors don't retire," Victor snorted.

"Only actresses," said Myrna Dustin Poole in an undertone not everybody at the table heard.

"Real actors don't," Eddie said, "guys like you who need applause like oxygen, but you told me once I was no actor, didn't you now?"

"If I said that, I was merely trying to spur you on."

"Hah! But you were right. If I *was* a real actor, I guess I'd be working on stage, memorizing two hours of dialogue at a time instead of two minutes."

"I never said movie actors weren't real actors, Eddie. Not exactly."

"Maybe I just need some more time off," Eddie said

casually. "After I get back from this promotion trip, I go right into my next roll of sausage, thing called *The King of the Tugboats*—almost step off the train and in front of the camera. Then it's *Stranger at the Door . . .*"

"We write only the best sausage," Van Hooper said with a grin. His wife looked a little startled that he'd deigned to speak at all, let alone facetiously, in this formidable company.

"Oh, no, that's not sausage. That's more like caviar. Hey, Van, Claudia, you kids turned out a swell piece of work there. Any actor'd be happy to say the great lines you wrote in that script." Claudia blushed, while Van looked unbecomingly smug. "But the way my pictures get churned out, one right after the other, doesn't let an actor prepare for that kind of a great role."

"Uh, Eddie," said Poole carefully, "I could certainly talk to Manny about putting someone else into *King of the Tugboats,* if you want more time to get yourself ready for *Stranger.* That's going to be a big picture—"

"You got me wrong," Eddie Carpenter said. "I *want* to do the tugboat flick. I act well with tugboats, always have. Their delivery and mine are just about as varied and expressive. But it's *Stranger* I'm not convinced I'm right for. You kids didn't write that part for a guy like me. You wrote it for a real actor."

That was my cue. Sounding like the good studio hack I was, I said, "Come on, Eddie, who could we ever get to do that D.A. part as well as you could?"

All eyes reflexively turned toward Victor Rasmussen, even Poole's, and we all laughed nervously in the awkward pause.

"Who's available for pictures, I mean," I added.

"Victor wouldn't be caught dead makin' a picture," Eddie said. "He wouldn't even go in front of a newsreel camera. It would ruin his standing as an *artiste.* Picture people are the dregs of the earth. You know, Van and Claudia, I'm surprised he'll even talk to you after you sold your play to Hollywood, and you're actually going out there to give your muse a sunburn. I'm surprised he'd even come to your apartment, Archer—afraid he might run into Clara Bow or Tom Mix."

"He knew he'd run into Myrna Dustin," Poole said lightly, smiling down the center of the table at his wife.

"But I had the good taste to quit," she replied, not nearly as lightly.

Victor was finding this all very funny. "I'm not that bad, Eddie. Remember how I congratulated you when you got your first picture contract?"

"Sure, because it got me off the stage. I should have been insulted. If you thought I was a real actor, you'd have said I was a traitor to the legitimate theatre."

I glanced at Rosey, and he raised his eyebrow in a gesture I took to mean things were going promisingly. I didn't know how much he'd managed to soften Victor up for what was coming, but it seemed obvious his client had mellowed a bit in his attitude toward Hollywood. Maybe the plan we'd worked out with Eddie was going to succeed.

By that time the main course (chateaubriand) had come along, and it was presented by the male servers with the kind of earnest attentiveness associated with a religious ritual. Conversation was momentarily silenced, and when it returned it centered on the tenderness of the beef, the almost artistic arrangement of the accompanying vegetables, and the body and flavor of the Clos Vougeot our host had selected to accompany the entrée. That the Pooles had a genius in their kitchen was only confirmed by the lemon soufflé that followed. There was also a bowl of fresh fruit and a cheese board presented. We did eat in those days.

In formal dinner party tradition, the ladies all trooped off after the dessert course to leave the gentlemen to their port and cigars, of both of which Archer Poole offered his guests only the best. After we heard about all the vintages, port *and* tobacco, the conversation got a little more frank and pointed. It also took a disconcerting turn.

"I know what you fellows are trying to do," Victor Rasmussen said. "You don't fool me for a minute."

With a broad wink at Archer Poole as if he were one of the conspirators (a clever touch), Eddie Carpenter said, "What are we tryin' to do, Vic?"

"Get me work. I'll admit I've been a bit financially strapped, but Rosey has a new play for me to go into, don't you, Rosey?"

The agent looked pained for a second, and I could imagine why. Rasmussen's overly frank statement had just knocked us conspirators out of the driver's seat. "They're not going to put it on, Victor," he muttered. "It's so tough to get financing these days. But there'll be other plays. The day I can't get work on Broadway for Victor Rasmussen, I'll take up another line."

"Or maybe I should." Rasmussen turned to Eddie Carpenter. "I could coach you in that role, Eddie."

For a second we didn't know what he was talking about. Eddie just gaped at him, and Victor mistook the meaning of his reaction.

"Not that you couldn't play it fine without me," he said quickly, "but if I could be of help, I'd be glad to."

This was not going right, and I could see Rosey was as surprised as I was. We had wanted it to appear that getting Rasmussen for the role would be a coup for Classic Pictures, but here Rasmussen was cheapening himself, acting less like a star than a guy begging for any work he could get. I glanced at Rosey. Hadn't he done *anything* to prepare Victor for this?

Archer Poole, obviously a man who thought before he spoke, had listened to all of this poker-faced. Finally, he said, "I think employing Victor as a coach for Eddie is a splendid idea. You're old friends who clearly have a personal rapport. And if Victor is confident of Eddie's ability to do the part, that makes me feel all the better about the chances of the picture." He looked at Eddie, Victor, and Rosey in turn. "If you are all agreed on this, I can make a long-distance call to Manny Grumbach in the morning and set things in motion."

None of us had anything to say to that. Victor had what

he wanted, at least apparently, and the rest of us were too stunned to know how to save the situation.

Archer Poole smiled. "Well, then, shall we join the ladies?"

I don't know what the ladies had been talking about, but they looked a lot jollier than we must have as we joined them in the living room. Rosey was especially tight-lipped and grim-faced, as if he'd been blindsided and couldn't decide how or by whom. We all managed to finish off the evening with small talk. Victor and Archer, back in mixed company, made no more mention of business matters, and Eddie, Rosey, and I would have no more to say on the subject until we could regroup and compare notes.

The party broke up about one A.M. Rosey and Victor went their separate ways in cabs, while Eddie and I walked the half-dozen blocks to our hotel. People of all kinds could be found on the Manhattan streets at any hour in those days, from elegant women with their close-fitting, helmet-style hats and hard-times-length dresses to apple and pencil sellers on the well-lighted corners to homeless beggars looking for a handout—with all the poverty and desperation that was around, the fear of crime just wasn't the same as it is now.

What about the murder, you say? I didn't even find out about it until the next morning, when a police detective came to ask us some questions.

In defiance of recent Manhattan history, a man who was *still* rich had hit the pavement at deadly speed. Archer Poole had jumped or fallen or been pushed from the window of his twelfth-story apartment and made a mess on the Park Avenue sidewalk.

The cop proved irritatingly uninformative, but the papers—and New York still had a bunch of dailies at that time—put together more of the story. Of the three possibilities, pushed was the favorite. There were several wounds on Poole's body, apparently made by a fireplace poker that had hit the concrete along with him. The overwrought articles reported that Poole's widow, former movie star Myrna

Dustin, had been in bed when she heard loud, masculine voices coming from her husband's study. She had been annoyed at first, but not particularly alarmed.

"Archer only slept four or five hours a night, so he often worked late. And it wasn't unusual for him to receive visitors at all hours."

Could Mrs. Poole hear what was being said? No, most of it was too muffled and indistinct. She had heard her husband say, "What are you doing back here?", which led her to think it was one of the guests at their dinner party earlier that evening. She hadn't recognized the voice of Poole's visitor, nor could she make out anything he said except for a couple of words: "parasite" and "vulture."

"At first I was going to get up and ask them to be quiet," Myrna went on, "but then the voices got louder and I became frightened. I heard a loud cry, running footsteps, a door slamming. I was petrified with fear. I must have stayed in my bed for several minutes before I could bring myself to do anything. Finally I gathered the courage to go to my husband's study. No one was there, but the window was wide open and the curtains blowing in the breeze. I looked down to the street below and saw a crowd of people around a body and an ambulance, and then I realized what must have happened."

The articles revealed that among the Pooles' guests had been Broadway star Victor Rasmussen and Hollywood star Edgar Carpenter. Lesser mortals like Rosey Patterson and Sebastian Grady were not mentioned.

Needless to say, Eddie Carpenter was not about to show himself in the lobby or on the streets with this added notoriety. We had room service bring lunch up to his suite and gave the bellhop a standing order for any new editions of the papers, which were the 1932 urban equivalent of the all-news radio and TV outlets today. Of course, I was considering the ramifications for Classic Pictures with the chairman dead, and I'd already placed a long-distance call to Manny Grumbach on the west coast. The most immediate concern was deciding what Eddie would say when the newshounds tracked him down, which was bound to happen, and soon.

I was energized but not really worried as I gobbled down my lunch. But I realized Eddie's reaction was more worrisome. He looked pale and uncertain, which was uncharacteristic. He wasn't eating, which was even more uncharacteristic.

"Eddie, if there's something you need to tell me, spill it," I said.

"It was me, Seb."

I looked up sharply. "What do you mean?"

"I couldn't sleep after we got in last night, so I went out for a walk. I walked back to Poole's apartment building, looked up at the windows for a while. Then I decided I had to talk to him."

"Did anybody see you?"

Eddie smiled humorlessly. "If they had, I'd be in the cooler by now, wouldn't I?"

"Not the number-one star of Classic Pictures," I said, with more confidence than I felt. The L.A. police were in the palm of the studios, but I couldn't be so sure about New York's finest.

"I slipped past the doorman and went up the stairs to his apartment," Eddie continued. "I tapped on the door, and Poole answered it himself. He normally has a live-in butler, you know, but it was the guy's night off and the cook and the rest of the live-out staff had been sent home, so only he and Myrna were in the apartment. He was surprised to see me, of course, but acted real cordial. He showed me into his study, started spouting about his goddamn first editions, but I wasn't in the mood for polite chitchat. I was mad."

"Why?"

"You know as well as I do that Poole profiteered after the crash, took advantage of all the investors who were losing their shirts to practically double his own fortune."

"I've heard the rumors," I said carefully.

"You could say that was just smart business. You could say anybody'd do the same if they had the opportunity.

Maybe I would. Maybe you would. But rubbing people's faces in it is another matter. Now I was lucky. I still had a big income, and I could pull myself out of it. But Victor lost his shirt too, and, spending so long between jobs, he was really hurting. A great star like him, offering himself up as a drama coach for a bum like me, and what does Poole do? He takes him up on it!"

"You might take that as a generous gesture," I said.

"You might take it that way, yeah, but I know better what kind of guy Poole is and how his mind works. So you could say I got mad. Hell, I erupted like a volcano, biggest scene I ever made when I wasn't stinko. And yes, I used the word 'parasite' and the word 'vulture,' just like his visitor was quoted in the paper. I really gave it to the bastard."

"But did you have to kill him, Eddie?"

He gaped at me. "*Kill* him? I didn't kill him."

"But you said you did it."

"Is that what you thought I was saying? I meant, I was up there and I said those things. He was alive when I left. But let's face it, if *you* assumed I did it, it's gonna sound that way to everybody else, too."

I believed Eddie Carpenter. As I said before, he wasn't that great an actor.

"If you didn't kill him, what happened? Did he commit suicide?"

Eddie shook his head. "Never, not him. He's not the type. He was thinking out his next move, but I don't see the guy killing himself."

"And there was that fireplace poker," I mused. "Somebody attacked him. If you didn't kill Poole, I guess it's pretty obvious who must have."

Eddie looked blank. "Who? Victor? Or Rosey?"

"Come on. You think another guest besides you just happened to make his way back to the apartment last night? That's too much to swallow."

"There are some desperate people out on those streets, Seb. If I could get in, so could one of them. Maybe Poole surprised a burglar, or just somebody who was hungry, or looking for a warm place to sleep."

I shook my head. "That's not what happened. This was what you might call an opportunistic murderer, and there's only one real possibility."

"Who?" Eddie said. I could hardly believe he could be so dumb. It had to be willful.

"Did you see Myrna when you were there?" I asked.

"No. Obviously, she must have been listening because she quoted me to the papers, but she never showed herself."

"What about the other statement she quoted? Did Poole ever ask you, 'What are you doing back here?' in a raised voice?"

"No, he never raised his voice at all. He was being real polite until I started laying into him, and even then he just seemed kind of stunned. He never yelled back at me."

"So Myrna lied about that."

"I guess—Seb, you don't think *she* did it, do you?"

"Who else? The servants were gone. She may have had reasons to want to kill him, and that angry argument she heard probably gave her the opportunity to do it. She comes into the study after you leave, takes him by surprise with the poker, starts flailing away at him, he backs up toward the open window, loses his balance. She either pitches the poker out after him or it flies out of her hand in one last frenzied blow."

Eddie shivered. "Why would she have killed him?"

"I don't know, but she resented the loss of her movie career. I could tell that from some of the things she said last night and some of the looks she gave her husband. Who knows what else might have built up over the years? Maybe he was seeing other women. She probably heard more of your conversation than she said, and she assumed someone as well-known as you would probably have been seen entering or leaving the building, so there was a built-in suspect available."

"Then she must have had it in for me, too."

"I guess so. Her story would handily pin the crime on you. She wouldn't even have to mention your name. Any reason why she *might* have it in for you?"

He paused too long to make any denial plausible. "We were, uh, involved with each other once."

"Before she married Poole?"

"Uh, mostly. Seb, you remember Sally Finley, don't you?"

"Sure." A cute kid but a lousy actress, she'd had what ballplayers would call a cup of coffee with Classic Pictures in the late twenties. "That was your second wife, right?"

"Uh, no, I never married her. But she did have something to do with initiating my first divorce, so your mistake is understandable. At the time Classic signed Sally, they'd been considering bringing Myrna back to the screen. Talkies were coming in, and you know what a great voice she has. But they picked Sally instead. She was younger and would cost them less. Myrna might have figured I'd used some influence there. To get Sally the job she thought *she* should have had."

"And did you?"

"You know me better than that, Seb. The decision not to sign Myrna came straight from Archer Poole, though Manny took the credit for it. I don't think Myrna ever knew her own husband nixed her return."

"Do you suppose she found out?"

The suite's telephone rang before he could answer, and I took that to mean the reporters had found Eddie. So what would we tell them? Not the truth, of course; that was never an option. I reached for the phone, thinking not as a road-company Philo Vance now but as a studio hack. I said the right things, and so did Eddie.

The full truth about Archer Poole's death never became public. Myrna was never charged with his death and nobody else was either. Over the years, though, I managed to piece some of it together, enough to convince me my guess was right. For all the money and wealth her marriage brought her, Myrna had bitterly resented the loss of her movie career. Archer's story to her was that the Hollywood boys really ran the studio, that he rarely had any influence on their decisions, and that he couldn't possibly be seen to unfairly favor his own wife. Shortly before our dinner party, she'd found a copy of a letter in his desk that revealed the truth. But instead of replacing her resentment of Eddie with anger at her husband, she'd just joined the two of them together and taken an opportunity when it presented itself.

"Eddie wound up playing the lead in *Stranger at the Door* after all," I told Ted Kaufman. "Victor finally did a few movie character parts through the late thirties, but never anything like his starring roles on stage. The Hoopers, you know, were in heavy demand as screenwriters till the sixties. I think she's still alive, at the Motion Picture Country House in Woodland Hills."

"What happened to Myrna?"

"Remarried just about as wealthily and moved to Florida. She kind of disappeared from the public eye. I couldn't say if she's alive or dead, but the chances are anybody I knew in those days is dead. The last time I saw Rosey Patterson, must have been in the mid-forties, we compared notes on the Poole case and learned we'd come to about the same conclusions. We talked about Myrna and her career, and whether she really was much of an actress. We couldn't decide. All there is on her is some silent film from 1912. If she'd only done some talkies."

California English professor Jon L. Breen flashes back to the infancy of Hollywood talkies in this mystery. Well-known as a mystery reviewer and short story writer, Breen also is the author of the Rachel Hennings series *(The Gathering Place* and *Touch of the Past)* and the Jerry Brogan series *(Listen for the Click, Triple Crown, Loose Lips,* and *Hot Air).*

Ways to Kill a Cat

Simon Brett

"There are more ways to kill a cat
than choking it with cream."
—old proverb

1. Putting the Cat Among the Pigeons

Seraphina Fellowes felt very pleased with herself. This was not an unusual state of affairs. Seraphina Fellowes usually felt very pleased with herself. This hadn't always been the case, but her literary success over the previous decade had raised her self-esteem to a level that was now almost unassailable.

Only twelve years before, she had been no more than a dissatisfied mousy-haired housewife, married to a Catholic writer, George Fellowes, whose fondness for "trying ideas out" rather than writing for commercial markets, coupled with an increasingly close relationship with the bottle, was threatening both his career and their marriage.

Seraphina clearly remembered the evening that had changed everything. Changed everything for her, that is. It hadn't affected George's fortunes so much, even though the original life-changing idea had been his. This detail was one of many that Seraphina tended to gloss over in media interviews about her success. George may have given her a little help in the early days, but he had long since ceased to have any relevance, either in her career or her personal life.

When the idea first came up, Seraphina hadn't even been Seraphina. She had then just been Sally, but "Sally Fellowes" was no name for a successful author, so that was the first of many details that were changed as she created her new persona.

Like an increasing number of evenings at that stage of the Fellowes' marriage, the pivotal evening had begun with a row. Sally, as she then was, had crossed from the house to the garden shed in which her husband worked and found George sprawled across his desk, fast asleep. Cuddled up against his head had been Mr. Whiffles, their tabby cat. Well, the cat was technically "theirs," but really he was George's. George was responsible for all the relevant feeding and nurturing. Sally didn't like cats very much.

It was only half past six in the evening, but already in George's wastepaper basket lay the cause of his stupor, an empty half bottle of vodka. That had been sufficient incentive for Sally to shake him rudely awake and pull one of the common triggers of their rows, an attack on his drinking. George's subsequent picking up and stroking the disturbed Mr. Whiffles had moved Sally on to another of her regular criticisms: "You care more about that cat than you do about me."

George had come back, predictably enough, with: "Well, this cat shows me a lot more affection than you do," which had moved the altercation inevitably on to the subject of their sex life—George's desire for more sex and more enthusiastic sex, his conviction that having children would solve many of their problems, and Sally's recurrent assertion that he was disgusting and never thought about anything else.

Once that particular storm had blown itself out, Sally had

moved the attack on to George's professional life. Why did he persist in writing "arty-farty literary novels" that nobody wanted to publish? Why didn't he go in for something like crime fiction, a genre that large numbers of the public might actually want to *read?*

"Oh, yes?" George had responded sarcastically. "What, should I write mimsy-pimsy little whodunits in which all the blood is neatly swept under the carpet and the investigation is in the hands of some heartwarmingly eccentric and totally unrealistic sleuth? Or," he had continued, warming to his theme and stroking Mr. Whiffles ever more vigorously, "why don't I make a cat the detective? Why don't I write a whole series of mysteries that are solved by lovable Mr. Whiffles?"

The instant he made the suggestion, Sally Fellowes' anger evaporated. She knew that something cataclysmic had happened. From that moment, she saw her way forward.

At the time, though the cat mystery was already a burgeoning sub-genre in American crime fiction, it had not taken much of a hold in England. Cat picture books, cat calendars, cat quotation selections, and cat greeting cards all sold well—particularly at Christmas—but there didn't exist a successful homegrown series of cat mysteries.

Sally Fellowes—or rather Seraphina Fellowes, for the name came to her simultaneously with the idea—determined to change all that.

George had helped her a lot initially—though that was another little detail she tended not to mention when talking to the media. She rationalized this on marketing grounds. The product she was selling was "a Mr. Whiffles mystery, written by Seraphina Fellowes." To mention the existence of a collaborating author would only have confused potential purchasers.

And George didn't seem to mind. He still regarded the Mr. Whiffles books as a kind of game, a diversion he took about as seriously as trying to complete the crossword. Seraphina would summon him by intercom buzzer from his shed when she got stuck, and he, with a couple of airy, nonchalant sentences, would redirect her into the next phase of the mystery. George was still, in theory, working on his "literary" novels, and regarded devising whodunit plots as a kind of mental chewing gum.

Seraphina proved to be a quick learner, and an assiduous researcher. She negotiated her way around library catalogues; she established good relations with her local police for help on procedure; she even bought a gun, which ever thereafter she kept in her desk drawer, so that she could make her descriptions of firearms authentic.

As the Mr. Whiffles mysteries began to roll off the production line, the summonings of George from his shed grew less and less frequent. While Seraphina was struggling with the first book, the intercom buzzer sounded every ten minutes, and her husband spent most of his life traversing the garden between shed and house. With the second, however, the calls were down to about one a day, and for the third—except to unravel a couple of vital plot points—Seraphina's husband was hardly disturbed at all.

The reason for this was that George had made the first book such an ingenious template that writing the rest was merely a matter of doing a bit of research and applying the same formula to some new setting. Seraphina, needless to say, would never have admitted this, and had indeed by the third book convinced herself that the entire creative process was hers alone.

As George became marginalized from his wife's professional life, so she moved him further away from her personal life. As soon as the international royalties for the Mr. Whiffles books started to roll in, Seraphina organized the demolition of George's working shed in the garden, and its replacement by a brand-new, self-contained bungalow. There her husband was at liberty to lead his own life. Whether that life involved further experimentation with the novel form or a quicker descent into alcoholic befuddlement, Seraphina Fellowes neither knew nor cared.

She didn't divorce George, though. His Catholicism put him against the idea, but Seraphina also needed him around to see that Mr. Whiffles got fed during her increasingly frequent absences on promotional tours or at foreign mystery conventions. Then again, there was always the distant possibility that she might get stuck again on one of the books and need George to sort out the plot for her.

Besides, having a shadowy husband figure in the background had other uses. When asked about him in interviews, she always implied that he was ill and that she unobtrusively devoted her life to his care. This did her image no harm at all. He was also very useful when oversexed crime writers or critics came on to her at mystery conventions. Her assertion, accompanied by a martyred expression of divided loyalties, that "it wouldn't be fair to George" was a much better excuse than the truth—that she didn't, in fact, like sex.

As the royalties mounted, Seraphina had both herself and her house made over. Her mousey hair became a jet-black helmet assiduously maintained by costly hairdressing; her face was an unchanging mask of expertly applied makeup; and she patronized ever more expensive couturiers for her clothes. The house was extended and interior designed; the garden elegantly landscaped to include a fishpond with elaborate fountain and cascade features.

And Seraphina always had the latest computer technology on which to write her money-spinning books. After taking delivery of each new state-of-the-art machine, her first ritual action was to program the "M" key to print on the screen: "Mr. Whiffles."

So, twelve years on from the momentous evening that changed her life, Seraphina Fellowes had good cause to feel very pleased with herself. The previous day she had achieved a lifetime ambition. She had rung through an order for the latest model Ferrari. There was a year-and-a-half waiting list for delivery, but it had given Seraphina enormous satisfaction to write a check for the full purchase price without batting an eyelid.

She looked complacently around the large study she had

had built on to the house. It was decorated in pastel pinks and greens, flowery wallpapers, and hanging swaths of curtain. The walls were covered with framed Mr. Whiffles memorabilia: book jackets, publicity photographs of the author cuddling her hero's namesake, newspaper best-sellers listings, mystery organizations' citations and awards. On her mantelpiece, amongst lesser plaques and figurines, stood her proudest possession, the highest accolade so far accorded to the Mr. Whiffles industry: an Edgar statuette from the Mystery Writers of America. Yes, Seraphina Fellowes did feel very pleased with herself.

But even as she had this thought, a sliver of unease was driven into her mind. She heard once again the ominous sound that increasingly threatened her well-being and complacency. It was the clatter of a letterbox and the solid thud of her elastic-band-wrapped mail landing on the doormat. She went through into the hall with some trepidation to see what new threat the postman had brought that day.

Seraphina divided the letters into two piles on her desk. The left-hand pile comprised those addressed to "Seraphina Fellowes, Author of the Mr. Whiffles Books"; the right-hand one was made up of letters addressed to "Mr. Whiffles" himself. A lot of those, she knew, would be whimsically written by their owners as if they came from other cats. In fact, that morning over half of Mr. Whiffles' letters had paw prints on the back of the envelopes.

But that wasn't what worried Seraphina Fellowes. What really disturbed her—no, more than disturbed—what really twisted the icy dagger of jealousy in her heart was the fact that the right-hand pile was much higher than the left-hand one. This was the worst incident yet, and it confirmed an appalling trend that had been building for the last couple of years.

Mr. Whiffles was getting more fan mail than she was!

The object of her jealousy, with the instinct for timing that had so far preserved intact all nine of his lives, chose that moment to enter Seraphina Fellowes' study. He wasn't, strictly speaking, welcome in her house—he spent most of his time over in George's bungalow—but Seraphina had had cat-flaps inserted in all her doors to demonstrate her house's cat-friendliness when journalists came to interview her, and Mr. Whiffles did put in the occasional appearance. To get to the study he'd had to negotiate four cat-flaps: from the garden into a passage, from the passage into the kitchen, kitchen to hall, and hall to study.

He looked up at his mistress with that insolence that cats don't just reserve for kings, and Seraphina Fellowes felt another twist of the dagger in her heart. She stared dispassionately down at the animal. He'd never been very beautiful, just a neutered tabby tom like a million others. Seraphina looked up at one of the publicity shots on the wall and compared the cat photographed five years previously with the current reality.

Time hadn't been kind. Mr. Whiffles really was looking in bad shape. He was fourteen, after all. He was thinner, his coat more scruffy, he was a bit scummy round the mouth, and he might even have a patch of mange at the base of his tail.

"You poor old boy," Seraphina Fellowes cooed. "You're no spring chicken any more, are you? I'm rather afraid it's time for you and me to pay a visit to the vet."

And she went off to fetch the cat basket.

At the surgery, everyone made a great fuss over Mr. Whiffles. Though he'd enjoyed generally good health, there had been occasional visits to the vet for all the usual, minor feline ailments and, as the fame of the books grew, he was treated there increasingly like a minor royal.

Seraphina didn't take much notice of the attention he was getting. She was preoccupied with planning the press conference at which the sad news of Mr. Whiffles' demise would be communicated to the media. She would employ the pained expression she had perfected for speaking about her invalid husband. And yes, the line "It was a terrible wrench, but I felt the time had come to prevent him future suffering" must come in somewhere.

"How incontinent?" asked the vet once they were inside the surgery and Mr. Whiffles was standing on the bench to be examined.

"Oh, I'm afraid it's getting worse and worse," said Seraphina mournfully. "I mean, at first I didn't worry about it, thought it was only a phase, but there's no way we can ignore the situation any longer. It's causing poor Mr. Whiffles so much pain, apart from anything else."

"If it's causing him pain, then it's probably just some kind of urinary infection," said the vet unhelpfully.

"I'm afraid it's worse than that." Seraphina Fellowes choked back a little sob. "It's a terrible decision to make, but I'm afraid he'll have to be put down."

The vet's reaction to this was even worse. He burst out laughing. "Good heavens, we're not at that stage." He stroked Mr. Whiffles, who reached up appealingly and rubbed his whiskers against the vet's face. "No, this old boy's got another good five years in him, I'd say."

"Really?" Seraphina realized she'd let too much pique show in that one, and repeated a softer, more relieved, more tentative, "Really?"

"Oh, yes. I'll put him on antibiotics, and that'll sort out the urinary infection in no time." The vet looked at her with concern. "But you shouldn't be letting worries about him prey on your mind like this. You mustn't get things out of proportion, you know."

"I am *not* getting things out of proportion!" Seraphina Fellowes snapped with considerable asperity.

"Maybe you should go and see your doctor," the vet suggested gently. "It might be something to do with your age."

Seraphina was still seething at that last remark as she drove back home. Her mood was not improved by the way Mr. Whiffles looked up at her through the grille of the cat basket. His expression seemed almost triumphant.

Seraphina Fellowes set her mouth in a hard line. The situation wasn't irreversible. There were more ways to kill a cat than enlisting the help of the vet.

2. Fighting Like Cats and Dogs

"Are you sure you don't mind my bringing Ghengis, Seraphina?"

"No, no."

"But I thought, what with you being a cat person, you wouldn't want a great big dog tramping all over your house."

A great big dog Ghengis certainly was. He must have weighed about the same as the average nightclub bouncer, and the similarities didn't stop there. His teeth appeared too big for his mouth, with the result that he was incapable of any expression other than slavering.

"It's no problem," Seraphina Fellowes reassured her guest.

"But he doesn't like cats." Seraphina knew this; it was the sole reason for her guest's invitation. "I'd hate to think of him doing any harm to the famous Mr. Whiffles," her guest continued.

"Don't worry. Mr. Whiffles is safely ensconced with George." The mastiff growled the low growl of a flesh addict whose fix is overdue. "Maybe Ghengis would like to have a run around the garden . . . to let off some steam?"

As she opened the back door and Ghengis rocketed out, Seraphina looked with complacency towards the tree under which a cat lay serenely asleep. "No, no!" her guest screamed. "There's Mr. Whiffles!"

"Oh dear," said Seraphina Fellowes with minimal sincerity. Then she closed the back door, and went through the passage into the kitchen to watch the unequal contest through a window.

The huge, slavering jaws were nearly around the cat before Mr. Whiffles suddenly became aware and jumped sideways. The chase thereafter was furious, but there was no doubt who was calling the shots. Mr. Whiffles didn't choose the easy option of flying up a tree out of Ghengis's reach. Instead, he played on his greater mobility, weaved and curvetted across the grass, driving the thundering mastiff to ever more frenzied pitches of frustration.

Finally, Mr. Whiffles seemed to tire. He slowed, gave up evasive action, and started to move in a defeated straight line towards the house. Ghengis pounded greedily after him, slavering more than ever.

Mr. Whiffles put on a sudden burst of acceleration. Ghengis did likewise, and he had the more powerful engine. He ate up the ground that separated them.

At the second when it seemed nothing could stop the jaws from closing around his thin body, Mr. Whiffles took off through the air and threaded himself neatly through the outer cat-flap into the passage, and then the next one into the kitchen.

Seraphina Fellowes just had time to look down at the cat on the tiled floor before she heard the splintering crunch of Ghengis hitting the outside door at full speed.

Mr. Whiffles looked up at his mistress with an expression that seemed to say, "You'll have to do better than that, sweetie."

As Seraphina Fellowes was seeing her guest and bloody-faced dog off on their way to the vet's, the postman arrived with the day's second post. The usual thick rubber-banded wodge of letters.

That day two-thirds of the envelopes had paw prints on the back.

3. Letting the Cat Out of the Bag

It was sad that George's mother died. Sad for George, that is. Seraphina had never cared for the old woman.

And it did mean that George would have to go to Ireland for the funeral. What with seeing solicitors, tidying his mother's house prior to putting it on the market, and other family duties, he would be away a whole week.

How awkward that this coincided with Seraphina's recollection that she needed to go to New York for a meeting with her American agent. Awkward because it meant that for a whole week neither of them would be able to feed Mr. Whiffles.

Not to worry, Seraphina had reassured George, there's a local girl who'll come in and put food down for him morning and evening. Not a very bright local girl, thought Seraphina gleefully, though she didn't mention that detail to George.

"Now, Mr. Whiffles is a very fussy eater," she explained when she was briefing the local girl, "and sometimes he's just not interested in his food. But don't you worry about that. If he hasn't touched one plateful, just throw it away and put down a fresh one—okay?"

Seraphina waited until the cab taking George to the station was out of sight. Then she picked up a somewhat suspicious Mr. Whiffles with a cooing "Who's a lovely boy then?" and opened the trapdoor to the cellar.

She placed the confused cat on the second step, and while Mr. Whiffles was uneasily sniffing out his new environment, slammed the trap down and bolted it.

Then she got into her BMW—she couldn't wait till it was a Ferrari—and drove to the Executive Parking near Heathrow, which she *always* used when she Concorded to the States.

Seraphina made herself characteristically difficult with her agent in New York. Lots of little niggling demands were put forward to irritate her publisher. She was just flexing her muscles. She knew the sales of the Mr. Whiffles books were too important to the publisher, and ten percent of the royalties on them too important to her agent, for either party to argue.

She also aired an idea that she had been nurturing for

some time—that she might soon start another series of mysteries. Oh yes, still cat mysteries, but with a new, female protagonist.

Her agent and publisher were both wary of the suggestion. Their general view seemed to be "If it ain't broke, don't fix it." An insatiable demand was still out there for the existing Mr. Whiffles product. Why put that guaranteed success at risk by starting something new?

Seraphina characteristically made it clear that the opinions of her agent and publisher held no interest for her at all.

On the Concorde back to London, she practised and honed the phrases she would use at the press conference that announced Mr. Whiffles' sad death from starvation in her cellar. How she would excoriate the stupid local girl who had unwittingly locked him down there in the first place, and then not been bright enough to notice that he wasn't appearing to eat his food. Surely anyone with even the most basic intelligence could have put two and two together and realized that the cat had gone missing?

There was indeed a press conference when Seraphina got back. The story even made its way onto the main evening television news—as one of those heartwarming end pieces that allow the newsreader to practice his chuckle.

But the headlines weren't the ones Seraphina had had in mind. "PLUCKY SUPERCAT SUMMONS HELP FROM CELLAR PRISON," "MR. WHIFFLES CALLS FIRE BRIGADE TO SAVE HIM FROM LINGERING DEATH," "BRILLIANT MR. WHIFFLES USES ONE OF HIS NINE LIVES AND WILL LIVE ON TO SOLVE MANY MORE CASES."

To compound Seraphina's annoyance, she then had to submit to many interviews, in which she expressed her massive relief for the cat's survival, and to many photographic sessions in which she had to hug the mangy old tabby with apparent delight.

Prompted by all the publicity, the volume of mail arriving at Seraphina Fellowes' house rocketed. And now almost all the letters were addressed to "Mr. Whiffles." Seraphina thought if she saw another paw print on the back of an envelope, she'd throw up.

4. Playing Cat and Mouse

In July 1985, in a speech to the American Bar Association in London, Margaret Thatcher said: "We must try to find ways to starve the terrorist and the hijacker of the oxygen of publicity on which they depend."

Seraphina Fellowes, a woman not dissimilar in character to Margaret Thatcher, determined to apply these tactics in her continuing campaign against Mr. Whiffles. His miraculous escape from the cellar had had saturation coverage. The public was, for the time being, slightly bored with the subject of Mr. Whiffles. Now was the moment to present them with a new publicity sensation.

She was called Gigi, and she was everything Mr. Whiffles wasn't. A white Persian with deep blue eyes, she had a pedigree that made the Apostolic Succession look like the invention of parvenus. Whereas Mr. Whiffles had the credentials of a street fighter, Gigi was the unchallenged queen of all she surveyed.

And, Seraphina Fellowes announced at the press conference she had called to share the news, Gigi's fictional counterpart was about to become the heroine of a new series of cat mysteries. Stroking her new cat, Seraphina informed the media that she had just started the first book, *Gigi and the Dead Fishmonger.* Now that "dear old Mr. Whiffles" was approaching retirement, it was time to think of the future. And the future belonged to a new, feisty, beautiful, young cat detective called Gigi.

The announcement didn't actually get much attention. It came too soon after the blanket media coverage accorded to Mr. Whiffles' escape and, though from Seraphina's point of view there couldn't have been more difference between the two, for the press it was "just another cat story."

The only effect the announcement did have was to increase yet further the volume of mail arriving at Seraphina Fellowes' house. At first she was encouraged to see that the majority of these letters were addressed to her rather than to her old cat. But when she found them all to be condemnations of her decision to sideline Mr. Whiffles, she was less pleased.

Seraphina, however, was philosophical. Just wait till the book comes out, she thought. That's when we'll get a really major publicity offensive. And by ceasing to write the Mr. Whiffles books she would condemn the cat who gave them their name to public apathy and ultimate oblivion. She was turning the stopcock on the cylinder that contained his oxygen of publicity.

So Seraphina Fellowes programmed the letter "G" as the shorthand for "Gigi" into her computer, and settled down to write the new book. It was hard, because she was canny enough to know that she couldn't reproduce the Mr. Whiffles formula verbatim. A white Persian aristocrat like Gigi demanded a different kind of plot from the streetwise tabby. And Seraphina certainly had no intention of enlisting George's help again.

So she struggled on. She knew she'd get there in time. And once the book was finished, even if the first of the series wasn't quite up to the standard of a Mr. Whiffles mystery, it would still sell in huge numbers on the strength of Seraphina Fellowes' name alone.

While she was writing, the presence—the existence—of Mr. Whiffles did not become any less irksome to her.

She made a halfhearted attempt to get rid of him by a plate of cat food laced with warfarin, but the tabby ignored the bait with all the contempt it deserved. And Seraphina was only just in time to snatch the plate away when she saw Gigi approaching it greedily.

Mr. Whiffles took to spending a lot of time in the middle of the study carpet, washing himself unhurriedly, and every now and then fixing his green eyes on the struggling author with an expression of derisive pity.

Seraphina Fellowes gritted her teeth and, as she wrote, allowed the back burner of her mind to devise ever more painful and satisfying revenges.

5. The Cat's Pajamas

"I've done it! I've finished it!" Seraphina Fellowes shouted to no one in particular, as she rushed into the kitchen, the passive Gigi clasped in her arms. The author was wearing a brand-new designer silk blouse. Mr. Whiffles, dozing on a pile of dirty washing in the utility room, opened one lazy eye to observe the proceedings. He watched Seraphina hurry to the fridge and extract a perfectly chilled bottle of Dom Perignon.

It was a ritual. In the euphoria of completing the first Mr. Whiffles mystery, Seraphina and George had cracked open a bottle of Spanish fizz and, even more surprisingly, ended the evening by making love. Since then the ritual had changed. The lovemaking had certainly never been repeated. The quality of the fizz had improved, but after the second celebration, when he got inappropriately drunk, George had no longer been included in the festivities. Now, when Seraphina Fellowes finished a book, she would dress herself in a new garment bought specially for the occasion, then sit down alone at the kitchen table and work her way steadily through a bottle of very good champagne. It was her ideal form of celebration—unalloyed pampering in the company she liked best in the world.

When her mistress sat down, Gigi, demonstrating her customary lack of character, had immediately curled up on the table and gone to sleep. So the new mystery star didn't hear the rambling monologue that the exhausted author embarked on as she drank.

Mr. Whiffles, cradled in his nest of dirty blouses, underwear, and silk pajamas, could hear it. Not being blessed with the kind of anthropomorphic sensibilities enjoyed by his fictional counterpart, he couldn't, of course, understand a word. But, from the tone of voice, he didn't have much problem in getting the gist. Continued vigilance on his part was clearly called for.

Seraphina Fellowes drained the dregs of the last glass and rose, a little unsteadily, to her feet. As she did so, she caught sight of Mr. Whiffles through the open utility room door. She stared dumbly at him for a moment; then an idea took hold.

Seraphina moved with surprising swiftness for one who'd just consumed a bottle of champagne, and was beside Mr. Whiffles before he'd had time to react. She swept up the arms of the silk pajama top beneath the cat and wrapped them tightly round him. Then she tucked the bundle firmly under her right arm. "You're getting to be a very dirty cat in your old age," she hissed. "Time you had a really good wash."

She was remarkably deft for someone who'd had a woman to come in and do all her washing for the previous ten years. Mr. Whiffles struggled to get free, but the tight silk tied in his legs like a straitjacket. Though he strained and meowed ferociously, it was to no avail. Seraphina's arm clinched him like a vise, and he couldn't get his claws to work through the cloth.

With her spare hand, she shoveled the rest of the dirty washing into the machine, finally pitching in the unruly bundle of pajamas. She pushed the door to with her knee, then turned to fill the plastic soap bubble.

Claws snagging on the sleek fabric, Mr. Whiffles struggled desperately to free himself. Somehow he knew that she had to open the machine's door once more, and somehow he knew that that would be his only chance.

The right amount of soap powder had been decanted. Seraphina bent down to open the door and throw the bubble in. With the sudden change of position, the champagne caught up with her. She swayed for a second, put a hand to her forehead, and shook her head to clear it.

"Quietened down a bit, have you?" she crowed to the tangled bundle of garments; then slammed the door shut. "Won't you be a nice clean boy now?" She punctuated the words with her actions, switching the dial round to the maximum number of rinses, then vindictively pulling out the knob to start the fatal cycle.

Seraphina Fellowes was a bit hung over when she woke the following morning. And the first thing that greeted her pained eyes when she opened them was a ghost.

Mr. Whiffles sat at the end of her bed, nonchalantly licking clean an upraised back leg.

Seraphina screamed, and he scampered lazily out of the bedroom.

She was far too muzzy and confused to piece together that Mr. Whiffles must have jumped out of the washing machine during the few seconds when the alcohol had caught up with her. She was too muzzy and confused for most things, really.

Her bleared gaze moved across to the chair, over which, in the fuddlement of the night before, she'd hung her new designer shirt.

The rich silk had been shredded into a maypole of tatters by avenging claws.

6. Cat on Hot Bricks

It was nine months later. A perfect summer day, drawing to its close.

On such occasions, a finely tuned heat-seeking instrument like a cat will always know where the last of the day's warmth lingers. Mr. Whiffles had many years before found out that the brick driveway in front of the house caught the final rays of sunlight and held that warmth long after the surrounding grass and flowerbeds had turned chilly. So, as daylight faded, he could always be found lying on the path, letting the stored heat of the bricks flow deliciously through his body.

Seraphina Fellowes felt very pleased with herself. Her self-esteem had taken something of a buffeting through the last months, but now she was back on course. She was on the verge of greater success than she'd ever experienced. And, to make her feel even better, she had taken delivery that morning of her new Ferrari.

Seraphina was driving the wonderful red beast back from the launch of *Gigi and the Dead Fishmonger,* and she felt powerful. The party had been full of literati and reviewers; the speech by her publisher's managing director had left no doubt about how much they valued their top-selling author; and everyone seemed agreed that the new series of books was destined to outperform even the success of the Mr. Whiffles mysteries.

Oh, yes, it might take a while for the new series to build up momentum, but there was no doubt that Mr. Whiffles would quickly be eclipsed forever.

Seraphina looked fondly down at Gigi, beautiful as ever, deeply asleep on the passenger seat. The cat had been characteristically docile at the launch, and the pair of them had been exhaustively photograpned. Gigi was much more of a fashion accessory than Mr. Whiffles could ever have been, and Seraphina had even begun to buy herself clothes with the cat's coloring in mind. One day, she reckoned, they could together make the cover of *Vogue.*

She leant across to give Gigi a stroke of gratitude, but her movement made the Ferrari swerve. She righted it with an easy flick of the steering wheel, and reminded herself to be careful. In the euphoria of the launch, she'd probably had more to drink than she should have done. Not the only occasion recently she'd overindulged. Must watch it. George was the one with the drink problem, not her.

The thought drove a little wedge of unease into her serenity. It was compounded by the recollection of a conversation she'd had at the launch with a major book reviewer. He'd expressed the heresy that he thought she'd never top the Mr. Whiffles books. Those were the ones for him; no other cat detective could begin to replace Mr. Whiffles in the public's affections.

The wedge of unease was now wide enough to split Seraphina's mind into segments of pure fury. That wretched mangy old cat was still getting more fan mail than she was! Bloody paw-prints over bloody everything!

Her anger was at its height as she turned the Ferrari into her drive. And there, lying fast asleep on the warm bricks, lay as tempting a target as Seraphina Fellowes would ever see in her entire life.

There was no thought process involved. She just slammed her foot down on the accelerator and was jolted back as the huge power of the engine took command.

Needless to say, Mr. Whiffles, alerted by some sixth or seventh sense, shot out of the way of the huge tires just in time.

The Ferrari smashed into a brick pillar at the side of the garage. Seraphina Fellowes needed five stitches in a head wound. Gigi, who'd been catapulted forward by the impact, hit her face against the dashboard and was left with an unsightly, permanent scar across her nose. For future publicity, the publishers would have to use the photographs taken at the launch; all subsequent ones would be disfigured.

And the Ferrari, needless to say, was a write-off.

7. Shooting the Cat

One morning a few weeks later, along with the rubber-banded brick of fan mail—almost all with bloody paw prints on the back—came an envelope from the publicity department of Seraphina Fellowes' publishers. She tore it open and, reading the impersonal note on the "With Compliments" slip ("These are all the reviews received to date"), decided she might need a quick swig of vodka to see her through the next few moments.

It wasn't actually that morning's *first* swig of vodka, but, Seraphina rationalized to herself, she had been under a lot of stress over the previous weeks. Once she got properly into the second Gigi book, she'd cut back.

Through the vodka bottle, as she raised it to drink, Seraphina caught sight of Mr. Whiffles, perched on her mantelpiece. The refraction of the glass distorted the features of his face, but the sneering curl to his lips was still there when she lowered the bottle.

Seraphina Fellowes firmly turned her swivel chair to face away from the fireplace, took a deep breath, and started to read the reviews of *Gigi and the Dead Fishmonger.*

She had had inklings from her publisher over the previous few weeks that the reaction hadn't been great, but still was not prepared for the blast of universal condemnation the cuttings contained. Setting aside the clever quips and snide aphorisms, the general message was: "This book is rubbish. Gigi is an entirely unbelievable and uninteresting feline sleuth. Get back to writing about Mr. Whiffles—he's great!"

As she put the bundle of clippings down on her desk, Seraphina Fellowes caught sight once again of the tabby on the mantelpiece. She would have sworn that the sneer on his face had now become a smirk of Cheshire cat proportions.

Seized by unreasoning fury, Seraphina snatched open her desk drawer and pulled out the gun she had bought all those years ago when researching the first book. Her wavering hand steadied to take aim at the cat on the mantelpiece. As she pulled the trigger, she felt as if she were lancing a boil.

Whether her aim was faulty, or whether another of Mr. Whiffles' extra senses preserved him, was hard to judge. What was undoubtedly true, though, was that the bullet missed, and before the echo of the shot died down, it had been joined by the panicked clattering of a cat-flap.

Mr. Whiffles had escaped once again.

Seraphina Fellowes' Edgar, however, the precious ceramic statuette awarded to her by the Mystery Writers of America, had been shattered into a thousand pieces.

8. All Cats are Gray in the Dark

What had started as a niggle and developed into a continuing irritation was by now a full-grown obsession. Seraphina couldn't settle down to anything—certainly not to getting on with the second Gigi mystery. The critical panning of the first had left her battered and embittered. It was a very long time since Seraphina Fellowes had felt even mildly pleased with herself.

She now spent her days lolling in the swivel chair in front of her state-of-the-art computer, gazing at the eternally renewed moving pattern of its screen saver, or drifting aimlessly around the house. She ceased to notice what clothes she put on in the mornings—or, as her sleep patterns got more erratic, afternoons. More and more white showed at the roots of her hair, but the effort of lifting the phone to make an appointment at her hairdresser's seemed insuperable. The vodka bottle was never far away.

And, with increasing certainty, Seraphina Fellowes knew that only one event could restore the self-esteem and success that were hers by right.

She could only be saved by the death of Mr. Whiffles.

One day she finally decided there would be no more pussyfooting. He was just a cat, after all. And if one believed in the proverbial nine lives, his stock of those was running very low. Seraphina decided that she really would kill him that day.

Bolstered by frequent swigs from the vodka bottle, she sat and planned.

George was away for the day, on one of his rare visits to hear his agent apologize about her inability to find a buyer for the latest George Fellowes "literary novel." So Seraphina went down to the bungalow, checked carefully that Mr. Whiffles wasn't inside, and locked the cat-flaps shut.

Then she looked in her house for Gigi. That didn't take long. The characterless, but now scar-faced, white Persian was, as ever, asleep on her mistress's bed. Seraphina firmly locked the bedroom door and the cat-flap that was set into it. The little fanlight window was still open, but Gigi would never overcome her lethargy sufficiently to leap up and climb through a fanlight.

Seraphina went down to the kitchen and prepared a toothsome plate of turkey breast, larded with a few peeled prawns. Then she sat down by the cat-flap, and waited.

In one hand she held the vodka bottle. In the other, the means that would finally bring about Mr. Whiffles' quietus.

After lengthy consideration of more exotic options, Seraphina had homed in on the traditional. From time immemorial, it had been the preferred way of removing unwanted kittens, and she saw no reason why it shouldn't also be suitable for an aging tabby like Mr. Whiffles.

She must've dozed off. It was dark in the kitchen when she heard the clatter of the outer cat-flap.

But Seraphina was instantly alert, and she knew exactly what she had to do.

It seemed an age while her quarry lingered in the little passage from the garden. But finally a tentative paw was poked through the cat-flap into the kitchen.

Seraphina Fellowes held her breath. She wasn't going to put her carefully devised plan at risk by a moment of impetuousness.

She waited as the metal flap slowly creaked open. And she waited until the entire cat outline, tail and all, was inside the room, before she pounced.

The furry body kicked and twisted, but the contest was brief. In seconds, the cat had joined the three bricks inside, and Seraphina had tied the string firmly round the sack's neck.

She didn't pause for a second. She allowed no space for

the finest needle of conscience to insert itself. Seraphina Fellowes just rushed out into the garden and hurled the meowing sack right into the middle of the fishpond.

It made a very satisfying splash. A few bubbles, then silence.

The next morning, Seraphina woke with a glow of well-being. For the first time in weeks, her immediate instinct was not to reach for the vodka bottle. Instead, she snuggled luxuriously under her duvet, feeling the comforting weight of Gigi across her shins, and planned the day ahead.

She would go up to London, for the first time in months. The morning she would devote to having her hair done. Then she'd visit a few of her favorite stores and buy some morale-boostingly expensive clothes. She wouldn't have a drink all day, but come back late afternoon, and at five o'clock, which she'd often found to be one of her most creative times, she'd start writing the first chapter of *Gigi and the Murdered Milkman.* Yes, it'd be a good day.

Seraphina Fellowes stretched languidly, then sat up, and looked down at the end of the bed.

There, licking unhurriedly at his patchy fur, his insolent green eyes locked on hers, sat Mr. Whiffles.

9. Cat's Cradle

After that, Seraphina Fellowes really did go to pieces. She didn't change her clothes, falling asleep and waking in the same garments, in a vodka-hazed world where time became elastic and meaningless. Her hair hung, lank and unwashed, now more white than black.

And the thought that drove all others from her unhinged brain was the imperative destruction of Mr. Whiffles.

Now that Gigi wasn't around—a sad, white, bedraggled lump had indeed been pulled out of the sack in the fishpond—there was no longer any limitation on the means by which that destruction could be achieved. There was no longer any risk of catching the wrong victim by mistake.

Mr. Whiffles, apparently aware of the murderous campaign against him, went into hiding. Seraphina cut off his obvious escape route by telling George the cat had died, and organizing a carpenter to board over the cat-flaps into the bungalow. George was very upset by the news, but Seraphina, as ever, didn't give a damn about her husband's feelings.

All through her own house, meanwhile, she organized an elaborate network of booby traps. "Network" was the operative word. Seraphina set up a series of wire snares around every one of the many cat-flaps. She turned the floors into a minefield of wire nooses, which, when tightened, would release counterweights on pulleys to yank their catch up to the ceiling. Designer-decorated walls were gouged out to accommodate hooks and rings, gleaming woodwork peppered with screws and cleats. The increasingly demented woman lived in a cat's cradle of tangled and intersecting wires. She ceased to eat, and lived on vodka alone.

And she waited. One day, she knew, Mr. Whiffles would come back into the death trap that had been her house.

And one day—or rather one evening—he did.

The end was very quick. Mr. Whiffles managed to negotiate the snares on the two cat-flaps into the house. He skipped nimbly over the waiting booby traps on the kitchen floor. But, entering the hall, he landed right in the middle of a noose, which, as he jumped away, tightened inexorably around one of his rear legs. He tried to pull himself free, but the wire only cut more deeply into his flesh. He let out a yowl of dismay.

At that moment, Seraphina, who had been waiting on the landing, snapped the light on, and shouted an exultant "Gotcha!" Mr. Whiffles, frozen by the shock of the sudden apparition, looked up at her.

Had Seraphina Fellowes by then been capable of pity, she

might have noticed how thin and neglected the cat looked. But her mind no longer had room in it for such thoughts—no room, in fact, for any thoughts other than felicidal ones. She reached across in triumph to free the jammed counter-weight that would send her captive slamming fatally up against the ceiling.

But, as she moved, she stumbled, caught her foot in a stretched low-level wire, and tumbled headfirst down the staircase.

Seraphina Fellowes broke her neck and died instantly.

Mr. Whiffles, jumping out of the way of the descending body, had moved closer to the anchor of the noose around his leg. Its tension relaxed, the springy wire loosened, and he was able to step neatly out of the metal loop.

And he started on his next set of nine lives.

10. The Cat Who Got the Cream

George Fellowes was initially very shocked by his wife's death. But when the shock receded, he had to confess to himself that he didn't really mind that much. And that her absence did bring with it certain positive advantages.

For a start, he no longer had the feeling of permanent, brooding disapproval from the house at the other side of the garden. He also inherited her state-of-the-art computer. At first he was a bit sniffy about this, but as he started to play with it, he quickly became converted to its many conveniences.

Then there was the money. In the press coverage of Seraphina Fellowes' death, her recent doomed attempt to start a new series of cat mysteries had been quickly forgotten. But interest in Mr. Whiffles grew and grew. All the titles were reissued in paperback, and the idea of a Hollywood movie using computer animation, which had been around for ages, suddenly got hot again. The agents of various megastars contacted the production company, discreetly offering their client's services for the year's plum job—voicing Mr. Whiffles.

So, like a tidal wave, the money started to roll in. And, because his wife had never divorced him, George Fellowes got the lot.

More important than all of this, Seraphina's death freed her Catholic husband to remarry. And there was someone George had had in mind for years for just such an eventuality.

The evening of Seraphina's funeral, George was sprawled across his desk, asleep in front of the evermoving screen saver of his late wife's computer, so he didn't hear the rattle of the reopened cat-flap. He wasn't aware of Mr. Whiffles' entrance, even when the old cat landed quietly on his desk top, but a nuzzling furry nose in his ear soon woke him.

"How're you, old boy?" asked George, reaching up with his left hand to scratch Mr. Whiffles in a favorite place, just behind the ear. At the same time, George's right hand reached out instinctively to the nearly full litre of vodka that stood on the edge of his desk.

Mr. Whiffles, however, had other ideas. Speeding across the surface, he deliberately knocked the bottle over. It lay sideways at the edge of the desk, its contents glugging steadily away into the wastepaper basket.

George Fellowes looked at his cat in amazement, as Mr. Whiffles moved across to the computer. One front paw was placed firmly on the mouse. (That bit was easy; for centuries cats have been instinctively placing their front paws on mice.) But, as the screen saver gave way to a white screen ready for writing, Mr. Whiffles did something else, something much more remarkable.

He placed his other front paw on the keyboard. Not just anywhere on the keyboard, but on one specific key. The "M."

Obedient to the computer's programming, two words appeared on the screen. "Mr. Whiffles."

George Fellowes felt the challenge in the old green eyes that were turned to look at him. For a moment he was undecided. Then, out loud, he said, "What the hell? I'm certainly not getting anywhere with my so-called 'literary' novels."

And his fingers reached forward to the keyboard to complete the title: "Mr. Whiffles and the Murdered Mystery Writer."

Simon Brett supplies a new and decidedly eccentric answer to the question, "There are more ways to kill a cat" in this rollicking tale of a desperate author and her smug feline. Brett, a former BBC producer, has written numerous mystery novels including two series featuring alcoholic actor Charles Paris and the widowed Mrs. Pargeter, and such nonseries mysteries as *A Shock to the System.*

Mea Culpa

Jan Burke

It was going to be my turn next, and I should have been thinking about my sins, but I never could concentrate on my own sins—big as they were—once Harvey started his confession. I tried not to listen, but Harvey was a loud talker, and there was just no way that one wooden door was going to keep me from hearing him. There are lots of things I'm not good at anymore, but my hearing is pretty sharp. I wasn't trying to listen in on him, though. He was just talking loud. I tried praying, I tried humming "Ave Maria" to myself, but nothing worked. Maybe it was because Harvey was talking about wanting to divorce my mother.

It was only me and Father O'Brien and Harvey in the church then, anyway. Just like always. Harvey said he was embarrassed about me, on account of me being a cripple, and that's why he always waited until confessions were almost over. That way, none of his buddies on the parish council or in the Knights of Columbus would see him with me. But later, I figured it was because Harvey didn't want anybody to know he had sins.

Whatever the reason, on most Saturday nights, we'd get into his black Chrysler Imperial—a brand-spanking-new soft-seated car, with big fins on the back, push-button automatic transmission and purple dashlights. We'd drive to church late and wait in the parking lot. When almost all the other cars were gone, he'd tell me to get out, to go on in and check on things.

I would get my crutches and go up the steps and struggle to get one of the big doors open and get myself inside the church. (That part was okay. Lots of other folks would try to do things for me, but Harvey let me do them on my own. I try to think of good things to say about Harvey. There aren't many, but that is one.)

I'd bless myself with holy water, then take a peek along the side aisle. Usually, only a few people were standing in line for confession by then. I'd go on up into the choir loft. I learned this way of going up the stairs real quietly. The stairs were old and wooden and creaked, but I figured out which ones groaned the loudest and where to step just right, so that I could do it without making much noise. I'd cross the choir loft and stand near one of the stained glass windows that faced the parking lot and wait to give Harvey the signal.

I always liked this time the best, the waiting time. It was dark up in the loft, and until the last people in line went into the confessional, I was in a secret world of my own. I could move closer to the railing and watch the faces of the people who waited in line. Sometimes, I'd time the people who had gone into the confessionals. If they were in there for a while, I would imagine what sins they were taking so long to tell. If they just went in and came out quick, I'd wonder if they were really good or just big liars.

Sometimes I would pray and do the kind of stuff you're supposed to do in a church. But I'm trying to tell the truth here, and the truth is that most often, my time up in that choir loft was spent thinking about Mary Theresa Mills. Her name was on the stained glass window I was supposed to signal from. It was a window of Jesus and the little children, and at the bottom it said it was "In memory of my beloved daughter, Mary Theresa Mills, 1902-1909." If the moon was bright, the light would come in through the window. It was so beautiful then, it always made me feel like I was in a holy place.

Sometimes I'd sit up there and think about her like a word problem in arithmetic: *Mary Theresa Mills died fifty years ago. She died when she was seven. If she had lived, how old would she be today, in 1959?* Answer: Fifty-seven, except if she hasn't had her birthday yet, so maybe fifty-six. (That kind of answer always gets me in trouble with my teacher, who would say it should just be fifty-seven. Period.)

I thought about her in other ways, too. I figured she must have been a good kid, not rotten like me. No one will ever make a window like that in my memory. It was kind of sad, thinking that someone good had died young like that, and for the past fifty years, there had been no Mary Theresa Mills.

There was a lamp near the Mary Theresa Mills window. The lamp was on top of the case where they kept the choir music, and that case was just below the window. When the last person went into the confessional, I'd turn the lamp on, and Harvey'd know he could come on in without seeing any of his friends. I'd wait until I saw him come in, then I'd turn out the lamp and head downstairs.

Once, I didn't wait, and I reached the bottom of the stairs when Harvey came into the church. A lady came down the aisle just then, and when she saw me she said, "Oh, you poor dear!" I really hate it when people act like that. She turned to Harvey, who was getting all red in the face and said, "Polio?"

I said, "No," just as Harvey said, "Yes." That just made him angrier. The lady looked confused, but Harvey was staring at me and not saying anything, so I just stared back. The lady said, "Oh dear!" and I guess that snapped Harvey out of it. He smiled real big and laughed this fake laugh of his and patted me on the head. Right then, I knew I was going to get it. Harvey only acts smiley like that when he has a certain kind of plan in mind. It fooled the lady, but it didn't fool me. Sure enough, as soon as she was out the door, I caught it from Harvey, right there in the church. He's no shrimp, and even openhanded, he packs a wallop.

Later, I listened, but he didn't confess the lie. He didn't confess smacking me, either, but Harvey told me a long time ago that nowhere in the Ten Commandments does it say, "Thou shalt not smack thy kid or thy wife." I wish it did, but then he'd probably just say that it didn't say anything about smacking thy stepkid. That's why, after that, I waited until Harvey had walked in and was on his way down the aisle before I came down the stairs.

So Harvey had been in the confessional for a little while before I made my way to stand outside of it. I could have gone into the other confessional, and I would, just as soon as I heard Harvey start the Act of Contrition—the last prayer a person says in confession. You can tell when someone's in a confessional because the kneeler has a gizmo on it that turns a light on over the door. When the person is finished, and gets up off the kneeler, the light goes out. But I knew Harvey's timing and I waited for that prayer instead, because, since the accident, I can't kneel so good. And once I get down on my knees. I have a hard time getting up again. Father O'Brien once told me I didn't have to kneel, but it doesn't seem right to me, so now he waits for me to get situated.

Like I said, I was trying not to eavesdrop, but Harvey was going on and on about my mom, saying she was the reason he drank and swore and committed sins, and how he would be a better Catholic if there was just some way he could have the marriage annulled. I was getting angrier and angrier, and I knew that was a sin, too. I couldn't hear Father O'Brien's side of it, but it was obvious that Harvey wasn't getting the answer he wanted. Harvey started complaining about me, and that wasn't so bad, but then he got going about Mom again.

I was so mad, I almost forget to hurry up and get into the confessional when he started the Act of Contrition. Once inside, I made myself calm down, and started my confession. It wasn't hard for me to feel truly sorry, for the first sin I confessed weighed down on me more than anything I have ever done.

"Bless me, Father, for I have sinned. I killed my father."

I heard a sigh from the other side of the screen.

"My son," Father O'Brien began, "have you ever confessed this sin before?"

"Yes, Father."

"And received absolution?"

"Yes, Father."

"And have you done the penance asked of you?"

"Yes, Father."

"You don't believe in the power of the Sacrament of Penance, of the forgiveness of sins?"

I didn't want to make him mad, but I had to tell him the truth. "If God has forgiven me, Father, why do I still feel so bad about it?"

"I don't think God ever blamed you in the first place," he said, but now he didn't sound frustrated, just kind of sad. "I think you've blamed yourself. The reason you feel bad isn't because God hasn't forgiven you. It's because you haven't forgiven yourself."

"But if I hadn't asked—"

"—for the Davy Crockett hat for your seventh birthday, he wouldn't have driven in the rain," Father O'Brien finished for me. "Yes, I know. He loved you, and he wanted to give you something that would bring you joy. You didn't kill your father by asking for a hat."

"It's not just that," I said.

"I know. You made him laugh."

I didn't say anything for a long time. I was seeing my dad, sitting next to me in the car three years ago, the day gray and wet, but me hardly noticing, because I was so excited about that stupid cap. We were going somewhere together, just me and my dad, and that was exciting, too. The radio was on, and there was something about Dwight D. Eisenhower on the news. I asked my dad why we didn't like Ike.

"We like him fine," my father said.

"Then why are we voting for Yodelai Stevenson?" I asked him.

See how dumb I was? I didn't even know that the man's name was Adlai. Called him Yodelai, like he was some guy singing in the Alps.

My dad started laughing. Hard. I started laughing, too, just because he's laughing so hard. So stupid, I don't even know what's so funny. But then suddenly, he's trying to stop the car and it's skidding, skidding, skidding and he's reaching over, he's putting his arm across my chest, trying to keep me from getting hurt. There was a loud, low noise—a bang—and a high, jingling sound—glass flying. I've tried, but I can't remember anything else that happened that day.

My father died. I ended up crippled. The car was totaled. Adlai Stevenson lost the election. My mom married Harvey. And just in case you're wondering, no, I never got that dumb cap, and I don't want one. Ever.

Father O'Brien was giving me my penance, so I stopped thinking about the accident. I made a good Act of Contrition and went to work on standing up again. I knew Harvey watched for the light to go off over the confessional door, used it as a signal that I would be coming out soon. I could hear his footsteps. He'd always go back to the car before I could manage to get myself out of the confessional.

On the drive home, Harvey was quiet. He didn't lecture to me or brag on himself. When I was slow getting out of the car, he didn't yell at me or cuff my ear. That's not like him, and it worried me. He was thinking hard about something, and I had a creepy feeling that it couldn't be good.

The next day was a Sunday. Harvey and my mom went over to the parish hall after Mass. There was a meeting about the money the parish needed to raise to make some repairs. I asked my mom if I could stay in the church for a while. Harvey was always happy to get rid of me, so he said okay, even though he wasn't the one I was asking. My mom just nodded.

The reason I wanted to stay behind was because in the

announcements that Sunday, Father O'Brien had said something about the choir loft being closed the next week, so that the stairs could be fixed. I wanted to see the window before they closed the loft. I had never gone up there in the daylight, but this might be my only chance to visit it for a while. As I made my way up the stairs, out of habit I was quiet. I avoided the stairs that creaked and groaned the most. I guess that's why I scared the old lady who was sitting up there in the choir loft. At first, she scared me, too.

She was wearing a long, old-fashioned black dress and a big black hat with a black veil, which made her look spooky. She was thin and really, really old. She had lifted the veil away from her face, and I could see it was all wrinkled. She probably had bony hands, but she was wearing gloves, so that's just a guess.

I almost left, but then I saw the window. It made me stop breathing for a minute. Colors filled the choir loft, like a rainbow had decided to come inside for a while. The window itself was bright, and I could see details in the picture that I had never seen before. I started moving closer to it, kind of hypnotized. Before I knew it, I was standing near the old lady, and now I could see she had been crying. Even though she still looked ancient, she didn't seem so scary. I was going to ask her if she was okay, but before I could say anything, she said, "What are you doing here?"

Her voice was kind of snooty, so I almost said, "It's a free country," but being in church on a Sunday, I decided against it. "I like this window," I said.

"Do you?" She seemed surprised.

"Yes. It's the Mary Theresa Mills window. She died when she was little, a long time ago," I said. For some reason, I felt like I had to prove to this lady that I had a real reason to be up there, that I wasn't just some kid who had climbed up to the choir loft to hide or to throw spitballs down on the pews. I told her everything I had figured out about Mary Theresa Mills's age, including the birthday part. "So if she had lived, she'd be old now, like you."

The lady frowned a little.

"She was really good," I went on. "She was practically perfect. Her mother and father loved her so much, they paid a lot of money and put this window up here, so that no one would ever forget her."

The old lady started crying again. "She wasn't perfect," she said. "She was a little mischievous. But I did love her."

"You knew her?"

"I'm her mother," the lady said.

I sat down. I couldn't think of anything to say, even though I had a lot of questions about Mary Theresa. It just didn't seem right to ask them.

The lady reached into her purse and got a fancy handkerchief out. "She was killed in an automobile accident," she said. "It was my fault."

I guess I looked a little sick or something when she said that, because she asked me if I was all right.

"My dad died in a car accident."

She just tilted her head a little, and something seemed different about her eyes, the way she looked at me. She didn't say, "I'm so sorry," or any of the other things people say just to be saying something. And the look wasn't a pity look; she just studied me.

I rubbed my bad knee a little. I was pretty sure there was rain on the way, but I decided I wouldn't give her a weather report.

"Is there much pain?" she asked, watching me.

I shrugged. "I'm okay."

We sat there in silence for a time. I started doing some figuring in my head, and realized that I had been in my car accident at the same age her daughter died in one.

"Were you driving?" I asked.

"Pardon?"

"You said it was your fault she died. Were you driving?"

"No," she said. "Her father was driving." She hesitated, then added, "We were separated at the time. He asked if he could take her for a ride in the car. Cars were just coming into their own then, you know."

"You mean you rode horses?" I asked.

"Sometimes. Mostly I rode in a carriage or a buggy. My parents were well-to-do, and I was living with them at the time. I don't think they trusted automobiles much. Cars were becoming more and more popular, though. My husband bought one."

"I thought you were divorced."

"No, not divorced, separated. We were both Catholics. We weren't even legally separated. In fact, the day they died, I thought we might be reconciling."

"What's that?"

"Getting back together. I thought he had changed, you see. He stopped drinking, got a job, spoke to me sweetly. He pulled up in a shiny new motor car, and offered to take Mary Theresa for a ride. They never came back. He abducted her—kidnapped her, you might say. She was his daughter, there was no divorce, and nothing legally barring him from doing exactly what he did."

"How did the accident happen?"

"My husband tried to put a great distance between us by driving all night. He fell asleep at the wheel. The car went off the road and down an embankment. They were both killed instantly, I was told. I've always prayed that was true."

I didn't say anything. She was crying again. I pulled out a couple of tissues I had in my pocket and held them out to her, figuring that lace hankie was probably soaked already.

She thanked me and took one of them from me. After a minute, she said, "I should have known! I should have known that a leopard doesn't change his spots! I entrusted the safety of my child to a man whom I knew to be unworthy of that trust."

I started to tell her that it wasn't her fault, that she shouldn't blame herself, but before the words were out of my mouth, I knew I had no business saying anything like that to her. I knew how she was feeling. It bothered me to see her so upset. Without really thinking much about what I was doing, I started telling her about the day my father died.

Since I'm being completely honest here, I've got to tell

you that I had to use that other tissue. She waited for me to blow my nose, then said, "Have you ever talked to your mother about how you feel?"

I shook my head. "She wanted me to, but since the accident—we aren't as close as we used to be, I guess. I think that's why she got together with Harvey. I think she got lonely."

About then, my mother came into the church, and called up to me. I told her I'd be right down. She said they'd be waiting in the car.

As I got up, the old lady put a hand on me. "Promise me that you will talk to your mother tonight."

"About what?"

"Anything. A boy should be able to talk to his mother about anything. Tell her what we talked about, if you like. I won't mind."

"Okay, I will," I said, "but who will you talk to when you start feeling bad about Mary Theresa?"

She didn't answer. She just looked sad again. Just before I left, I told her which steps to watch out for. I also told her to carry an umbrella if she went out that evening, because it was going to rain. I don't know if she took any of my good advice.

In the car, I got worried again. I was expecting Harvey to be mad because I kept them waiting. But he didn't say anything to me, and when he talked to my mom, he was sweet as pie. I don't talk when I'm in a car anymore, or I might have said something about that.

Harvey went out not long after we got home. My mother said we'd be eating Sunday dinner by ourselves, that Harvey had a business meeting he had to go to. I don't think she really believed he had a business meeting on a Sunday afternoon. I sure didn't believe it. My mom and I don't get to be by ourselves too much, though, so I was too happy about that to complain about Harvey.

My promise to Mary Theresa's mother was on my mind, so when my mother asked me what I was doing up there in the choir loft, I took it as a sign. I told her the whole story, about the window and Mary Theresa and even about the accident. It was the second time I had told it in one day, so it wasn't so rough on me, but I think it was hard on her. She didn't seem to mind, and I even let her hug me.

It rained that night, just like my knee said it would. My mom came in to check on me, saying she knew that the rain sometimes bothered me. I was feeling all right, though, and I told her I thought I would sleep fine. We smiled at each other, like we had a secret, a good secret. It was the first time in a few years that we had been happy at the same time.

I woke up when Harvey came home. When I heard him put the Imperial in the garage, I got out of bed and peeked from behind my bedroom door. I knew he had lied to my mom, and if he was drunk or started to get mean with her, I decided I was gonna bash him with one of my crutches.

He came in the front door. He was wet. I had to clamp my hand over my mouth to keep from laughing, because I realized that he had gone out without his umbrella. He looked silly. The rain and wind had messed up his hair, so that his long side—the side he tries to comb over his bald spot—was hanging straight down. He closed the front door really carefully, then he went into the bathroom near my bedroom, instead of the one off of his room. At first I thought he was just sneaking in and trying not to wake up my mom, but he was in there a long time. When he came out, he was in his underwear. I almost busted a gut trying not to laugh. He tiptoed past me and went to bed. The clock was striking three.

I waited until I thought he might be asleep, then I went into the bathroom. There was water all over the place. He hadn't mopped up after himself, so I took a towel and dried the floor and counter. It was while I was drying the floor that I saw the book of matches. It had a red cover on it, and it came from a place called Topper's, an all-night restaurant down on South Street. I picked up the matchbook. A few of the matches had been used. The name "Mackie" was written on the inside, and just below that, "1417 A-3." I closed the cover and looked at the address for Topper's. 1400 South Street. I knew Harvey's handwriting well enough to know that he had written that name and address.

What was he doing with matches? Harvey didn't smoke. He hated smoke. I knew, because he had made a big speech about it on the day he threw away my dad's pipes. I had gone into the trash and taken them back out. I put them in a little wooden box, the same one where I kept a photo of my dad. I never looked at the photo or the pipes, but I kept them anyway. I thought my mom might have found the place I hid them, but so far, she hadn't ratted on me.

I opened the laundry hamper. Harvey's wet clothes were in there. I reached in and pulled out his shirt. No lipstick stains, and even without lifting it close to my nose, I could tell it didn't have perfume on it. It could have used some. It smelled like smoke, a real strong kind of smoke. Not like a fire or anything, but stronger than a cigarette. A cigar, maybe. I had just put the shirt back in the hamper when the door flew open.

"What are you doing?" Harvey asked.

I should have said something like, "Ever heard of knocking?" or made some wisecrack, but I was too scared. I could feel the matchbook in my hand, hot, as if I had lit all the matches in it at once.

Luckily, my mom woke up. "Harvey?" I heard her call. It sounded like she was standing in the hall.

"Oh, did I wake you up, sweetheart?" he said.

My jaw dropped open. Harvey never talked to her like that after they got married.

"What's wrong?" she asked.

"I was just checking on the boy," he said. He looked at me and asked, "Are you okay, son?"

Son. That made me sick to my stomach. I swallowed and said, "Just came in to get some aspirin."

"Your leg bothering you because of this rain?" he asked, like he cared.

"I'll be all right. Sorry I woke you up."

My mom was at the door then, so I said, "Okay if I close the door? Now that I'm up . . . well, you know . . ."

Harvey laughed his fake laugh and put an arm around my mom. He closed the door.

I pulled a paper cup out of the dispenser in the bathroom. I turned the cup over and scratched the street numbers for Mackie and Topper's, then put the matchbook back where I found it. By now, I was so scared I really did have to go, so I didn't have to fake that. I flushed the toilet, then washed my hands. Finally, I put a little water in the cup. I opened the door. I turned to pick up the cup, and once again thought to myself that one of the things that stinks about crutches is that they take up your hands. I was going to try to carry the cup in my teeth, since it wasn't very full, but my mom is great about seeing when I'm having trouble, so she said, "Would you like to have that cup of water on your nightstand?"

I nodded.

Harvey watched us go into my bedroom. He went into the bathroom again. My mom started fussing over me, talking about maybe taking me to a new doctor. I tried to pay attention to what she was saying, but the whole time, I was worrying about what Harvey was thinking. Could he tell that I saw the matchbook? After a few minutes he came back out, and he had this smile on his face. I knew the matches wouldn't be on the floor now, that he had figured out where he had dropped them and that he had picked them up. He felt safe. I didn't. I drank the water and saved the bottom of the cup.

The next morning I got up early and went into the laundry room. Harvey's clothes were still in the bathroom, but I wasn't interested in them anyway. I put a load of his wash in the washing machine, checking his trouser pockets before I put them in. I made sixty cents just by collecting his change. I put it in my own pocket, right next to the waxy paper from the cup.

I had just started the washer when my mom and Harvey

came into the kitchen. My mom got the percolator and the toaster going. Harvey glared at me while I straightened up the laundry room and put the soap away.

"You're gonna turn him into a pansy, lettin' him do little girl's work like that," he said to my mom when she brought him his coffee and toast.

"I like being able to help." I said, before she could answer.

We both waited for him to come over and cuff me one for arguing with him first thing in the morning, but he just grunted and stirred a bunch of sugar into his coffee. He always put about half the sugar bowl into his coffee. You'd think it would have made him sweeter.

That morning, it seemed like it did. Once he woke up a little more, he started talking to her like a guy in a movie talks to a girl just before he kisses her. I left the house as soon as I could.

Before I left, I told my mom that I might be home late from school. I told her that I might catch a matinee with some of the other kids. I never do anything with other kids, and she seemed excited when I told her that lie. I felt bad about lying, even if it made her happy.

All day, I was a terrible student. I just kept thinking about the matchbook and about Mary Theresa's father and Harvey and leopards that don't change their spots.

After school, I took the city bus downtown. I got off at South Street, right in front of Topper's.

The buildings are tall in that part of town. There wasn't much sunlight, but up above the street, there were clotheslines between the buildings. The day was cloudy, so nobody had any clothes out, although I could have told them it wasn't going to rain that afternoon. Not that there was anything to rain on—nothing was growing there. The sidewalks and street were still damp, though, and not many people were around. I was a little nervous.

I thought about going into Topper's and asking if anybody knew a guy named Mackie, but decided that wouldn't be too smart. I started down the street. 1405 was the next address. Linden's Tobacco Shop. I had already noticed that sometimes they skip numbers downtown. I stopped, thinking maybe that was where Harvey got the smoke on his clothes. Just then a man came out of the door and didn't close it behind him as he left the shop. As I stood in the doorway, a sweet, familiar smell came to me, and I felt an ache in my chest. It was pipe tobacco. It made me think of my father, and how he always smelled like tobacco and Old Spice After-Shave. A sourpussed man came to the door, said "No minors," and shut it in my face. The shop's hours were painted on the door. It was closed on Sundays.

I moved down the sidewalk, reading signs, looking in windows. "Buzzy's Newsstand—Out-of-Town Papers." "South Street Sweets—Handmade Chocolates," "Moore's Hardware—Everything for Home and Garden," "Suds-O-Mat—Coin-Operated Laundry." Finally, I came to "The Coronet—Apartments to Let." The address was 1417 South Street. The building looked older than Mary Theresa's mother.

Inside, the Coronet was dark and smelled like a mixture of old b.o. and cooked cabbage. There was a thin, worn carpet in the hallway. A-3 was the second apartment on the left-hand side. I put my ear to the door. It was quiet. I moved back from the door and was trying to decide what to do when a man came into the building. I turned and pretended to be waiting for someone to answer the door of A-4.

The man was carrying a paper sack and smoking a cigar. The cigar not only smelled better than the hallway, it smelled exactly like the smoke on Harvey's clothes. It had to be Mackie.

Mackie's face was an okay face, except that his nose looked like he had run into a wall and stayed there for a while. He was big, but he didn't look clumsy or dumb. I saw that the paper sack was from the hardware store. When he unlocked his door, I caught a glimpse of a shoulder holster. As he pulled the door open, he saw me watching him and gave me a mean look.

"Whaddaya want?" he said.

I swallowed hard and said, "I'm collecting donations for the Crippled Children's Society."

His eyes narrowed. "Oh yeah? Where's your little collection can?"

"I can't carry it and move around on the crutches," I said.

"Hmpf. You won't get anything there," he said, nodding toward the other apartment. "The place is empty."

"Oh. I guess I'll be going then."

I tried to move past him, but he pushed me hard against the wall, making me drop one of my crutches. "No hurry, is there?" he said. "Let's see if you're really a cripple."

That was easy. I dropped the other crutch, then reached down and pulled my right pant leg up. He did what anybody does when they see my bad leg. They stare at it, and not because it's beautiful.

I used this chance to look past him into his apartment. From what I could see of it, it was small and neat. There was a table with two things on it: a flat, rectangular box and the part of a shot they call a syringe. It didn't have a needle on it yet. You might think I'm showing off, but I knew it was called a syringe because I've spent a lot of time getting stuck by the full works, and sooner or later some nurse tells you more than you want to know about anything they do to you.

Mackie picked up my crutches. I was trying to see into the paper sack, but all I could make out was that it was some kind of can. When Mackie straightened up again, his neck and ears were turning red. Maybe that's what made me bold enough to say, "I lied."

His eyes narrowed again.

"I'm not collecting for Crippled Children. I was just trying to raise some movie money."

He started laughing. He reached in his pocket and pulled out a silver dollar. He dropped it into my shirt pocket. "Kid, you earned it," he said and went into his apartment.

I leaned against the wall for another minute, my heart

thumping hard against that silver dollar. Then I left and made my way to the hardware store.

No other customers were in there. The old man behind the counter was reading a newspaper. I cleared my throat. "Excuse me, sir, but Mackie sent me over to pick up another can."

"Another one? You can tell Mackie he's got to come here himself." He looked up at me and then looked away really fast. I'm used to it. "Look," he said, talking into the newspaper, "I'm not selling weed killer to any kid, crippled or no. The stuff's poisonous." That's the way he said it: "crippled or no." Like I had come in there asking for special treatment.

I had too much on my mind to worry about it. I was thinking about why a guy who lived in a place like the Coronet would need weed killer. "What's weed killer got in it, anyway?" I asked.

He folded his newspaper down and looked at me like my brain was as lame as my leg. "Arsenic. Eat a little of that and you're a goner."

At home that night, I kept an eye on Harvey. I noticed that even though he was still laying it on thick with my mom, he was nervous. He kept watching the clock on the mantle. My mom was in the kitchen, making lunches, and he kept looking between the kitchen and the clock. When the phone rang at eight, he jumped up to answer it, yelling, "I got it." To the person on the phone, he said, "Just a sec." He turned to me and said, "Get ready for bed."

I thought of arguing, but changed my mind. I went into the hallway, and waited just out of sight. I hoped he'd talk as loud as he usually did.

He tried to speak softly, but I could still hear him.

"No, no, that's too soon. I have some arrangements to make." He paused, then said, "Saturday, then. Good."

That night, when my mom came in to say good night, I told her not to let Harvey fix her anything to eat, or take anything from him that came in a rectangular box. "He wants to poison you, Mom," I whispered.

She laughed and said, "That matinee must have been a detective movie. I was waiting for you to tell me about your afternoon. Did you have a good time?"

It wasn't easy, but I told her the truth. "I didn't go to a movie," I said.

"But I thought . . ."

"I went downtown. To South Street."

She looked more scared than when I told her that her husband wanted to poison her.

"Please don't tell Harvey!" I said.

"Don't tell Harvey what?" I heard a voice say. He was standing in my bedroom door.

"Oh, that he got a bad grade on a spelling test," my mom said. "But you wouldn't get angry with him over a little thing like that, would you, dear?"

"No, of course not, sweetheart," he said to her. He faked another laugh and walked off.

Although I don't think Harvey knew it, she hadn't meant it when she called him "dear." And she had lied to him for my sake. Just when I had decided that meant she believed me about the poison, she said, "You and I will have a serious talk very soon, young man. Good night." She kissed me, but I could tell she was mad.

That was a terrible week. Harvey was nervous, I was nervous, and my mom put me on restriction. I had to come straight home after school every day. I never got far enough in the story to tell her what happened when I went downtown; she just said that where Harvey went at night was his business, not mine, and that I should never lie to her again about where I was going.

We didn't say much to one another. On Friday night, when she came in to say good night, I couldn't even make myself say good night back. She stayed there at my bedside and said, "We were off to such a good start this week. I had hoped . . . well, that doesn't matter now. I know you're angry with me for putting you on restriction, but you gave me a scare. You're all I have now, and I couldn't bear to lose you."

"You're all I have, too." I said, "I don't mind the restriction. It's just that you don't believe anything I say."

"No, that's not it. It's just that I think Harvey is trying to be a better husband. Maybe Father O'Brien has talked to him, I don't know."

"A leopard doesn't change his spots," I said.

"Harvey's not a leopard."

"He's a snake."

She sighed again. She kept sitting there.

All of a sudden, I remembered that Harvey had mentioned Saturday, which was the next day, and I sat up. I hugged her hard. "Please believe me," I said. "Just this once."

She was startled at first, probably because that was two hugs in one week, which was two more than I'd given her since she married Harvey. She hugged back, and said, "You really are scared, aren't you?"

I nodded against her shoulder.

"Okay. I won't let Harvey fix any meals for me or give me anything in a rectangular box. At least not until you get over this." She sounded like she thought it was kind of funny. "I hope it will be soon, though."

"Maybe as early as tomorrow," I whispered, but I don't think she heard me.

I hardly slept at all that night.

The next morning, Harvey left the house and didn't come back until just before dinner. He wasn't carrying anything with him when he came in the house, just went in and washed up. I watched every move he made, and he never went near any food.

"C'mon," he said to me after dinner, "let's go on down to the church."

A new thought hit me. What if the weed killer was for someone else? What if Harvey had hired Mackie to shoot my mom? "I don't want to go," I said.

"No more back talk out of you, buster. Let's go. Confessions will be over if we don't get down there."

I looked at my mom.

"Go on," she said. "I'll be fine."

As Harvey walked with me to the car, I kept trying to think up some way to stay home. I knew what Mackie looked like. I knew he carried his gun in a shoulder holster. I knew he liked silver dollars, because I had one of his in my pocket. I knew—

I looked up, because Harvey was saying something to me. He had opened the car door for me, which was more than he usually did. "Pardon?"

"I said, get yourself situated. I've got a surprise for your mother."

Before I could think of anything to say, he was opening the back door and picking up a package. A rectangular package. As he walked past me, I saw there was a label on it. South Street Sweets.

My mother took it from him, smiling and thanking him. "You know I can't resist chocolates," she said.

"Have one now," he said.

I was about to yell out "No!", thinking she'd forgotten everything I said, but she looked at me over his shoulder, and something in her eyes made me keep my mouth shut.

Harvey followed her glance, but before he could yell at me, she said, "Oh Harvey, his knee must be bothering him. Be a dear and help him. I'm going to go right in and put my feet up and eat about a dozen of these." To me, she said, "Remember what we talked about last night. You be careful."

All the way to the church, Harvey was quiet. When we got there, he sent me in first, as usual.

"But the choir loft is closed," I said.

"It hasn't fallen apart in a week. They haven't even started work on it. Go on."

I went inside. He was right. Even though there was a velvet rope and a sign that said, "Closed," it didn't look like any work had started. I wanted to be near Mary Theresa's window anyway. But as I got near the top of the stairs, I noticed they sounded different beneath my crutches. Some of the ones that were usually quiet were groaning now.

I waited until almost everyone was gone. By that time I had done more thinking. I figured Harvey wouldn't give up trying to kill my mom, even if I had wrecked his chocolate plan. He wanted the house and the money that came with my mom, but not her or her kid. I couldn't keep watching him all the time.

I turned the lamp on and waited for him to come into the church. As usual, he didn't even look toward me. He went into the confessional. I took one last look at the window and started to turn the lamp off, when I got an idea. I left the lamp on.

I knew the fourth step from the top was especially creaky. I went down to the sixth step from the top, then turned around. I held on to the rail, and then pressed one of my crutches down on the fourth step. It creaked. I leaned most of my weight on it. I felt it give. I stopped before it broke.

I went on down the stairs. I could hear Harvey, not talking about my mom this time, but not admitting he was hoping she was already dead. I went into the other confessional, but I didn't kneel down.

I heard Harvey finish up and step outside his confessional. Then I heard him take a couple of steps and stand outside my confessional door.

For a minute, I was afraid he'd open the door and look inside. He didn't. He took a couple of steps away, and then stopped again. I waited. He walked toward the back of church, and I could tell by the sound of his steps that he was mad. I knocked on the wall between me and Father O'Brien.

"All right if I don't kneel this time, Father?" I asked.

"Certainly, my son," he said.

"Bless me, Father, for I have sinned. I lied three times, I stole sixty cents, and . . ."

I waited a moment.

"And?" the priest said.

There was a loud groaning sound, a yell, and a crash.

"And I just killed my stepfather."

He didn't die, he just broke both of his legs and knocked himself out. A policeman showed up, but not because Father O'Brien had told anyone my confession. Turned out my mother had called the police, showed them the candy, and finally convinced them they had to hurry to the church and arrest her husband before he harmed her son.

The police talked to me and then went down to South Street and arrested Mackie. At the hospital, a detective went in with me to see Harvey when Harvey woke up. I got to offer Harvey some of the chocolates he had given my mom. Instead of taking any candy, he made another confession that night. Before we left, the detective asked him why he had gone up into the choir loft. He said I had left a light on up there. The detective asked me if that was true, and of course I said, "Yes."

The next time I was in church, I put Mackie's silver dollar in the donation box near the candles and lit three candles: one for my father, one for Mary Theresa Mills, and one for the guy who made up the rule that says priests can't rat on you.

After I lit the candles, I went home and took out my wooden box. I put my father's pipes on the mantle, next to his photo. My mom saw me staring at the photo and came over and stood next to me. Instead of thinking of him being off in heaven, a long way away, I imagined him being right there with us, looking back at us from that picture. I imagined him knowing that I had tried to save her from Harvey. I thought he would have liked that.

My mom reached out and touched one of the pipes very carefully. "It wasn't your fault," she said.

You know what? I believed her.

California resident Jan Burke proves that confession is good for someone's soul in this departure from her mysteries featuring newspaper reporter Irene Kelly. *Goodnight, Irene; Dear Irene; Sweet Dreams, Irene;* and *Remember Me, Irene*. *Goodnight, Irene* was nominated for Anthony and Agatha awards for Best First Novel in 1993.

The Gentleman's Gentleman

Dorothy Cannell

"I've been thinking, Dickie." Lady Felicity Entwhistle, known to her friends as Foof, pursed her cherry red lips and looked soulful.

"Bad idea, old thing, likely to give you a confounded headache," her twenty-four-year-old companion on the stone bench under the arbor smiled at her fondly. "Doesn't do, you know, to get yourself stirred up. Not with the wedding only three weeks away. Stupid idea of Mother's, having a house party this weekend. And she shouldn't have shown you those photos of Great Uncle Wilfred last night." Mr. Richard Ambleforth looked decidedly downcast. "The thought of any of our children inheriting his nose rather takes the icing off the cake."

"But that's the whole point, Dickie." Foof fussed with the strand of beads that hung to what would have been the waist of her green voile frock, if current fashion had not dictated that ladies' garments forgo shape in favor of showing what would once have been considered an unconscionable amount of leg.

"Can't say I see what you're getting at." Dickie reached

into his pocket for his cigarette case and lit up. "Spill the beans, Foof. What is the whole point?"

"That we won't be having any children." She hung her head so that her dark, silky hair swung over her ears, and even in the midst of feeling nervous and upset, part of her reveled in the tragedy of the moment. There was no denying that the grounds of Saxonbury Hall, with its formal rose gardens, rock pools, and darkly beckoning maze made a fitting setting for beauty in distress. The wind murmured mournfully among the trees and the sun slipped tactfully behind a cloud.

"No children?" Dickie took a moment to assimilate this piece of information. "Well, I don't suppose that matters, but are you sure?" He stubbed out his cigarette and placed an arm around his betrothed's dropping shoulders. "Been to see a doctor, have you? Things not quite right in the oven, is that it?"

"Oh, really, Dickie!" Foof could not keep the exasperation out of her voice even as a sob rose in her throat. "You do have a way of putting things, and I do still love you in a way, darling, but the reason we won't be having any children is that I can't marry you."

"Mother been at you again?" Dickie wore what was for him an unamiable expression. "Shouldn't take any notice if I were you, old thing. Won't have to see her if you don't like after we are married. The Pater has managed to avoid her for the best part of thirty years. Nothing to it in a house this size. And, anyway, most of the time we'll be living in the London flat."

"No, we won't." Foof stood up, but managed to resist stamping her foot. "You're making this most frightfully difficult, but the truth is I'm in love with someone else. One of those bolt of lightning things. I hate having to hurt you, but there it is. You will be a sport about it, won't you, Dickie? He's frightfully keen that you and I stay friends. That's the sort of person he is, absolutely noble, besides being the handsomest man alive." Foof clasped her hands together and her eyes took on a glow that would have rivaled the stars had this not been midafternoon.

Dickie was looking up at the sky. He decided it had turned remarkably chilly for July. "You must have drunk too much wine at lunch. Yes, that's it." He nodded his head vigorously. "You were trying to keep up with George, which is always a mistake. Never knew such a chap for knocking it back. Now, I don't say I blame him today, with Mrs. Bagworthy droning on about nothing and that ghastly girl, Madge, ogling him across the table, although one would think old George was used to that sort of thing. Girls tend to make the most alarming twits of themselves where he's concerned. He isn't the one, is he?" Dickie lit another cigarette with a determinedly steady hand. "You've not gone and fallen in love with George?"

"Betray you with your best friend?" Foof flushed a deep rose. "Honestly, Dickie! I understand your being cross with me and all that, but one would think you'd know I'd never sink that low. It's not as though I've been keeping things from you. I haven't known," her voice took on a dazed quality, "my beloved very long."

"How long?" Dickie ground out the words along with his cigarette.

Foof avoided his eyes. "Well, I know it sounds silly," she said, "but we only met this afternoon."

"You're pulling my leg!"

"I told you it was like a bolt of lightning. But you never do listen. I came out into the garden after lunch, when you were playing billiards with George. If you must know, I wanted to get away from your mother, who was buttering up to Madge like anything and making it as plain as day that she would far rather have her for a daughter-in-law. And," Foof sat back on the bench, drew up her knees and cupped her chin in her hands, "there he was, getting out of a taxi."

"A what?"

"Oh, Dickie, you're such a snob. Not everyone has to flaunt around in a chauffeur-driven car. And, looking back, I realize it was his simplicity that immediately attracted me."

Foof smiled dreamily. "Our eyes met and we moved towards each other. Just like that, Dickie, we both knew that fate had brought us irrevocably together."

"Does this blackguard have a name?"

"Of course he does. You don't think I'd fall in love with just anyone, do you?" Foof reached for his hand. "His name is Lord Dunstairs."

"What?" Dickie bounced up and almost lost his balance as one foot slid sideways on the mossy path. "You can't be serious! He has to be donkey's years old. And you can forget about fate. It was Mother who invited him for the weekend. She's been curious as all get-out about Lord Dunstairs ever since he moved down here last year. All those stories about his being a miserly recluse, living alone in that rambling old house at Barton-Among-The-Reeds got her all fired-up to bag him for one of her house parties."

"He's *not* old." Foof sat spinning her beads. "If you must know, Dickie, Lord Dunstairs isn't a day over thirty-five. And he doesn't live alone in a ramshackle way as you make it sound. He has servants like everyone else. There's a housekeeper and a valet. The housekeeper is getting a bit past it, but his man is a gem. Every bit as good as your indispensable Woodcock, from the sound of it. Sometimes, you know," Foof tossed her silky head, "I've wondered why you didn't decide to marry Woodcock instead of me; but there it is, Dickie. Don't let's have any hard feelings. Lord Dunstairs isn't the old crackpot people assumed. He's a mature man who doesn't need to be always off at his club or out shooting with his friends." Foof paused to let these words sink in. "He enjoys the quiet pleasures of his library and his wine cellar. And what it comes down to, Dickie, is that there's room in his life for a woman to matter in a terribly vital sort of way. I don't mean to be cruel and go on about him, because, really, I do love you and always shall in a way. So you will," Foof squeezed his hand, "be a brick and wish me joy?"

"I'll be damned if I'll do anything of the sort." Dickie flounced to his feet. "And anyway, aren't you being a bit premature? Surely the blighter hasn't proposed to you already?"

"No, but he did kiss me under that weeping willow over there before going into the house to meet your mother and father. And I know, fantastic as it sounds, that it's just a matter of time until he does ask me to marry him. Oh, darling, don't look at me like that. You'll find someone else. Who knows, it could even be Madge Allbright. You're wrong about her making eyes at George. It's that squint of hers that's so confusing. I've known for ages that Madge is absolutely dotty about you."

"I have to get out of here, Foof, before I choke you with those beads." Dickie could feel his own face turning suffocation red. "And that would be a pretty daft thing to do when I should be saving my energy to do in the real villain of the piece."

"Wait." Foof tugged at her finger. "I must give you the ring back."

"So I can throw it into the rock pool?" Upon this surly response Dickie retreated with all the wounded dignity he could muster, and upon entering the gloomy splendor of his ancestral home encountered his mother in the hall.

Mrs. Ambleforth was one of those deceptively comfortable-looking women, rather like an overstuffed sofa that gives no hint at first glance of the springs poking up through the upholstery. "What ever is the matter, my dearest boy?" she asked as she bustled towards her one and only offspring. "Has Foof been upsetting you?"

"If you must know, Mother," Dickie addressed one of the portraits hung upon the wainscoting, "she has broken off the engagement."

"Oh, my poor love," Mrs. Ambleforth pressed a hand to her maternal bosom, "but perhaps it is all for the best. Naturally, I never said a word, but it was clear to me from the word go that Foof was not the girl for you. And your father thought exactly the same."

"Thanks for the boost, Mother." Dickie was already

trudging up the oak stairs. "I'd prefer not to discuss the matter further."

"Of course, dear. Much wiser to put the whole foolish business out of your mind." Mrs. Ambleforth dabbed at her eyes. "Foof never deserved you. A willful creature if ever I saw one. Always flapping about and saying whatever silly thing came into her head. One dreads to think what your life would have been like with her. Now, a girl like Madge Allbright is a different story altogether! Impeccable manners and the gentlest nature."

"And about as much sex appeal as one of these banisters."

"Dickie! Really, you shouldn't say such things. Such a vulgar expression. But there, I do understand you are not thinking clearly at the moment."

"And neither are you, Mother," Dickie looked down at her from the top stair, "or instead of gloating you'd be planning what to say to people when word gets out that your son has been ditched by the lovely Lady Felicity Entwhistle."

"Good heavens!" Mrs. Ambleforth paled. "You don't suppose anyone could possibly concoct nasty stories suggesting *I'm* the cause of her backing out of the marriage? Oh, but surely not! No one who knows me could think I haven't done everything within my power to embrace Foof as a daughter. What did the tiresome girl say? What reason did she give for breaking the engagement?" Mrs. Ambleforth's voice followed her son along the upper gallery, and even when he closed his bedroom door behind him he still heard its distant vibrations.

"Ah, there you are, sir," Woodcock's voice was as soothing as massaging lotion without being the least bit oily. The consummate gentleman's gentleman, he could tell without turning round from the wardrobe, where he was putting away some freshly laundered shirts, that something was not right with his young master. "Shall I run you a bath, sir?"

"I should say not." Dickie flopped down on the four-poster bed and glowered up at the tapestry canopy. "It's hours until I need to change for dinner."

"I beg your pardon." Woodcock crossed the room with the aplomb of a prime minister. "Perhaps a glass of sherry would be in order."

"Not unless you put poison in it."

"That's one liberty you may be assured I would never take, sir."

Dickie ignored this response. "Although I don't know why," he grumbled, "I should choose to do away with myself, when it's that blasted Lord Dunstairs I should be plotting to put underground."

"The gentleman who arrived after luncheon?" Woodcock bent to remove his employer's shoes and, after a swift investigation to ascertain they had suffered no recent scuff marks, placed them on a table designated for the purpose. "Am I to assume, sir, that you did not take to Lord Dunstairs?"

"That's rum!" Dickie vented a bitter laugh. "The taking has all been on Lord Dunstairs' part!"

"I'm afraid I don't quite follow you, sir."

"Well, it's quite simple. The blighter has stolen Lady Felicity's heart. Love at first sight and all that rot. They met in the garden, and the next thing you know she is breaking off our engagement."

"Surely not, sir," Woodcock poured whiskey from a decanter, having deemed sherry insufficient to the circumstances, and upon Dickie's sitting up handed him the glass. "I have not seen Lord Dunstairs, but I had attained the impression of a gentleman well advanced in years."

"Not according to Lady Felicity, unless of course you view the age of thirty-five or so as being on the brink of decrepitude."

"Hardly, sir, given that I am myself no spring chicken."

"Rubbish," Dickie drained his glass and set it down, "you never get any older. *I'm* the one who's aged ten years in the last hour. Perhaps I should go ahead and shoot myself. The thought of her ladyship wallowing in guilt until the end of her days does rather cheer me up."

"Sir, if I might presume . . ."

"Oh, by all means, presume away." Dickie waved a languid hand, sending the whiskey glass onto the carpet.

"It occurs to me, sir," Woodcock retrieved the glass and removed it to safety, "that her ladyship may have fallen prey to the wiles of Lord Dunstairs during a period of uncertainty. Young ladies, as I understand it, are inclined to require reassurance by way of florid protestations of devotion from the gentlemen to whom they are affianced. And, if you will pardon the impertinence, sir, I am inclined to the opinion that, with your not being a person much given to effusion . . ."

"No need to go on like a confounded dictionary." Dicky sounded decidedly testy.

"Very well, sir. Shall I say that you may have failed to provide Lady Felicity with the desired assurance that you are one hundred percent—if you will pardon the vulgarism—" Woodcock cleared his throat, "bonkers about her?"

"But she *must* know." Dickie got off the bed and began pacing up and down, shoulders hunched, hands sunk deep in his pockets. "Dash it all, Woodcock, I asked her to marry me, didn't I? Not the sort of thing a chap does if he isn't enamored. Told her I would get her a spaniel bitch for her birthday. Not particularly keen on spaniels myself. Much rather have a bull mastiff, but what's a small sacrifice here and there? And I'll say this," Dickie gave the wardrobe a thump of his fist for emphasis, "the biggest sacrifice of all has been not kissing her as much as I would have liked. Never know where that sort of thing will lead, Woodcock. And you see," Dickie's voice reduced to a mutter, "for all she's so up-to-the-minute in lots of ways, Felicity's a complete innocent and only an out-and-out cad would take advantage of her. Damn Dunstairs! I'm back to thinking I'll have to bump him off. But if I understand you, Woodcock,"

Dickie sank down on the wing chair by the window, "your advice is that I try to win Lady Felicity back by fair means."

"I wouldn't go that far, sir." Woodcock smoothed out the bedspread and adjusted the angle of a reading lamp. "Certainly I would suggest that you present yourself in the most appealing light when next encountering her ladyship, but I see nothing amiss in attempting to discover if Lord Dunstairs may not be all that is desirable in a suitor. Happily, it occurs to me that the new gardener, a man by the name of Williams, came to use after working for his lordship and I will be happy to have a tactful word with him, if you should wish, sir."

"Sounds a topping idea." Dickie bounded to his feet like a man rejuvenated. "You're the best of good chaps, Woodcock. And I don't know what I would do without you. Now tell me if I have this straight. I'm to let Felicity know that I'm dashed miserable. Perhaps have a bunch of flowers sent up to her room?"

"An admirable start, sir, but I do suggest going the extra mile. Poetry, I have been given to understand, has a remarkably softening effect on the female, and if you were to exert yourself to pen a few verses . . ."

"I suppose I could try," Dickie looked doubtful, "but I've always been most awfully thick when it comes to that sort of thing. And anyway, other people have already bagged most of the best lines. I suppose it would be cheating to write 'Come into the garden, Foof, I am here at the gate alone'?"

"I am afraid so, sir."

"I can't help thinking that it might be simpler to order Lord Dunstairs from the house."

"Unwise, if I may say so, sir. Far better to trust that, during his visit here, his lordship will show himself up in such a way as to lower him in Lady Felicity's esteem."

"Yes, there is always that." With this, Dickie took himself from the room, intent on retreating to the library and thumbing through volumes of poetry in hopes of inspiration. However, he was circumvented in this plan by colliding with his friend George Stodders at the top of the stairs.

"By gad," said that gentleman, looking very sporting in knickerbockers and knee-length socks, "don't seem to be able to get away from you, old chap."

"What's that supposed to mean?" Dickie suddenly bore a striking resemblance to the portrait of his grim-faced great-grandfather hanging on the wall to his left.

"Keep your shirt on," answered George. "All I meant is that I've been stuck with the impossible Madge for the last half hour, listening to her rant on about what a sublime fellow you are. The poor girl is in a bad way for you, Dickie. Thinks it's her little secret. But head over heels in love with you."

"Well, I suppose I should be glad someone is."

"I say, what's this all about?" George's pale blue eyes narrowed. "Can see now you look a bit glum. Problems with Foof?"

"She's broken off the engagement." Dickie had always considered himself the reticent sort, and here he was spilling the beans for the third time since entering the house.

"You must be joking!" George leaned against the banister rail and produced his cigarette case.

"Only wish I were," Dickie reached for his lighter; they both lit up, and even as he determined not to say any more, the words tumbled out. "Foof has fallen hook, line, and sinker for Lord Dunstairs."

"Don't think I know him."

"Neither did Foof until just after lunch. He's here for the weekend at Mother's invitation."

"And you're telling me that he and Foof hadn't laid eyes on each other until an hour or so ago?"

"Precisely."

George's lips parted in a soundless whistle, but after a few seconds he managed to ask if Dickie had broken the news to his mother that she had invited a serpent into their midst.

"I told her the engagement was off but I didn't explain why, and she was so relieved she forgot to ask." Dickie puffed resolutely on his cigarette. "And after talking with

Woodcock just now, I'm glad I didn't give Mother the full story, because even though she's not overly keen on Foof, I'm sure she wouldn't appreciate having me, and herself in the process, made ridiculous and would insist on Father giving Lord Dunstairs the boot."

"And what would be so bad about that?" George tapped out his cigarette in a potted plant.

"Let's say I prefer to handle Lord Dunstairs in my own way."

"Going to call him out?"

"I haven't made up my mind what I'm going to do." Dickie's expression now made his great-grandfather's painted physiognomy look positively amiable by comparison. "But let me assure you," Dickie ground out his cigarette, "I intend to do whatever it takes to get Foof back."

"That's the spirit, old man!" George beamed at him. "And as your best friend, I'll do my damnedest to help out. How would it be if I suggest a game of poker after dinner and fleece the lining out of Lord Dunstairs' pockets?"

"Decent of you. But I'd rather you left things to me."

"No, no! Insist on doing my bit."

Deciding it was pointless to argue, Dickie said he was in need of solitude and wended his way downstairs to the library where he poured over the Oxford Book of English Verse for a full minute before tossing it aside and himself down on the leather sofa under the window. What he should be doing, he realized, was seeking out Lord Dunstairs and sizing up the opposition, but Dickie had the sinking feeling that so doing would only succeed in making him wish that he were taller, with a thicker head of hair and the daunting manner of a man to whom Latin and women came easily. Rather than face his rival in person, Dickie settled for an imaginary conversation in which he wiped the floor with Lord Dunstairs and afterwards turned to find Foof tearfully repentant and positively desperate to become re-engaged to him. After replaying this scenario a half dozen times, Dickie dozed off and was awakened by the chiming of the carriage clock on the mantelpiece to the realization that he had less than ten minutes in which to change for dinner.

Woodcock sped him into his dinner jacket with a minimum of commentary and Dickie set off for the dining room looking slightly more cheerful than a man about to be hanged. His palms were sweating as he pushed open the door, and it took a few seconds for the roaring inside his head to sort itself out into the voices of the people gathered in the room. Then came the necessity of shuffling the faces out of deck to get a clear view of who was present.

His mother, wearing a puce-colored frock, was standing at the far end of the table talking to the large woman in black brocade and pearls who was Mrs. Bagworthy. His father, looking rumpled and distracted as always, was endeavoring to attend to whatever George was saying to him. And, Dickie's throat tightened, there by the fireplace was Foof, looking unquestionably ravishing in a silvery frock with fringe at the hem and a glittering band encircling her forehead. It required a couple of gulps for Dickie to steady himself sufficiently to size up the man engaged in animated conversation with Lady Felicity. On the bright side, Lord Dunstairs was neither possessed of great height nor an imposing physique, but the most critical observer would have been obliged to concede that he was a not a man ever to be overlooked in a crowd. He had the dark good looks of a film star and, Dickie decided bleakly, all the assurance of a man who could charm the birds off the trees. There are times when it is good to feel invisible, and Dickie was savoring the heartwarming realization that no one appeared to have noticed his entrance, when the door banged into him from behind, shooting him several feet into the room, and Madge Allbright's voice ripped through the hum of conversation.

"I'm late again, aren't I?" She was addressing the group at large but looking at Dickie, her squint very much in evidence. "Really, I don't know why you put up with me, I'm quite impossible. Yesterday I kept you waiting and the soup was cold because I couldn't find the sash to my frock, and today it was my amber beads."

Poor Madge, thought Dickie. She's so thoroughly irritating, the kind of girl who seems to go to great lengths to make herself look as unappealing as possible. That lank hair and the frumpy frock! But she looks almost as unhappy as I am, and that makes us temporarily kindred spirits.

"Don't worry, Madge dear," Mrs. Ambleforth said in her cozy voice, "we're having a chilled soup this evening. Ah, there you are, Dickie!" She crossed the room towards her son and, under the guise of planting a kiss on his cheek, whispered to him, "I was worried, son, when you didn't come to the drawing room for drinks. And I haven't known how to behave to Foof. So difficult trying to put a brave face on things and not spoil Lord Dunstairs' visit after waiting so long to meet him. Oh, I don't think," Mrs. Ambleforth's voice returned to normal levels, "that you two have met. Lord Dunstairs!"

His lordship responded instantly to her beckoning finger. And Dickie put on his bravest face as he uncurled his fist and shook hands. "Good to have you at Saxonbury." The words were forced out between his teeth. It was impossible not to glance at Foof. "Everything to your liking, Lord Dunstairs?"

"Couldn't be better." His lordship produced what Dickie deemed a well-oiled smile, providing a glimpse of excellent teeth. "Having a bang-up time. Such a pleasure to meet everyone. And Lady Felicity was kind enough to take me through the maze."

"Don't suppose you found that a dead end."

"Meaning?" His lordship's smile now appeared decidedly malicious.

"Yes, exactly what are you getting at, Dickie?" Foof came up alongside him, a rhinestone-studded cigarette holder tucked between two fingers and her dark hair dancing about her chin.

"Just a joke." He had been effectively reduced to the

status of petulant schoolboy, and his discomfiture was only increased when Madge piped up.

"You've always been such a wit, Dickie."

"Absolutely," George had to stick in his oar. "Would keep a barrel of monkeys laughing."

"There, my dearest," Mrs. Ambleforth squeezed her son's elbow, "isn't it nice to know how fond everyone, or, I should say," shooting a furious look at Foof, "*most* people are of you?"

"What I'm fond of," Mr. Ambleforth spoke up from across the room, "is having dinner served on time." His untidy appearance, capped by hair better suited to a mad scientist, would not have created the impression that he was a slave to routine. Sometimes it seemed that the passion in his life was neither his wife nor his son but his bee-keeping activities; any unnecessary time spent away from his hives was torture. "Allow me, Mrs. Bagworthy," he said, offering his arm to that lady, "to see you to your place at table, and if the rest will be seated, my wife will ring for Mercer to bring in the first course."

There followed a scraping back of chairs and a settling of damask napkins on knees. Dickie, seated across from Foof, tried to take a particle of solace in the fact that she was still wearing her engagement ring and that Lord Dunstairs was on his side of the table, between Madge and Mrs. Bagworthy. His mother gave the bell rope a tug before assuming her place and almost instantly the door opened and a trolley was wheeled into the dining room by Woodcock.

"My goodness." Mrs. Ambleforth turned an inquiring look upon him. "Where is Mercer?"

"He is unwell, Madam. A sudden attack of lumbago. And he hopes it will not be inconvenient for me to take his place this evening." Woodcock removed the lid from the soup tureen, and while giving the contents a stir with the ladle briefly caught Dickie's eye.

"I wouldn't put up with that kind of thing," boomed Mrs. Bagworthy before Mr. or Mrs. Ambleforth could respond.

"A butler giving in to twinges! Where is this world headed? My late husband was a stickler when it came to the servants. And I still refuse to have any slacking at Cobblestone Manor."

"Have you lived there long, Mrs. Bagworthy?" Lord Dunstairs crumbled the roll on his bread and butter plate. "I've had the feeling ever since being introduced to you that I know you from somewhere. You don't by any chance originate from Butterfield, a village just outside Reading? I know the place quite well. There's quite a decent pub, The Black Horse, where I've stopped in for a drink on occasion."

"Well, I'm sure you didn't see *me* there." Mrs. Bagworthy flushed all the way down her neck and shifted in her chair, with the result that Woodcock narrowly missed spilling her soup into her lap. "I don't frequent public houses and I'm sure I've never been anywhere near," she took a deep breath, "Buttergate or whatever the place is called."

"I say! Isn't life full of surprises?" George reached for the pepper pot. "It seems people around here have had you pegged all wrong, Lord Dunstairs. I heard you didn't get out and about much and that you were . . ."

"A bit of a nutter?" His lordship smiled over the rim of his soup spoon. "Quite true, I'm afraid. I'm a regular Bluebeard, with a dozen or more wives buried under my cellar floor."

"Oh, how horrible!" Madge shrank into her chair.

"Don't be such a goose," said Foof.

"What's that?" Mr. Ambleforth started as if stung by his bees. "Goose, you say? I thought we were having rack of lamb."

"So we are, dear." His wife's laugh vibrated on the edge of irritation. "My husband has his head in the clouds half the time," she told Lord Dunstairs.

"Happens to all of us as we advance in years." His smile was exclusively for Foof. "I could have sworn I sent a note accepting your gracious invitation, Mrs. Ambleforth, and I arrive to find everyone amazed to see me."

"You really mustn't worry about it."

"But I do. I am not usually an oblivious man." Lord Dunstairs was again looking at Foof, who blushed rosily.

"I'm sure there is some perfectly simple explanation," Mrs. Ambleforth said, sounding as though she had just discovered she was sitting on a pin. "There usually is."

"Nice of you to let me off the hook so easily." Lord Dunstairs dipped his spoon into his soup and drew it to his lips. "And I do suppose the likeliest explanation is that my housekeeper forgot to post the letter. She's not the brightest woman alive, but as I'm sure you'll all agree," looking around the table, "it's almost impossible to get decent servants these days."

Dickie felt himself go hot under the collar, and was about to speak when Woodcock appeared at his side and, in handing him another roll, placed discreet pressure on his arm. The room was thus left for a few moments in uncomfortable silence, and the mood of those seated around the table never seemed to pick up during the rest of the meal. George made the liveliest attempt at conversation, but nobody paid him much attention, so with equal goodwill he began concentrating his energies on his wine glass. Madge sat fidgeting with the front of her frock as if feeling for the amber beads she had misplaced. Mrs. Bagworthy's usually unassailable appetite seemed to have failed her. Mr. Ambleforth was mainly silent, and his wife a little disjointed in her conversation. Dickie didn't want to think about what Foof had on her mind as she pushed her food around on her plate. As for Lord Dunstairs, Dickie ground his teeth and pictured what the man would look like with an egg custard sitting on his head.

At last the ladies withdrew, leaving the gentlemen to their port, and after staring glumly at the unlit cigar in his hand, Dickie excused himself, saying he had the most confounded headache. Over George's protestations that he would feel better for a game of cards, Dickie went up to his room. Twenty minutes later Woodcock joined him.

"Very clever of you," Dickie looked up from the chair in

which he was reclining, "persuading Mercer that he didn't feel up to snuff so that you could take his place at dinner."

"A liberty, sir,"

"So, what did you think of his lordship?"

"A remarkably good-looking man." Woodcock poured his employer a glass of brandy.

"That's all you can say?" Dickie glowered. "I felt like tearing his tongue out when he made that remark about it being impossible to find good help, and I would have done so if you hadn't pinched my arm."

"It was not my place to take offence, sir," Woodcock handed over the glass, "and I intended only to brush a fly off your sleeve. I do, however, most humbly beg your pardon."

"Oh, cut the cackle, you old poser!" Dickie downed half the brandy and leaned back in his chair. "If you saw nothing amiss with his lordship I'm sure I'm no end delighted. I've obviously been overreacting to his pursuit of my fiancée, and I suppose it was my blasted imagination that made me think that every time he looked at me he did so with the most gloating of expressions. Get me a refill, Woodcock," he said, handing back his glass, "while I make a mental note not to make snap decisions about people in future."

"Very wise, sir."

"Well, I wonder what his lordship is up to at this moment. Kissing Lady Felicity in the garden springs to mind, but I'm such a pessimist."

"I believe, sir," said Woodcock, lifting the decanter, "that he has engaged to play cards with Mr. Stodders. But at the moment, he may be in discussion with Mrs. Bagworthy. I saw his lordship talking with her in the alcove to the right of the stairs as I was proceeding down the gallery to this room, sir."

"Always said you're a positive mine of information." Dickie forced a smile.

"I endeavour to be of use." Woodcock dabbed around the rim of the brandy glass with a white cloth before returning it to his employer. "Is there anything more you will be needing? Because if not, sir, I would very much appreciate your permission to use the telephone. You have my assurance that I will leave fourpence in the box on the table."

"I suppose you had better," said Dickie, "even though I've never known you to use the phone before. Father often gets a bee in his bonnet (goes with the hobby), and now he's come up with the idea of making everyone—including myself and Mother—pay for our calls. Oh, stuff, perhaps it's as well Felicity won't marry me. What with Uncle Wilfred's nose and Father's nutty episodes, our children could be a sorry bunch."

During the rest of the evening, Dickie endeavored to resign himself to his lot by looking for other reasons that would indicate that being jilted was a cause for celebration. By the time he retired for the night he had drunk sufficient brandy to enable him to fall asleep after only half an hour of tossing from one side to the other. He woke once or twice during the small hours to a feeling of uneasiness, but each time fell back asleep before sorting his way through the layers of consciousness to the source. And when he sat up in bed the next morning, the only thing that was crystal clear to him was that he had the worst headache.

"Woodcock!" Dickie bellowed, but there was no response. And when he rang the bell it was one of the chambermaids, a cheeky girl by the name of Gladys, or it might have been Daisy, who popped her head round the door.

"No, I haven't seen Woodcock, sir," she responded in answer to his inquiry. "But I'll have a look and send him right up."

"No need," said Dickie. Feeling abandoned on all sides and heartily sorry for himself, he descended half an hour later to the dining room, where he found his parents sitting in state at the long table with their breakfast of bacon, kidneys, and fried mushrooms on their plates.

"Your father is in one of his moods and I can't get out of him what's the matter," said Mrs. Ambleforth as Dickie, after an unenthusiastic glance at the dishes set out on the sideboard, took his seat.

"Not keen on some of our guests." Mr. Ambleforth glowered at his wife.

"So you keep saying, dear," his wife buttered a slice of toast, "but that's not very specific, is it?"

"Well, I'm not talking about Foof. Like that girl, always have. Dickie's lucky to get her, and I won't stand for your becoming the heavy handed mother-in-law, Alice."

Before Mrs. Ambleforth could respond to this admonition, the door opened and George Stodders slunk into the room. From his unearthly pallor, Dickie concluded that his friend had a devil of a hangover, and this was borne out when George collapsed into a chair and gripped the table edge as if in hope he could stop it from spinning.

"Is there any black coffee?" he asked in a croak and, when Dickie obliged by fetching him a cup, said, "I don't know whether to drink this or drown myself in it."

"It looks to me," said Mrs. Ambleforth in her deceptively cozy voice, "that you stayed up till all hours, George, playing cards and drinking more than was good for you."

"Spot on!"

"Oh, I'm late again," bleated a voice from the doorway, and Madge blundered into the room—all elbows and darting eyes. "May I sit next to you, Dickie, since Foof isn't here?"

"Delighted."

No sooner was Madge in her seat than the door opened again to admit Mrs. Bagworthy, and coming in right behind her was Foof, looking so desperately pale that Dickie did not need to hear her whisper his name to leap to his feet and follow her out into the hall.

"Not here." She gripped his arm so tightly that her nails dug through his jacket sleeve. "Come into the library, where no one can hear us. And don't you dare say anything," she told him through quivering lips when they entered that room and she had closed the door as if bolting them in against an enemy army. "Not a word, Dickie, until I'm finished talking, unless . . ." tears spilled down Foof's cheek, "you can find it in your heart to tell me you still love me."

"Of course I do. Always have and always will." Dickie's voice sounded ludicrously high-pitched, but it was necessary to speak up in order to be heard over the pounding of his heart. "Don't cry, you silly goose." He pulled her into his arms and kissed her fiercely. "You had me worried yesterday, but I needed to be brought to my senses. Woodcock said as much. And he was right, as he almost always is. I haven't let you know, not properly," he kissed her again, "that I'm absolutely nuts about you, Foof. And my mother can go to perdition if she doesn't like it."

"I'll make her like me, I'll do anything, Dickie! Oh, if ever a girl was born a fool, it was me! It's true I wanted to shake you up, darling. Make you jealous. As if it wasn't enough to know you're the dearest man alive. Well, I've been punished." Foof stepped back from him and pressed her hands to her throat in an attempt to hold back a sob. "He has to be the most evil creature alive . . ."

"Did he," Dickie strove for some measure of control, because the last thing his beloved needed was for him to go to pieces, "did Lord Dunstairs . . . ?"

"No," said Foof, "he didn't take advantage of me, at least not in the way you mean. But oh, it was horrible. I got up early, you see, and went out into the garden. I had to clear my head after not sleeping hardly at all for wishing I hadn't been so silly—letting him kiss me after talking to him for five minutes, and then talking all that rubbish to you about being in love with him. He *is* handsome and—I'll admit it, Dickie—I *did* get in a bit of a flutter over him at first. But at dinner I realized I didn't like him at all, and when I saw him in the garden this morning, I felt sick remembering I'd let him kiss me like that. I kept thinking about what he'd said about being a Bluebeard and burying numerous wives in the cellar. And perhaps he read all that in my face, because . . ."

"Because what, Foof darling?"

She shuddered and clung to him for a moment before straightening up. "It was as though he'd finished playing one game and had started on another. He said he was leaving and asked me to thank your parents and the rest for providing him with a most amusing time. And then, Dickie, it got to be really horrible. He started ticking off on his fingers what he called the high points of his visit."

"Which were?" Dickie held Foof's hands tight but could not stop their trembling.

"Fleecing George at cards last night. He got several hundred pounds out of him. And he also got a nice little sum out of Mrs. Bagworthy, playing what he called another sort of game."

"Meaning?"

"Blackmail." Foof sat down on the nearest chair. "That's what anyone but him would call it. It seems he recognized her and knew that before she came here, having come into a large legacy, she used to be a barmaid at a pub. He said she cried when he asked how she would feel if people found out she was a 'jumped-up,' and she begged him to let her write him out a cheque."

"My God!"

"And he stuck his claws into Madge in a different way. He got her alone and told her it stuck out a mile that she was in love with you, and asked if she could imagine how people were laughing behind her back at her."

"Damnable."

"Dickie, remember how she said she couldn't find her amber beads? Well, he had them in his pocket. He pulled them out and showed them to me. And that's not all. He said he'd even helped himself to the telephone money—from that little box your father put on the table. And then he laughed in a way that made me wish I could be sick. 'Wouldn't you say I've made the most of my visit to Saxonbury Hall?' That's what he said. I told him he'd be laughing on the other side of his face when we sent for the police."

"That was very brave of you," said Dickie, "but awfully risky, Foof. What if he'd hit you over the head with a brick? It doesn't bear thinking about."

"I was afraid for a minute that he would go for me, because it was as clear as day that he was completely wicked.

But do you know, Dickie, I think what he did was just as scary. He just smiled and said nobody was going to ring up the police because doing so would mean all those nasty little secrets coming out, and we wouldn't want that, would we?"

"So now we know," said Dickie, "why his lordship doesn't get out and about much. Who'd want him for a house guest? And I'm willing to bet that those servants of his are employed by some relative or other to keep him under lock and key." He was about to say more when a disturbance was heard in the corridor outside: upraised voices, and a screech that sounded as if it could have come from Madge. Seconds later, the door burst open and a wild-eyed George brought Dickie and Foof to their feet.

"You won't believe it," he cried. "The gardener just came running into the house to say that he was doing a bit of trimming and found Lord Dunstairs, dead as a doornail, inside the maze. Your father's ringing up the police, because," George took a deep breath, "it appears his lordship was strangled. Oh, I say! What's wrong with Foof?"

"She fainted, you clot!" Dickie had caught his beloved before she could slump to the floor. "Get out of here, George, and don't let anyone in here, least of all my mother."

"Aye, aye, sir!"

The door closed and Foof opened her eyes as Dickie lowered her onto the leather sofa. "I didn't," she clutched at his jacket lapel, "truly, I didn't kill him."

"Of course you didn't, darling!"

"But the police will think I did! They're fiendishly clever, Dickie. They'll ask all sorts of innocent-sounding questions and get it out of me that Lord Dunstairs played me for a silly little fool."

"He made monkeys out of everyone here. And one of them killed him. Oh, my God! What if it was my father, Foof? He's got a few spokes missing when it comes to such things as his bees and the telephone money. He could have seen Dunstairs emptying the box and gone after him in a blind rage. And there's my mother! I'm sure she noticed the looks he was giving you last night! What if she suddenly saw herself as a lioness protecting her one and only cub?"

"Oh, you poor darling!" Foof sat up and reached for his hand. "What a fix to be in, because of course we can't spill the beans about everyone having a motive to do away with that monster. It simply isn't done, turning in one's friends. I'll just have to let them take me away and hope like anything the judge is a kind old man, with a soft spot for pretty young women. It would be quite awful to be hanged; but, God willing," her voice broke, "I suppose I would get used to prison food in time, even though I am the most dreadfully picky eater."

"You're trying to make me laugh." Dickie kissed her cherry lips and stroked her silky dark hair back from her forehead. "And I adore you for being brave, but there's really no need. Don't you see, my treasure, I am the obvious suspect. I've talked about wanting to kill Lord Dunstairs for tampering with your affections."

"Oh, darling." Foof clung to him as if fearing he would be torn away from her by the arms of the law at any moment. "I don't believe any sensible person could seriously suspect you. And it would be too cruel, when I so desperately want us to get married and have a dozen children, even if they all have Uncle Wilfred's nose. Surely the real murderer will own up. It would be the only decent thing to do."

"I beg your pardon for the intrusion," Woodcock's voice jerked them apart, "but I thought you would wish to know that the body, covered with some sacking so as not to alarm the ladies, has been brought into the house and placed in the study. And I thought, sir," he said, looking keenly at Dickie, "that you might wish to make a positive identification before the police arrive. They tend to be sticklers, and might deem the gardener to be a man who flusters easily and not, therefore, to be entirely relied on in such a matter."

"Oh, for heaven's sake," Dickie said crossly, "isn't it abundantly clear that I have to stay with Lady Felicity?"

"I'll come with you. No, really." Foof got to her feet. "I

think I need to see him to convince myself that he really is dead and not just pretending."

"If you will excuse the liberty, your ladyship," Woodcock looked at her with troubled eyes, "I do believe it would be wiser to leave this to Mr. Ambleforth."

"Rubbish," she retorted roundly, and Dickie knew she would only stay put if he tied her to the sofa—an impossibility given that he had no rope handy. So he took her arm and led her in Woodcock's wake to the study. He felt her sway against him for a fraction of a second before standing up very straight and staring unflinchingly at the desk, which was sufficiently sizable for the body (covered in sacking, as Woodcock had described) to have been laid out on its leather top.

"Pull that stuff back, please, Woodcock," she said in a tight little voice, "and let us take a look."

"As you wish, my lady." He moved to one end of the desk and turned back a corner, sufficient for them to view the face of the dead man.

"But it isn't him." Foof and Dickie almost fell over each other as they leaned closer.

"Isn't whom?" responded Woodcock.

"Lord Dunstairs."

"If you will pardon the impertinence, I have to disagree with you. This *is* his lordship."

"But he is an old man." Foof looked quite exasperated. "And I have most certainly never seen him before in my life."

"But Williams the gardener has, and as I mentioned to Mr. Ambleforth last night, he worked for his lordship until recently, before coming here, and he was in no doubt as to this gentleman's identity."

"Then who . . . ?" Dickie watched, spellbound, as Woodcock replaced the triangle of sacking.

"Who was the so-called gentleman who came here under false pretenses? It is my belief, sir, that he was Lord Dunstairs' valet. A man by the name of Villers. I had my suspicions that he was not the genuine article when you mentioned to me that he had arrived in a taxi. That struck me as decidedly odd. Gentlemen of Lord Dunstairs' sort do not usually arrive in taxis. And then last night, when I was serving dinner, I was struck by the way the supposed Lord Dunstairs partook of his soup. Rather than lifting his spoon away from him in a backwards motion, as is considered proper, he lifted it directly to his lips as," Woodcock smiled without amusement, "I myself might do. Given my suspicions, I asked your permission, sir, to make a telephone call."

"So, you did," said Dickie.

"I was able to reach Lord Dunstairs' housekeeper. A sensible and quick-witted woman from the sound of her. And in the course of our conversation I ascertained that his lordship had that afternoon given his valet notice, after discovering that the man had not been dealing honestly with him."

"So that's who turned up here." Foof stood very still. "Yes, I can imagine him delighting in pulling such a stunt for the sheer malicious thrill of it. All that talk at dinner about his letter accepting your parents' invitation going astray, Dickie. I don't suppose his lordship ever wrote a response."

"The housekeeper was quite sure he hadn't," said Woodcock. "She explained to me that her employer had been in failing health for some time, and was besides of a reclusive nature, who rarely opened any of his post. She told me she would not wake him to relay my suspicions as he was already in bed for the night, but would speak to him first thing in the morning. I must assume she did so, and that, thoroughly outraged, his lordship got into his car, a risky business in his infirm state, and drove over here at the crack of dawn."

"Where he met Villers in the garden after I went back into the house." Flora looked sadly at the desk. "Oh, how I hope the police catch up with your murderer, Lord Dunstairs."

"I am convinced they will, your ladyship," said Woodcock. "I just now took the liberty of telephoning Police

Constable Jones, an acquaintance of mine, and put him in possession of the facts. One of which is that there is no sign of his lordship's car, which would indicate that Villers made away in it after hiding the body in the maze, where it might not have been discovered for some time had the gardener not been working on it."

"You never cease to amaze me." Dickie managed a smile while wondering if Foof was inwardly doing battle with the realization that, among her other woes, she had been kissed by a valet, but he decided he had in all likelihood done her an injustice when she left his side to press her bright lips against Woodcock's cheek.

"I know you feel awful about Lord Dunstairs," she said, "but you mustn't blame yourself in any way for his death, and I want you to know that if I weren't promised to Dickie I would definitely set my cap at you, dearest Woodcock."

"Thank you, my lady." The usually imperturbable gentleman's gentleman looked suspiciously moist around the eyes. "I feel entirely undeserving of your appreciation, given the fact that this morning I overslept, not having slept well last night, and for the first time failed in my morning duties to Mr. Ambleforth."

"Shocking," said Dickie with a severe expression and a wink at Foof. "I think I may have to replace you, Woodcock, but not for thirty or forty years. It's not easy these days to find help who can save a chap from being sent up on a charge of murder."

In this story, transplanted Brit and Illinois resident Dorothy Cannell provides another of her hilarious send-ups of the English country house mystery. Author of the Ellie Haskell series *(The Thin Woman, Down the Garden Path, The Widow's Club, Mum's the Word, Femmes Fatal, How to Murder Your Mother-in-Law),* Cannell won an Agatha for Best Short Story in 1995 for "The Family Jewels."

Malice Among Friends

Sarah Caudwell

Veronica I recognized at once. If I hesitated to cross the room and greet her with the warmth usually shown by a novelist to a distinguished literary critic, it was because of a moment's disconcerting doubt about her companion, who looked so much like—and yet could not possibly be—so amazingly like Rosemary.

Once, certainly, they had been friends. Until halfway through our second year at Oxford they had wandered constantly in and out of each other's rooms, making each other coffee, sharing suppers of burnt scrambled eggs, exchanging books, records, and confidences. The friendship between them—Veronica dark, angular, and reserved, Rosemary an effervescent blonde—seemed a striking example of the attraction of opposites. It had ended, however, in a degree of rancor that the passage of a mere twenty years could not be expected to assuage.

A man, I need hardly say, was the cause of the trouble—one Geoffrey, reading English at Balliol—though not altogether in the usual way. Neither his attachment to Rosemary nor its reciprocation would have caused Veronica any resentment. There was, however, another factor in the equation: the editorship of *Abattoir*—an undergraduate journal doubtless now long forgotten, but whose columns we thought then a sure stepping-stone to intellectual glory. Geoffrey desired it above all things; so did Veronica.

Geoffrey was the favorite for the post, Veronica an almost hopeless outsider. The members of the committee responsible for the appointment, though supporters to a man of women's liberation, felt that to choose a woman would somehow be . . . inappropriate. A woman, at that, not notable for personality or glamour; Veronica had not in those days the style and confidence of her later years, and presented an appearance verging on dowdiness.

A sensitive woman, in Rosemary's position, might have suffered from conflicting loyalties. Rosemary evidently did not. She devoted herself wholeheartedly to the campaign for Geoffrey's appointment—a campaign not of honest debate but of subtle and stealthy denigration, of damning innuendo slipped artlessly into coffeehouse gossip. She did not forget her friendship with Veronica; she remembered it all too well, lending to every scrap of malicious rumor the authority of the personal confidante. Friends of Veronica with less claim to intimacy were left powerless in rebuttal.

Veronica's unglamorous exterior, whispered Rosemary and rumor, was a mask for her true character. It concealed a woman of unprincipled and insatiable sensuality, knowing neither shame nor scruple in pursuit of her desires. The list of her conquests was too scandalous to be spoken aloud. Were she appointed editor, the contributors would doubtless be drawn from among her lovers; but never mind, said Rosemary and rumor—that would not unduly restrict the field, and some of them were quite distinguished.

With the photograph, the campaign at last overreached itself.

I happened myself that evening to be in the bar of the Eastgate, and saw Geoffrey and Rosemary at a table in the far corner, with several members of the committee crowded around them. Something was passing from hand to hand, productive of gasps and guffaws. Someone called out to me to come and look.

The photograph showed Veronica reclining on a bed, disposed in attitude of languorous abandon and draped in folds of gauzy nylon more subtly revealing than mere nudity. Though not in any obvious sense compromising—she was alone on the bed—it could not be taken for the portrait of an innocent.

"Isn't it amazing," said Rosemary, "how attractive Veronica can look when she really wants to? No, honestly, Geoffrey, I can't possibly say who took it, that's absolutely confidential. No, it wouldn't be fair—after all, he is a senior member of the University, and married and so on, and I don't suppose it was his fault, poor chap. When Veronica wants a man, she gets him."

At that moment, by some lucky or unlucky chance—she was not an habitué—Veronica came into the bar.

Rosemary admitted, in the rather appalling scene that followed, that she herself had taken the photograph, having roused Veronica, late one night, to assist in experiments with a new flashlight. She admitted also, under a tempest of questioning, to a number of other lies. She had done it all, she said tearfully, to please Geoffrey. Geoffrey, in scarlet rage, denied all responsibility for her behavior, called her by several disagreeable names, and walked out. She followed him, weeping.

For Veronica, it might be said, the affair ended not unhappily. Contempt for Geoffrey and sympathy for her might not in themselves have sufficed to ensure her appointment. Ironically, it seemed to be the notion (especially prevalent among those who had seen the photograph) that there must after all have been a grain of truth in the stories, and that Veronica was a woman with hidden depths, which was finally decisive in her favor. For the remainder of their time at Oxford, however, she and Rosemary were never again known to speak to each other.

No—even after twenty years, it certainly could not be with Rosemary that Veronica, champagne glass in hand, was now conversing with such intimacy and animation. And yet, when they turned, smiling, in response to my greeting, I saw that it certainly was.

It occurred to me then that they had never ceased to be friends. I felt, for the first time, rather sorry for Geoffrey.

In this rare short story, Sarah Caudwell tells of duplicity among Oxford students. Author of the gender-bending Hilary Tamar series *(Thus Was Adonis Murdered, The Shortest Way to Hades, The Sirens Sang of Murder),* Caudwell is a former barrister and daughter of the late Claud Cockburn, noted left-wing activist and author.

True Confessions

Kate Charles

Celia Rusbridge wasn't the sort of woman who ever went to church. Neither was she the sort of woman to be involved in a sensational murder case, but that came later.

Church. To Celia, it meant weddings. "Till death us do part," and all of that. She and Edmund had been married in church, of course, as people of their sort always were—registry offices were so sordid, and churches provided such a suitable background for photos. Her friends were all married in church, and in due course their friends' children were as well, though these days things had changed a bit. Apart from the weddings, Celia could have counted the number of times she'd been inside a church on the fingers of one hand. One or two christenings of friends' children—Celia and Edmund had never had any children of their own—and once on Christmas, when Edmund had fancied it.

Looking back later, she was never sure exactly what had drawn her into the church that day. She'd been shopping for a new frock to wear to a party on the weekend; her search had taken her from Knightsbridge back to Sloane Square, and she'd run into her best friend Trish in Harvey Nichols.

They'd gone to the General Trading Company for a bite of lunch, at Trish's suggestion. Over the salmon fishcakes the reason came out: Trish's husband had fallen in love with another woman—a younger woman—and wanted a divorce. Trish was devastated; Celia listened sympathetically. She'd always been a sympathetic listener.

And so it was Trish, and Richard, and the unnamed bimbo in Richard's life who dominated Celia's thoughts as she walked past the church. She supposed she'd probably walked past the church, just a few streets off Sloane Square and not far from her house, a hundred or even a thousand times before, and had never paid any particular attention to it. But on that day, for whatever reason, she stopped outside the church, looked at the notice board, and without any conscious decision to do so, she pushed on the door and went inside.

Even a non-churchgoer like Celia could tell that this church was what was known as "High." A gilded statue of a Madonna and Child stood near the door, draped in a lace mantilla and surrounded by flickering votive candles on an iron stand. The distant altar, bedecked in gold, was surmounted by six candlesticks of immense height, and a faint whiff of incense hung in the air, mingling with the waxy scent of the burning candles. If the sign outside had not said "Church of England," Celia might have been forgiven for assuming that it was Roman Catholic.

There was no one in sight. Celia, still without thinking about what she was doing, put down her shopping bags in a pew near the statue and sat down, staring as if mesmerized at the golden folds of the Madonna's gown.

She was startled from her absorption by the sound of a soft, hesitant voice just behind her. "Are you . . . all right?" Celia turned to see a tall man bending towards her with a concerned expression. He was wearing a long black garment, which she only later learned was called a cassock.

"Why, yes, I'm perfectly fine," said Celia, confidently. She lifted a hand to smooth her hair back from her cheek, and to her surprise encountered the traces of a tear marring the perfection of her makeup. She had been crying—and she hadn't even known it. The realization horrified her, and resulted in still more tears, a trickle that soon turned into a flood. "Oh! I don't know what's the matter with me," she gulped, hoping that the man would go away.

He didn't go away; instead, he sat down beside her and offered her a handkerchief. Celia accepted it gratefully, doing her best to stanch the flow without causing any more damage to her makeup. When the storm had subsided, as quickly as it had come, he remained, silent, a strangely comforting presence.

"Sorry," said Celia as soon as she felt she could trust her voice. "And thank you for the handkerchief." She put it back in his hand and half-rose, as if to go.

"Wouldn't you like to tell me about it?" the man invited. "That's what I'm here for, you know."

Of course, realized Celia. He was a priest. She looked at him more closely: a narrow, intelligent face and wisps of thinning hair. Middle-aged. Opening her mouth to say that she had to be going, she found herself telling him instead, "That's very kind of you . . . Father. I'm just so worried about my friend."

"Your friend?" Dark eyes looked into hers and encouraged her to go on.

"My friend Trish. She and Richard have been married as long as Edmund—my husband—and I have. And now Richard's fallen in love with someone else—a young woman."

"I see."

"Poor Trish. What is she supposed to do?" Celia went on. "It happens so often. Trish isn't the first of my friends to have something like this happen. Why are middle-aged men so silly about young women?" This last was a fierce outburst, almost involuntary; Celia, embarrassed, looked down at her hands, then up into the priest's face.

He was smiling to himself, as if at a private joke. "Middle-aged men *can* be silly about young women," he agreed. "It often comes with the territory—call it a mid-life crisis, if you like. But if it's any consolation, they often get over it. Give your friend a few months and see what happens."

Richard *did* get over it, as it transpired. Or perhaps the bimbo did. But three months later things had returned to normal, as Trish told Celia over tea at Peter Jones in Sloane Square.

"Just like old times," she said smugly. 'In fact, things are better than ever. Richard is so guilty for what he put me through that he can't do enough to make up for it. Maybe he's afraid," she added, with a sly smile, "that I'll take a page out of his book. Find myself another man."

"But you wouldn't do that!" Celia protested.

Trish raised her eyebrows. "Don't be so sure. It would serve him right, you know."

On the way home, Celia stopped in the church once again. She hadn't been back in the intervening months, but as she drew near she found herself looking forward to seeing the priest again, to telling him the latest developments. She was sure that he'd be pleased to know that he'd been right about Richard.

To her disappointment, though, there was no sign of him. Celia lingered in the empty church for a quarter of an hour, leafing through the tracts on the book stall and wandering up one aisle and down the other. Though she'd never done such a thing before, she lit a candle in front of the statue of the Madonna; it seemed the right thing to do somehow.

It became Celia's habit, after that, to drop into the church whenever she was passing by and light a candle. Eventually, of course, she ran into the priest again. Almost literally, in fact: fresh from Christmas shopping, she was headed down the side aisle laden with carrier bags as he emerged from behind a purple curtain.

"Oh!" said Celia, startled. She'd looked for him in vain so often that she scarcely knew what to say when he appeared.

The priest recognized her; he stopped and smiled at her. "How nice to see you again," he said. "I hope I didn't frighten you, popping out like that."

Celia looked at the curtain. "I *was* a bit surprised."

"Confession," he explained. Perceiving Celia's incomprehension, he amplified, "Sacramental confession, that is. Just before Christmas is a busy time for confessions. But I don't suppose that's why you've come."

"No," said Celia awkwardly, brandishing her carrier bags. "Christmas shopping. And I . . . just thought I'd stop by."

Sensing her nervousness, and trying to put her at her ease, the priest gave her a conspiratorial smile. "Did you buy anything nice, then?"

Celia reached into a bag at random and produced a box. "Cufflinks for my husband," she said, opening the box to show him. "I had them made specially, with his initials. ER."

"Not to be confused with the Queen," the priest laughed. "You've just made me feel terribly guilty, I'm afraid. I haven't even begun to think about what to buy my wife for Christmas."

Conversations about confession were one thing, but on the subject of shopping Celia felt on firm ground. "You want to go to Peter Jones," she said confidently. "They have something for every budget."

Celia went to church at Christmas, and found it thrilling: the candles, the clouds of incense, the rich cloth-of-gold vestments. In the new year she started attending services every Sunday morning, and occasionally during the week.

Edmund, of course, thought it was daft, and said so. "Only old women with nothing better to do, and emotional weaklings, go to church," he scoffed. "I'll be charitable, and blame it on your time-of-life."

And Trish, too, found Celia's new enthusiasm completely incomprehensible. "I suppose the priest is dishy," she surmised to her friend during one of their weekly Friday morning sessions at the hairdresser's. "That would explain it. You must fancy him."

"Not at all," Celia said defensively. "You just don't understand. The Church is important to me. I know that it never used to be, but I've . . . changed." She refrained from pointing out that Trish, too, had changed. In the months since Richard had come crawling back to her, Trish had become noticeably more glamorous: her drab hair was now colored an expensive—and flattering—shade of gold, she'd lost weight, and her wardrobe had been revamped. Gone was the dowdy, if well-to-do, matron, garbed in serviceable tweeds; in her place was a beautiful and stylish woman. Celia wondered whether Trish had indeed found herself another man; it seemed likely, but she wouldn't have dreamed of asking. Sooner or later, she was sure, Trish would confide in her.

"Well," said Trish, with a considering look at the new shade of nail polish that the manicurist had just applied to her left hand, "if you ask me, Celia, you're quite mad."

But neither Trish's incomprehension nor Edmund's scorn kept Celia from church. It was the classic case of the new convert who couldn't get enough of something she'd lived without for so many years. She herself wasn't sure exactly what it was that attracted her, but it certainly wasn't that she fancied the priest. He was anything but dishy; he was, however, a man she could talk to, and he encouraged her developing spirituality. They talked often, and she began to think of him as a friend.

It was natural enough, therefore, that she eventually formed the idea that Edmund—and Trish—should meet him, and should come to share her regard for him. They certainly weren't going to come to him, so she should have to take him to them instead.

A dinner party, Celia decided. A small dinner party, for six. The priest and his wife, Trish and Richard, and herself and Edmund. The invitations were extended and accepted, and careful preparations were made. The menu, the flowers—Celia saw to them all herself, anxious that everything should be just perfect.

It was a disaster, of course. It could never have been anything else. Edmund radiated contempt for the priest, and was barely civil to him. He spent the evening talking to Trish, who was looking particularly glamorous, and who, in fact, flirted with him in an outrageous and forthright way. Richard, as a consequence, sulked quietly, refusing to talk to anyone. This left Celia to entertain the priest and his wife on her own.

The priest's wife was a surprise—Celia hadn't met her before, and had envisioned her as a typical clergy wife, mousy and badly dressed in castoffs from the jumble sale, holy and immersed in good works. But she was none of these things: she was a young woman with model-like beauty and a figure to match, very long legs and a very short skirt. She was also not, it would seem, very intelligent, and she declared herself not at all interested in the Church. Celia understood, suddenly, why the priest had smiled in that particular way as he'd said, "Middle-aged men can be silly about young women." He'd known what he was talking about, it was clear.

The realization might have lessened Celia's respect for the priest, but in an odd way it did the opposite. It showed him to be fallible, human, rather than a holy man with his head in the clouds, and Celia found herself turning to him even more in the weeks that followed the disastrous dinner party.

The two of them never talked about that evening, by unspoken common consent. Celia had been so humiliated at Edmund's conduct—and Trish's as well—that she wanted to pretend that it had never happened, and the priest seemed to concur. At least, she thought gratefully, he didn't seem to hold it against her. There was, needless to say, no talk of a reciprocal invitation. Their relationship—friendship, as Celia thought of it—was now clearly defined as one taking place within the confines of the church, with no question of any further social interaction.

It wasn't too long after the dinner party that the priest suggested that Celia had reached a point in the development of her spiritual life when she might find sacramental confession helpful. "It's not something that the Church forces on us," he explained to her. "Rather, it's a tool that is available to those who want it. 'None must, all may, some should' is the phrase that's often used to describe it."

"You think that *I* should, Father? And that I'm ready?" Celia was flattered.

"I think you might find it helpful," he replied. He gave her a book to read that explained the theology behind confession, outlined the procedure, and provided some useful advice on preparing oneself for making a confession.

Celia read the book. She understood the theology, which was much as the priest had explained it to her, but was unsure about the practical benefits for her personally. "I mean," she said to the priest, "it's not as if I've done anything terrible that I need to confess. I've never killed anyone, I've never . . . committed adultery. . . ."

"That's just exactly why it's important for you to examine yourself, to be rigorous with your conscience," the priest pointed out. "The sins of spiritual pride are just as bad as the more . . . physical . . . sins, though most people don't look at it that way. We're *all* sinners, Celia."

And so Celia began going to confession. She found it very difficult at first; her sins seemed far too trivial to be occupying the time of the priest. She had forgotten to leave a tip when she and Trish had lunched at the General Trading Company, she had crossed the street to avoid a disreputable-looking man who was selling "The Big Issue" outside Peter Jones, she had snapped at the daily for not dusting the top of the mantelpiece properly. Trivial sins for a trivial life, she thought sadly. But the priest encouraged her to persevere.

"Examine your thoughts," he urged her, "not just your actions."

In the following weeks Celia's conscience went into overdrive. She analyzed her every motivation, probed the dark corners of her mind, and brought out the results for the priest's inspection. "I feel superior to people who aren't as lucky as I am," she admitted. "People who don't have as much money, or as big a house."

"Pride," diagnosed the priest.

It went on from there. Celia's weekly confession, at three o'clock on Thursday afternoons, became as immutable a feature of her life as her Friday appointment at the hairdresser's. She both dreaded and looked forward to it: dreaded the feeling of self-loathing that came with the scrupulous examination of her conscience, but looked forward to the enormous relief when it was all over, and the priest pronounced absolution. Clean and pure, she felt, as she left the confessional each week. Ready to go home and face Edmund's scorn.

It must be explained at this point that Edmund Rusbridge was a gentleman, in the old sense of the word: that is, he did not have to work for a living. He didn't even find it necessary, as so many of those of his class do, to pretend to work, or to find employment for his own self-satisfaction. No, Edmund Rusbridge was content to remain at home, as idle as he pleased. He had his hobbies, of course, but they did not necessitate his leaving the house very often. That was one reason, Celia knew, that he resented her newfound attachment to the Church. He preferred having her at home with him, occasional shopping forays and lunches with Trish excepted.

Edmund Rusbridge was also a well-preserved man for his age. In his idleness, he had managed to keep a good figure, and his dark hair wasn't even thinning on top, let alone going gray. He had been considered handsome in his youth—quite a catch for Celia, everyone said—and now, in his middle age, he knew that he had nothing to be ashamed of in the looks department.

Celia loved Edmund, but realized, in her weeks of self-analysis, that she probably took him for granted. She was always, herself, well-groomed and expensively dressed, but she had no illusions of youth. She didn't, like the new Trish, color her hair or try to pretend that she was anything but a middle-aged woman.

She began to think about this one day when she returned home from her weekly confession, and Edmund was not at home. She couldn't imagine where he might be: if he were going out, on some rare occasion, to lunch at his club or visit his tailor, he would always warn her well in advance. But he had said nothing, and she was worried.

He arrived home a few minutes after Celia, slightly out of breath and a bit flushed, and offered no explanation for his absence. "Don't you think it's time for some tea?" he demanded instead.

Other departures from his usual behaviour, slight in themselves but significant to one who knew him as well as his wife, troubled Celia over the following weeks.

A further cause of concern was her relationship with Trish. There had been no row, no open rift between them, but somehow Celia seemed to see very little of Trish these days. They hadn't had lunch together for what seemed like months, and Trish had changed her weekly appointment at the hairdresser's from Friday to Thursday morning.

Trish was her oldest friend; they had known each other as schoolgirls, and had shared a great deal through the years. They had been bridesmaids at each other's weddings, and Celia was godmother to Trish's daughter. Why were they now drifting apart? Celia pushed to the back of her mind the suspicion that Trish was deliberating avoiding her. She knew that Trish didn't understand, and didn't approve of, her attachment to the Church; perhaps that explained it. Perhaps she was uncomfortable with, embarrassed by, Celia's newfound religious zeal, and was afraid that Celia would try to convert her.

On impulse, Celia picked up the phone and rang Trish. "I

was wondering if we might have lunch one day," she suggested brightly.

Trish's voice was cool, detached. "I'm frightfully busy at the moment," she said. "I'll give you a ring when things are back to normal, shall I?"

Celia put the phone down, her hand shaking. There was no mistaking it: Trish *was* avoiding her. What had she done to offend her friend? She thought back to their last meeting, running through their conversation in her mind; she hadn't said anything out of the ordinary, she was sure. And she hadn't forgotten Trish's birthday, or her goddaughter's birthday, or even Richard's birthday.

And then it came to her, in a blinding flash of insight so painful that she caught her breath. Of course! It was so simple, so clear. Trish was having an affair . . . with Edmund.

Now that she'd realized the truth, Celia wondered how she could have blinded herself to it for so long. There were so many giveaways: Trish's newfound glamor; the way she had flirted with Edmund at the disastrous dinner party—and he had flirted back; Trish's avoidance of her; Edmund's odd behavior. All of those little things became pieces of a jigsaw puzzle that had suddenly, monstrously, dropped into place, and the picture it showed was not a pretty one. Celia even recalled, now, that Trish had fancied Edmund long ago, had, in fact, gone out with him for a time before he'd settled on Celia. Over the years, Trish had occasionally joked about it with Celia, had said things like, "If you ever get tired of Edmund, let me know," or "I should have held on to Edmund when I had the chance." Celia had always laughed, smugly; now, though, it didn't seem very funny.

Celia brooded over this for several days. When the time came for her confession on Thursday, she considered telling the priest of her turmoil, but decided against it; it was too raw, too painful.

On her return home that afternoon, she found, once again, that Edmund was out. Now she understood why, and if any further confirmation were needed, she discovered it when he came in: there was a minute dab of lipstick on his shirt collar, and one blond hair on the lapel of his suit. Celia said nothing.

The following Thursday she could contain herself no longer. When she'd finished the usual litany of her sins and failings, she added, "And there's something worse, Father. Jealousy. I've discovered that Edmund is having an affair, and I just can't control my jealousy about it."

The priest was startled. "An affair?" he said sharply. "You're sure about that?"

She wept then, as she had on their first meeting, but this time her tears were for herself and her own disintegrating marriage. And she told the priest of her suspicions and then her certainty about Edmund and Trish. "It was that blond hair that convinced me," she sobbed. "And the lipstick. He said he'd been to his club, but he certainly didn't get those at his club."

Once again the priest proffered his handkerchief. "But how dreadful for you."

"And one of the worst things about it, Father, is that he's doing it on Thursday afternoons, when he knows that I'm here with you! It's the one time of the week, apart from Friday morning, that he can be sure I won't be at home! I mean, to think that at this very moment . . . they're together!" Her tears showed no sign of abating. "Oh, Father. I just don't know what do to."

On the next Thursday, Celia went to the church as usual. But the priest was not in the confessional, nor anywhere else to be seen. She waited for some time, then went home, assuring herself that he'd been held up by some unavoidable parish emergency. Someone sick in hospital, someone dying.

Edmund wasn't at home, which by now was no surprise to Celia; she made some tea and waited for him to come home from his assignation with Trish. But Edmund didn't come home.

* * *

He'd caught them in the act. *In flagrante,* as the tabloids liked to put it: Edmund Rusbridge and his beautiful, young, blond wife. And he'd killed them both. A crime of passion, said the tabloids. An old-fashioned crime of passion. Unpremeditated. He'd come home unexpectedly and found them at it, and in the grip of an uncontrollable rage had killed them both.

That was only partly right, of course. But only the priest, and possibly his own confessor, knew the whole truth: that he had known very well what he would find when he went home on that Thursday afternoon instead of going to the church. Celia had told him herself, though she hadn't realized it, and he'd had no doubt about it. There was the blond hair, and something else that Celia didn't know about: that distinctive cufflink with the initials "ER," which he'd found under his bed a fortnight before. So Celia could be forgiven for reaching the wrong conclusion, for not realizing the significance of the fact that Thursday afternoon was the one time when they were *both* sure to be occupied.

But perhaps, in time, Celia guessed the whole truth. After all, Celia knew—and had known for a long time—the truth about middle-aged men, and how silly they could be about young women.

An American who now makes her home outside London, Kate Charles provides dubious comfort for the heroine of this story and her fascination with a priest. Her series of mysteries feature a close look at the Anglican church and solicitor David Middleton-Brown *(A Drink of Deadly Wine, The Snares of Death, Appointed to Die, A Dead Man Out of Mind, Evil Angels Among Them).*

Abstain from Beans

Lindsey Davis

For Lisa Cody, Co-founder of the Milo Appreciation Society

Dawn in the Mediterranean: sunlight twinkled to perfection on the Ionian Sea. Dolphins cavorted in the stinging blue waves. White marble glittered like a cliché on a dramatic seashore temple. On a promontory in the far south of Italy stood the little Greek outpost of Croton. It would have been idyllic, but for the nasty pall of black smoke hanging over the town.

The time was the sixth century B.C. Not that the Crotonians would consider they were living *before* anything, or anyone. For them, Croton was It. Top town. Top town in any league.

Its credentials were impeccable: founded by Achaeans, redoubtable Greeks despatched overseas by the famous Oracle at Delphi. They had established this jewel, with the only harbor on the hot eastern seaboard of the toe of Italy. It grew. It became home to the finest proponents of both athletics and philosophy. In the Greek world, that covered almost everything. Then, to enrich their reputation further, the Crotonians proved themselves warlike as well, beating up the rival town of Sybaris so thoroughly that its very location would soon vanish from the map. For a small town that tended to smell of fish, Croton had done well.

That applied until yesterday. Something extremely unpleasant had happened at Croton last night.

On the outskirts of town, facing across pleasant fields and with a dazzling view towards the ocean, had stood a delightful villa—clearly built as the home of a major personality. There had been cool rooms, peaceful colonnades, and a courtyard with a fig tree. But this secluded location was the source of today's choking smoke. Last night, rioters had caused devastation. Through the acrid fug that remained, fallen columns and roof tiles could be glimpsed in hot, haphazard piles. Doors and furniture, heated to charcoal, still glowed menacingly. Alone in the tragic wreck of his home stood its owner. As he surveyed the remains of the villa that had been gifted to him by a grateful town, his swelling anger made him inconsolable.

Rage was a dangerous emotion in a man of such strength. He was built on a colossal scale. Double the body weight of most of his fellow townfolk, or even the small-holders and fishermen nearby who earned their living by physical labor. None of his bulk was fat. His neck was as wide as his head. Little of the neck seemed visible, for a heavy scarf of muscle—where most men had none—buried the top vertebrae of his spine. Huge shoulders and arms strained the seams of this athlete's tunic. Compared to his shoulders' width and power, his legs appeared normal. But these were the strongest legs in the world. When he kicked angrily at a scorched roof beam, a whole tree trunk that had resisted the heat of the fire, it exploded under the blow, shedding its charred exterior surface like powder.

His name was Milo. He was a wrestler. The most famous wrestler ever. Milo of Croton had won both the Olympic Games and the Pythean Games, six times each. He came home, still seeking bigger and better trials of strength. When he helped destroy the rival town of Sybaris, Croton had given him this villa. Its gracious proportions and civilized amenities had seemed an incongruous setting;

Milo had preferred to spend his time in the gymnasium in town, though he was generous and offered the use of his fine home to others. Even when he himself was absent, the villa had represented local recognition of his astonishing talent, and his high status in Croton. Now somebody had burned it to the ground.

After a long while standing silent in the ruins, Milo left the smoldering remains. He walked around the grounds with the slow, purposeful movements of a powerful man who was holding his emotions under control. Milo was looking for a focus for his rage.

Eventually he came upon a failed philosopher, sitting in a beanfield, beside a corpse.

Somebody—a large group of people—had made quite a mess of the field. Out here in the open, the tang from the low pall of smoke still caught in the throat. In addition, a damp, sordid scent of crushed vegetation also hung in the warm air. Trampled bean haulms lay in huge tangles, like fishing nets after a violent storm. Amongst this horticultural disaster lay the dead body of an elderly man.

The corpse had a striking face and flowing white hair. His beard jutted boldly from the chin. He wore a long, white gown, now stained by the wrecked bean haulms; it was the sort of robe philosophers wrapped themselves in while they aired their thoughts in the porticos of the gymnasia where athletes trained. At Croton, philosophers and athletes rarely deigned to notice one another.

Alongside the corpse the seated mourner cut an unimpressive figure: spindly legs wearing untidy sandals, knobbly knees beneath a tattered tunic, a mat of unwashed hair, a pathetic attempt at a beard. He was in his twenties, but had the pallor and pustules of adolescence.

The great athlete, who had always eaten well, who spent his days exercising in the clear, open air and his nights in deep sleep, surveyed this tormented human grub with amazed contempt. "What's your name?"

"Helianthos."

"Very pretty! I'm Milo."

"I was afraid of that."

Helianthos tried to forget the legendary stories of Milo's fabulous strength: destroying Sybaris almost single-handedly, rendering an army unnecessary. And that famous tale about him carrying a heifer around the stadium on his shoulders, killing the beast with a blow of his fist, then eating it raw. That was Milo when he was happy and triumphant. Best not to think of such a man's behavior if he was annoyed.

He was extremely annoyed now.

"Who has done this?" Milo felt dissatisfied with the question. He turned it over slowly, then tried more informally: "Who did it?" Still not quite right, but closer. A combination of the two phrases came to his mind unbidden: *who done it?* . . . But to a son of a democratic Greek city this was unacceptable. Even athletes were taught grammar in Greek schools.

Any lad who was big enough and strong enough to look like a promising champion could generally find a place in a Greek school. And no one who went to a Greek school grew up afraid of asking questions. "Who is this man?" he boomed.

"That Man."

"What man?"

The mourner's voice sank to a horrified whisper: *"That* man . . ."

Milo considered the daft answer for a moment. Then he stared at the corpse. "Oh! Pythagoras. The *triangle* man."

His companion flinched. Everyone was supposed to know that the name of Croton's superstar mathematician and philosopher was never to be spoken by ordinary people. Mind you, Helianthos reflected, even the master would have allowed that the mighty athlete should not be called "ordinary." Not in a face-to-biceps confrontation, anyway. Besides, Milo had been the great philosopher's landlord. He had a keen interest in the fire that ended the tenancy.

"So you were one of his lot?" Milo demanded.

Helianthos shook his head miserably. "Deemed unworthy," he squeaked. Milo could believe it.

Pythagoras' unworthy disciple had been grieving without tears, but now, in the presence of another human being, he sought to express his emotions in a wilder outburst. "Oh, this is terrible! He's gone!"

Milo glared. "He's dead all right. That's the end of him."

"Oh, not dead!" exclaimed the younger man. "Nothing ends. His soul has returned to the circle of life as a higher or lower being—"

Milo interrupted in a dry tone that gave the impression he had heard about, and did not support, the concept of reincarnation: "It had better not be promotion. It's due to him I've lost my house."

Helianthos looked up quickly, intending to retort that a mere house mattered nothing when the greatest mind in circulation had just been snuffed out and possibly reallocated to a slug. He realized he was looking up at a stomach that could flatten fences with a gentle nudge. Meekly, he apologized. "I'm sorry about your house."

"You should be." Milo started complaining bitterly. "I was told your lot would be ideal tenants. A peaceful group. Thinkers who despise women, never drink, and don't even eat meat because you can't bear to kill animals. Dreamers, who would spend all their time meditating, and not break up the furniture. The reborn souls of lettuce leaves and butterflies."

Helianthos deduced that when Milo saw a fly he swatted it—and did not care whether in a previous incarnation it might have been his grandmother. He tried to win Milo's sympathy. "It was a beautiful villa. I can understand that you needed tenants. You wanted to prevent squatters—"

"Too right. Bloody goatherds—probably with their bloody goats."

"I'm really sorry about this."

"Thanks. Still, nothing ends, you tell me. Perhaps at this very moment Pythagoras is being reborn as a stonemason who can rebuild my place."

"He's already been the son of Apollo."

"Somehow I didn't think your great man would have seen himself as the son of a drain-cleaner."

Helianthos made no answer. Young people who attach themselves to unusual cults soon learn to ignore ridicule.

The followers of Pythagoras had once been welcomed to Croton as an educational sect who would raise the tone—or at least, as wealthy newcomers, who would bring in business. More recently they had had to face unpleasantness. The trouble was that Pythagoras had raised the tone of his own parts of Croton so high he tended to look down on the original inhabitants. The Greeks of Croton liked to sneer at the native Italians whom they had pushed back into the hills, but in their own agora they expected to swank. The philosopher's arrogance towards them was insulting. They responded with spirit. Some threw rocks.

To tell the truth, that was why the master had looked around for a secluded out-of-town villa where he could expound his great theories in private.

"I want to know who did it," Milo exclaimed. He held out a hand; Helianthos made the mistake of taking it. As he was pulled to his feet, all the bones in his fingers were subjected to excruciating pressure. He had never felt such pain. "I'm a wrestler," said Milo. "I live by coordination and speed—and power, of course." Of course. "You're the man who was trained by his brain. You'll have to help me work this out."

Helianthos, who had reckoned his best ploy was to run very fast to another area, found himself nodding obediently.

As the sun climbed, bees came to forage in the beanfield. Other insects were exibiting a more doubtful interest in the fresh corpse of Pythagoras. The two men retreated to sit on a hurdle beside the dusty track. They made an incongruous partnership, the extremes of humanity: one triumphal body and one totally inadequate personality. "We need to establish what happened," Milo decreed.

Helianthos might have failed at philosophy, but he had mastered the unexpected reply: "I can tell you what happened."

"Oho! How? Were you here?"

"No. I was in a tavern in town."

"Were you drunk?"

"As drunk as I could get."

Not very, Milo decided. "Why?"

"Despair!" Noticing that this proud cry had failed to impress the wrestler, Helianthos continued shyly. "People rushed in shouting. *A gang of lads have gone up to Milo's house to see off Pythagoras!"*

"So you went with them?"

"No. I kept my head down and had more to drink. This morning I came up to see what was what. And I found him, lying here. He hated beans. He must have refused to cross the field with the others. He could have got away with them, but because of his principles he stood bravely to meet his fate. The attackers hacked him to pieces without mercy—"

"This hardly counts as an eyewitness report," Milo broke in, dismissing the sensational aspects. "It doesn't fit the facts. The man appears to have been killed with one efficient blow to the head. A hard one, which spilt his skull."

Helianthos looked surprised. "You're very observant!" Milo gave him a dry smile.

Time to get tough. Milo put it to the lad bluntly: "Was there anyone at your tavern who'll be able to confirm you were there all night?"

"I had nothing to do with this!" Helianthos was a realist; that was why he had been deemed unsuitable for Pythagorean philosophy. Even so, he felt put out. "Whatever are you suggesting?"

Unperturbed, Milo stated, "A rejected follower is the obvious suspect."

"I wasn't the only one!" Helianthos panicked. "And I don't know any gang of lads. Whoever destroyed your house definitely had help." Once he calmed down, Helianthos did possess basic good sense (in fact, he was *completely* unsuitable for any sort of academic life). "Still, I'd better come up with an alibi. Well, the woman who runs the tavern will remember me clearly: I'm not used to drinking. I was extremely sick. Then I passed out for the rest of the night. I've got bruises from the people who stepped on me."

Milo stamped his foot with delight. A stadium's length away across the fields licorice plants trembled. "So it's not you. Well, are there any other intellectual rejects hanging around the neighborhood?"

"Once they're turned down as students they tend to slink off to their own cities. The people of Croton are very unfriendly."

"They get tired of being sneered at," explained Milo. "Don't blame us. It was your lot who looked down their noses. Who even refused to shake our hands."

The rejected pupil still clung to old loyalties. "You don't understand. The master was different from other people—"

"Oh, yes! He was a demigod, the rest of us were dust. Says he!"

As an athlete, Milo naturally wished to keep sport separate from politics (except when he was asking for a civic contribution to pay for his training or his travel to sporting venues). He liked to pretend he had no idea what was going on in Croton, yet Helianthos was beginning to suspect that was a pose.

Milo spent his days relentlessly exercising and practicing at the gymnasium. Even in the dry heat and cold rooms of the baths, few people cared to engage Milo in casual chat. But when the spectators were standing on the raised walkways watching him, or while he silently scraped off the oil and sand that wrestlers applied as a protective second skin, other men talked to each other—and then Milo listened. He had heard the rumbles of unrest over the Pythagoreans' love of mystery and their snobbery.

One subject of the mutterings was the razing of Sybaris. Since he had helped to flatten the town (though not to put its citizens to the sword), Milo particularly listened to that.

Attacking Sybaris had been strongly urged by Pythagoras. He had convinced the civic elders of Croton that their neighbors were too carefree. (The Sybarites were the kind of easygoing folk who banned cockerels from their town to avoid being woken up early.) The Sybarites had been glamorous, sophisticated—and happy. Now there were people in Croton who whispered that happiness was a feature of democracy, which only barbarians would destroy.

"Let's consider," said Milo, "who had a reason to go for Pythagoras—a motive," he added, feeling pleased with the terminology. It sounded businesslike. "You lived in the commune. Tell me about it. If it wasn't an outcast who did this, the next consideration must be an inside job."

"The whole community adored him," declared Helianthos.

"Explain it. What made him such a celebrity?"

"He was an extraordinary man."

"So what did he win his prizes for?"

Helianthos faced up to the question seriously. "His learning—"

"Such as?"

"His first study was how to perform miracles." At this Milo showed a definite interest, but he made no comment. So Helianthos continued. "Then he turned to mathematics. He was taught mysteries by the priests of the great temples of Egypt. He learned astrology, logistics, geometry, and occult lore. He traveled widely—Egypt, Phoenicia, and the Chaldees. After that, he turned his abilities to teaching, starting as tutor to the son of Polycrates of Samos—"

"That old ruffian!" One of the perks of athletics was free trips to Greece, sponsored by your hometown. As a traveler, Milo had heard all about the piratical king of Samos. "How did your prudish master fit in with riotous living among poets, girls, and pretty youths?"

"He was deeply offended. So he accepted an invitation to cross the ocean to Croton and to found a school here." Helianthos was remembering how he himself had been drawn to it. "People came from all over the world. He accepted about three hundred students, who were allowed to live with him in an exclusive school, devoting their days to his precepts—"

"Which were?"

"Oh, that's an absolute secret! I couldn't possibly reveal them!"

"I think you'd better," Milo suggested, not even bothering to inflate his mighty chest.

Helianthos sighed. "I don't know much. Pupils at the school lived together, holding all things in common—" Milo knew most of the pupils had come from wealthy homes, arriving at Croton with well-stuffed travel packs. He was thinking how useful their money must have been for Pythagoras. Helianthos pressed on bravely. "They were divided into two groups: the mathematicians, who had a rightful access to knowledge, and the rest. I'm afraid I was in the second category. Our only duty was to obey the rules."

"What rules?"

"I am sworn not to tell."

"A man has been killed," Milo commented. "That may not be important, of course. But property has been destroyed. That's *very* important. Tell me about the rules!"

"They won't make much sense to an uninitiate," Helianthos warned defensively. "Well, things like, not to leave the imprint of your body on the bedclothes on rising, not to look into a mirror beside a light—and the main one was, never to eat beans."

Milo breathed heavily. "I won't ask what the point was."

"Of abstaining from beans?"

"Oh, I can see that! You don't want three hundred people farting all night." He could see *some* point in all of it: drilling the pupils with an unusual routine, so they could be controlled. Every fake demigod who ever lived—and some athletic trainers—knew that trick. It *was* a trick of course. He wondered how much else had been.

"Milo, every night we had to ask ourselves three questions: What evil have I done? What good have I done? What have I omitted to do?"

Milo gazed at him, giving Helianthos an uncomfortable feeling. "So while you were getting out of bed very carefully and watching your diet, what were the mathematicians up to?"

"I really can't tell you that. They had a secret language, devised by the master, based on symbols and codes—"

"Surprise me!" growled Milo. "So I suppose you have no idea what the great man was teaching them?"

At this juncture Helianthos began to look more sheepish. He was beginning to be interested in solving the mystery. "Well, I did keep my ear to the ground."

"Smart boy!"

"There were three main areas of thought being discussed: transmigration of the soul—"

"I think we'll skip that one," sneered Milo. A fly flew too close and he killed it: one rapid movement of his lower leg. A heel-kick that would have knocked the knee from under any other town's champion in the wrestling ring.

Helianthos tried not to quake. "His other principal interests were the theory of numbers, and cosmology—the universe."

"Numbers? You mean that stuff about the sides of the triangle?"

"Well, the Hypotenuse Theorem was one practical by-product. The main thrust of the master's teaching was more all-enveloping. He said that numbers are the essential element of matter. Where other thinkers have maintained that everything is composed of fire, or air, or water, the master taught that numbers have substance and everything is composed of them. Some are more powerful than others. The number ten is divine, and one, two, three, and four have special qualities. Their sum equals ten, and they form the divine configuration." Helianthos risked drawing it in the dust:

*
**
***
****

Seeing Milo's expression, he erased it hastily.

Milo asked frankly, with a grin that said a lot, "You mean, according to Pythagoras, I could have saved myself bother if I'd known the right number? I could have walked out into the arena at Olympia, for example, and defeated my opponent just by shouting 'thirty-two!' Or whatever?"

"Everything depends on the law of Harmony," Helianthos rushed on. "This controls the universe. The master observed that there is a relation between the length of a lyre string and the sound produced; that gave rise to his ideas about the Music of the Spheres—the ten heavenly bodies, or planets, whose continual sweet sounds mankind cannot hear—"

Milo whistled. It sounded derisive, though his manner was humble.

Helianthos paused, then began again. "The master said that in the beginning was Chaos, then numbers were created to give relationships between lines and points, and Harmony produced the Cosmos, which is Order."

"In this part of the Cosmos, Order seems to have broken down," Milo interrupted with one of his wry put-downs, waving an arm towards the smoking villa and the body in the beanfield.

"But we're here to reimpose Harmony!" Helianthos retaliated weakly. "If we ask the right questions, we'll be able to draw a line straight to the culprits . . . Look, I'm not competent to explain it. I'm just illustrating what I secretly overheard."

"Was it convincing when *he* told it?"

"Oh, absolutely!" The young man's face lit with remembered fervor. "His evening lectures were riveting. People came from everywhere to hear him. He never let strangers see him—even initiates were not allowed that privilege until they had passed through all the mysteries. He sat behind a curtain expounding his doctrines, and it was—" He sought for words. "Magical!"

"Ah!" Milo said. "Well, he had studied under the Egyptians and the Chaldeans."

Helianthos felt Milo had something on his mind. "Whenever he taught his first words would be: 'I swear by the air I breathe and the water I drink that I shall never suffer censure on account of that which I am about to say'—"

"Big-headed bugger!" Milo commented. "Hasn't got a lot to say for himself now." Pythagoras, being dead in the beanfield, for once proposed no argument.

Pythagoras would be known for centuries, even if his theories were discredited. Milo, as an athlete, would have no future once his strength started to fail, but he could enjoy a very decent present. When a wrestler had won the Pythean and the Olympic Games six times each, he got a villa in the sun, free beef for life, more laurel wreathes than he could find space for—and a reputation that might also last for a couple millennia. By then, even though he was famous for brawn not brain, he knew a thing or two. He reached the question he had been quietly saving. "Tell me about the miracles."

Helianthos blushed. "The master had a golden thigh."

"Is that the truth?"

"Well, it's a myth." Helianthos was catching the wrestler's skeptical attitude. "He killed a deadly snake by biting it. He held conversations with a bear, over many years—"

"I'd like to hear the bear's side of that story!"

"He persuaded a heifer to refrain from eating beans. He was seen at the same time in both Croton and Metapontium—"

"Don't go on."

"I'm just telling you what people said."

"No one can be in two places at once. Not even if they're composed of harmonious numbers and they reckon they were once Apollo's son."

Helianthos drew a deep breath. "Don't let's argue."

"I'm not arguing. I'm just thinking about those devious buggers, the Egyptians and the Chaldeans." The phrase "all done with mirrors" sprang unbidden to Milo's mind. He rebuffed it. Mirrors in those days—even the finest polished Etruscan mirrors—were not shiny enough for conjuring. Tricks had to be worked by sleight of hand, by deceiving the eye—or by the simple use of stand-ins.

Helianthos was worried by the sudden silence. "None of this is helping you decide who burned down your house."

"Or who killed Pythagoras! Tell me more about the cult."

"The school, you mean?"

"The school then. So what do you know about Pythagoras and his school?"

"Is this a time to be considering achievements?"

"Stuff his achievements. Tell me how he lived while he was at my villa. I want to know what he did to irritate somebody so intensely that they came mob-handed with torches, then smoked him out of his hidey-hole and kicked in his brains."

Helianthos shuddered. "Do you have to be so graphic?" Then, when Milo merely shrugged, he found enough spirit to reprimand him. "Those, Milo, were very particular brains! Those brains—"

"They're offal now," disagreed the wrestler. "And my house is ash! So what was it like, at the commune in the final days?"

"Tense. Everything was going wrong. There was a terrible sense of approaching disaster. One student, whose name was Hippasus, had caused a lot of trouble. He revealed the existence of irrational numbers."

"Do I need to understand that?"

"All you need to know is that it strikes at the heart of the master's theories about numerical harmony—"

"Proves him wrong, you mean?"

"A blasphemer might say so."

"So what happened to the brave, outspoken Hippasus? Is he a suspect for the killing?"

"He's dead himself, Milo. The master cursed him. He was

so terrified he fled, plunged into the sea, and was drowned a few miles from shore."

"Had word got out about what he had said?"

"Oh, certainly. He was hopeless; he went around telling everyone."

"So he had thoroughly undermined the master's theory. Was it possible Pythagoras may have felt his term was up?"

"He had certainly considered relocating the school. I believe there was talk of disbanding from Croton and moving—Metapontium had been suggested."

"It sounds as if the whole mystic edifice was on the verge of collapse. Were the pupils aware of this?"

"They didn't want to believe it. Sometimes there was hysterical talk. The main threat came from the town. There was serious opposition in Croton. People had begun to hate having mysteries on their doorstep. What happened at Sybaris alarmed them. That was when the pupils became agitated, and even talked of all taking hemlock together—Whatever had been decided, what was done last night overtook it. This came from outside."

"Well, it looks that way. Did Pythagoras have any particular enemies?" Milo felt pleased with this question. It had a sound feel, a rightness: order out of chaos. He liked it better than the one about who had done this.

"Oh I'm sure he didn't." Whenever Helianthos seemed to have grasped reality, his innocence and good nature had a habit of breaking through.

"So," commented the wrestler, in a rather facetious mood, "he was perfectly well-liked—except by bean farmers, rejected philosophy students, and the entire city of Sybaris?"

Helianthos nodded.

"Well, we can rule out the Sybarites; none of them were left alive. So let's look again for someone who had reason to be jealous of the school. Somebody local, who could assemble a gang. Who was the latest would-be student to be shown the door?"

"Probably Chilon. He's from Croton."

"Was Chilon very upset at being chucked out?"

"Furious. He is of high birth and violent nature."

"Oh, *that* Chilon!" Milo had remembered him. "He dabbled with weight training before his daddy bought him a set of philosophy lessons. Useless. No discipline. He's a spoiled thug. I can imagine his reaction if anybody told him that." Someone as arrogant as Pythagoras had probably had no qualms about telling him frankly.

"Does he have any friends?" Helianthos asked.

"He goes around in a group of other rich brats. They like to make a racket. Always pushing and shoving in the marketplace."

"They sound the sort who might decide to pick on an unpopular group."

"Oh, they'd love it! Especially if the unpopular group were ethereal types who could be relied on not to come out fighting. So, you reckon when Chilon was turned down by the school, he went away, downed a few consoling drinks, then came roaring out swearing vengeance? I should have realized the obvious candidate was some crazy aristo."

"Why's that?" asked Helianthos.

"A poor man couldn't afford the drinks."

"Maybe he and his friends were just angry," Helianthos suggested.

"They were drunk," Milo insisted.

"No, it could have been high spirits that went wrong." Helianthos still pursued the issue, now wanting the master's death to be more than a sudden act of violence in the midst of a drunken brawl. "They had to bring torches with them, as the night was dark, but maybe it was an accident that they burned down the house. Young men could be forgiven for carelessness—"

"Not at *my* house!" Milo boomed. Helianthos fell silent. "You want me to believe Chilon's intentions were perfectly peaceful? He just intended to back Pythagoras against a wall and have a quiet word?"

"Explain that his opinions had become unwelcome in

Croton, then show him the quickest route out of town?" Helianthos contributed.

Milo had become sarcastic. "Well, I wouldn't want to slander Chilon, if we've got it wrong!" Chilon's father was a big man in Croton. "But I might ask whether it would not have been more considerate to set Pythagoras on the road by daylight. And it's easy to envisage a scene where Chilon and his friends arrived at the villa in a bawdy throng, called for the philosopher, who sensibly refused to emerge, then they torched the place to flush him out."

"His pupils fled for their lives across country," Helianthos now agreed sadly.

"Pythagoras himself refused to cross a field of beans. So he stood and met his death."

"That seems a logical explanation." Helianthos felt like a philosopher who was losing faith in logic.

The two men rose quietly and went again to survey the corpse.

"Just one more question," Milo said, as if it were an afterthought. "You identified the body. If no one was allowed to see him at close quarters, how are you so sure this is Pythagoras?"

Helianthos felt taken aback. "I had glimpsed him from a distance. Initiates had described him. Who else could it be?"

Milo smiled. "Good question!" He was thinking again about the lore and the mysteries of the Egyptians and Chaldeans. Masters of cunning. Past masters of deception and fakery. "Put it this way: if by any chance you should hear in the near future that Pythagoras has reappeared somewhere else, you'll naturally assume it is another miracle."

"I will! But you sound doubtful?"

"Oh, far be it from me to dabble in mysteries."

"But?"

Milo made a self-deprecating gesture. "But it seems to me, something doesn't add up."

"Things always add up," the ex-student replied gravely.

"The problem is they don't always add up the way you want them to."

"Maybe someone has deliberately decided how things should work out here."

"What are you suggesting?"

"Just this: that a man who kept his appearance secret, yet who made a practice of being seen in two places at once, might just have helped the myth along by employing a stand-in."

Helianthos discovered he was not as shocked as he would once have expected to be. "You mean the *stand-in* is dead?"

Below the promontory the Ionian Sea stretched to the bright horizon, a blue so clear it hurt the eyes, variegated with mysterious swaths of darker hues. Dolphins played. Bees hummed in what was left of the beanfield. Helianthos seemed to have matured ten years. The effect was cheering. "But if you are right, Pythagoras escaped to safety after all. Chilon and the others found the poor old man dead and abandoned the chase—"

"Being a stand-in isn't much of a life. Maybe he had been promised his soul would be rewarded with a better existence next time," suggested Milo, in his scathing mood.

"Who killed this man?"

"What do you think?" asked Milo.

"I think—" Helianthos sucked his teeth, then could not face the answer.

"It was perfect," said Milo. "A conjuring trick: the philosopher vanishes, yet he's lying here dead."

The two men walked slowly down the track, leaving the burned-out villa and the fly-blown corpse. They were drawing near to Croton. Milo clapped an arm over the younger man's shoulders, causing him to buckle slightly at the knees. "So, what will you do now?"

Helianthos managed to keep walking despite the pressure. "Return to my own people and try to lead a useful life."

"Good lad. If I was you, I'd try and get more exercise.

And take care of your diet. Raw steak would fill you out a bit. But pulses are full of goodness," instructed Milo, with a comfortable smile. "You know—peas, lentils, that sort of thing."

Helianthos smiled back. "Are you recommending beans, Milo?"

Milo of Croton shrugged his massive shoulders peacefully. The failed student had really grown up. He had learned to make jokes.

"So . . . who killed the old man? Who stood to gain?" asked Milo quietly.

"Pythagoras." Helianthos had found an expression of wry acceptance that mirrored the wrestler's own. "But of course," he said, "we know that cannot be possible, because Pythagoras could not bring himself to kill any living thing."

"Philosophy's wonderful," Milo agreed.

Lindsey Davis departs from ancient Rome to explore the murder of Pythagoras—of Theorem fame—among the ancient Greeks in Italy. Her series of mysteries featuring wiseguy "informer" Marcus Didius Falco *(Silver Pigs, Shadows in Bronze, Venus in Copper, Poseidon's Gold, The Iron Hand of Mars, Last Act in Palmyra, Time to Depart)* won a "Dagger in the Library" award in 1995 from the British Crime Writers Association.

Time's Wingéd Chariot

Marjorie Eccles

Retirement had loomed large for Spencer Harrison during the last twelve months, considerably more so for his wife, Eunice. Inevitably, it was now here, and to celebrate, Spencer had put two bottles of champagne on ice. He and Eunice lay on garden chairs in the hot sunshine, waiting to drink it. The salmon mayonnaise and the raspberries and cream to follow stood ready in the fridge.

"I think," Spencer said, "I can run the track fairly easily round that maple."

Eunice wasn't listening. She lay back in the garden chair, hoping they could get this business over quickly so that she could go back to her summer pruning. Leaning over, she tugged at a daisy between the paving. The state of her hands was deplorable, but she didn't care for wearing gloves. She enjoyed the cool, green feeling of tiny plants and the sensuousness of sweet, crumbling earth between her fingers. She was large and placid, with a fair, bland face and a patient, plodding walk.

The garden had daunted other buyers, twenty years ago. Disproportionately large in relation to the size of the house, and encompassing to one side a steep and desolate jungle, bramble and weed-infested, where once stone had been gouged from the hillside, it had, however, rejoiced Eunice's heart with its challenges and possibilities. Spencer had bought the house for Eunice even before his first wife—Eunice's best friend, as it happened—had astonished him and left him, without so much as a word or a note, but at least sparing him the inconvenience and expense of the divorce he would never have got around to asking for.

Behind the house now stretched smooth lawns and herbaceous borders, while to the side the old quarry cascaded with rock plants in season, intersected by winding paths. High up, a small ornamental bridge crossed a narrow crevasse, down which a bright, natural stream tumbled from above, providing moisture for the heathers, rhododendrons, and azaleas that bordered it. All the work had been done by Eunice. She was a strong woman and lifted large rockery stones or wheeled heavy barrowloads of timber for constructing the bridge more easily—or, at any rate, more willingly—than Spencer would have done. He did not share her obsession.

The garden was indeed beautiful, but above all it was quiet, blessedly quiet. Apart from the gentle splash of the stream, the sounds were all of bees buzzing, leaves falling, birdsong in the springtime and the wind in the trees. Not a clock within earshot.

If Eunice's passion was gardening, Spencer's was clocks. Twenty-three at the last count, disposed in various parts of the house: the grandfather—which she must remember to call the long-case clock—in the hall, the Viennese wall clock halfway up the stairs, the French carriage clock, whose moods varied with the temperature, the sheep's-head country clock, whose wooden works were riddled with worm, the skeleton clock in the dining room, the hideous black marble and ormulu mantelpiece set. Spencer was incapable of doing things by halves.

The clocks were the only things ever seriously to disturb Eunice's placidity. The relentless chimes and strikes counting and measuring out the quarter-hours of her life drove her mad, while their constant ticking was like the Chinese water torture to her. Throughout the day, throughout the night, they ticked and chimed and struck, the silvery tones of the walnut bracket clock vying with the loud bong of the kitchen wall clock and the double strike and the slow, measured thunk of the grandfather—the long-case—not to mention the Westminster chimes on the landing and the Whittington ones in the study.

It was no use stopping them while Spencer was out at work, because starting them again put the chimes and strikes out of kilter. Spencer's rage when this happened made even the noise of the clocks seem easy to bear. He had been a British Army sergeant once, and still wore a stiff mustache and a bristly haircut. He was compact and muscular. His temper was nasty when roused.

The years with Spencer had, after all, been no big deal, and Eunice sometimes wondered if the clocks were a punishment for the wrong done to his first wife. But at least now she was spared the worst atrocity of the lot: a wooden wall clock decorated with garish Highland scenes and "A Souvenir from o'er the Border" painted around the face, with the long and repetitious tune of "The Bluebells of Scotland" marking the quarters. Several years ago they'd been burgled and it had been lost, along with some ugly Victorian silver that had belonged to Spencer's mother. The police, thank God, had found neither clock nor silver.

Spencer lifted the first bottle of champagne from the bucket, uncorked it faultlessly and poured it so they might toast his future retirement. He could have stayed on until he was sixty-five, but he'd elected to go at sixty. "Well, you please yourself," Eunice had said, "but you, retiring at sixty? You're a young man yet."

He wasn't going to disagree with that, but she hadn't fooled him. She didn't want him under her feet all day, keeping her from her confounded garden. *Their* garden, upon which his own eye had now lit.

He wasn't going to be idle, he told her. He had plans for his retirement. Weekly trips to the library. Auctions where he might find the odd clock bargain. Visits to stately homes. Railway museums. He didn't mention the holidays abroad; he knew she'd never be persuaded to leave her garden.

He was full of the little economies they might make, too, and began to list them as the wine loosened his tongue. Eunice could dispense with the services of Mrs. Cathcart, who presently came twice a week, because he wasn't a man who was afraid of turning his hand to a bit of help with the housework. And he would make their own wine, he added, gazing reflectively into his Sainsbury's champagne-type bubbles. Of course, they'd get rid of Eunice's car—not that they'd get anything for it, B reg and all that, but they'd save on the tax and insurance.

Eunice, who'd heard all this before and had succeeded in coming to terms with what was going to happen by so far ignoring it, sipped her wine. She was totally unprepared when Spencer dropped his bombshell. "I think," he remarked, evidently continuing something he'd begun earlier, "the track can run along there—" pointing to her herbaceous border—"and come along to the tunnel, which I'll make here."

There appeared to go smack through the middle of the magnificent clump of *Lilium regale* that had taken years to establish. *Here* was just where the small rockery was, a little beyond the flagged path outside the French windows. Looking at it, Eunice's heart, not normally a volatile organ, jumped about like a wild thing inside her rib cage. She felt sick. The moment she'd dreaded for years was here.

"Track?" she echoed faintly. "What track?"

"My steam railway track. I knew you weren't listening." He repeated what he'd said before, and outlined its proposed route through the peonies, skirting the Japanese maple, with a little station, maybe, at that point, there . . . where this year *Nevada* excelled herself in a huge, arched spread of white fragrance. "I've always wanted a steam railway, ever since I was a lad."

Eunice's horrified mind took in the enormity of what he was saying, and what she was going to have to do. She looked around at her beautiful garden. "You have? I never knew."

"Oh, yes, dear, I've been planning it for years," he said.

The next morning Eunice went into town to do some shopping. Before she went, she announced that if the track was to go through the rockery by the French window, the stones and some of the plants would need to be moved, and she'd do it on Tuesday.

"Isn't it a bad time of year for moving plants?"

"I'll settle them in plenty of peat—they won't realize they've been moved. There's a nice shady place for them on the other side of the bridge."

Spencer was very busy while she was out. Afterwards, he cleaned up the tools and put them all back in place so that she wouldn't notice they'd been used.

It was raining the next day, but that didn't prevent Eunice starting on the job. He watched her from the kitchen window, monolithic in a shapeless old waterproof garment and gumboots, patiently trudging up the steep, narrow path of the quarry with her first barrowload of stones.

He knew how she hated his precious clocks, though she'd long ago given up saying so. After that burglary, in fact. She'd been very shifty about it, and he'd suspected for years why the police had never been able to trace any of those stolen goods—the Scottish clock and the silver, taken while he was away on a business trip. It had been fairly obvious, knowing Eunice as he did, that to get rid of them she'd bury them somewhere in the garden, but where, in a garden this size? He'd known that one day, if he waited, she'd give herself away and he'd find out what she'd done with them.

She'd gone white when he'd mentioned tunneling under that rockery.

There was the second bottle of champagne left from Sunday, nearly full. Eunice had suddenly seemed to lose her taste for it after his announcement about the rockery. He'd corked it up again with one of those gizmos that was supposed to keep it drinkable, and put it back in the fridge. It shouldn't be too bad.

He took it out and poured a glass, holding it in readiness as Eunice came to the bridge with the heavy barrow. She paused and lowered it, and he began to sweat. She wasn't going to cross after all. But after a moment, she lifted the barrow again, and moved. When she reached the middle, the planks he'd loosened yesterday gave with the heavy weight, and he watched his wife, jerked forward and off balance as the barrow tipped, tumble down the steep crevasse of the stream, with the barrowload of stones on top of her. He smiled and lifted his glass. Now he could go out and finish the job she'd started. No chance of salvaging anything much of his clock by this time, but at least he'd have proof of her perfidy, and justification for what he'd done. He tipped the glass and drained the champagne.

The clocks all over the house began to chime eleven o'clock as Spencer Harrison died from the paraquat put into the champagne bottle by his wife. Outside, under the aubretia and alyssum and miniature junipers by the French windows, the first Mrs. Harrison, put there by Eunice before she constructed her rockery twenty years ago, slept on undisturbed.

This story from Marjorie Eccles describes the dark prospect of impending retirement for an elderly couple. Among her numerous novels is her mystery series featuring Detective Chief Inspector Gil Mayo, including *A Species of Revenge* (September 1996). Eccles lives in a village on the edge of the Chilterns.

Alternative Reality

Anthea Fraser

Sybil came across the salon purely by chance; but then, chance had governed her life these last few weeks. She had no more volition than a leaf blown before the wind, her sole concern being to get through each endless day as best she could.

She'd set out in the car as she had fallen into the habit of doing, simply to get out of the house. It was raining, and summer rain, intensified by the heavy, dripping foliage, seemed somehow so much more depressing. Even though her wipers were on double speed, great globules cascaded down the windscreen, then, with the impetus of the car's motion, flew back up again. Like tears flowing back into eyes.

Well, she thought desolately, he was gone, and all the tears in the world wouldn't bring him back. She wasn't the first whose husband had fallen for a younger woman and she wouldn't be the last, though the knowledge brought little comfort. But the way he'd told her—so calmly and matter-of-factly, even adding that he'd arranged a three months' leave of absence from the office, "to give us all a chance to adjust." As if she could rebuild her shattered world in three months! Was it any wonder she'd reacted as she had?

If only they'd had children, she thought wistfully. Robert had brought up the subject once, in the early days, but she'd cut him short. She was perfectly happy as she was, she'd insisted, free to go with him on business trips and entertain his clients. But the real reason, unadmitted even to herself, was that she was too possessive to share his love, even with their own child. There was irony in that.

Had she reacted differently, those children would now be in their twenties. A daughter, perhaps, to gossip with, to accompany on shopping trips and to the theatre; a son, who would cosset her and buy her flowers. Now, she had need of them, and regretted denying them their existence.

What names would they have had, these mythical children? Charles, perhaps, after her father? And Rosemary? That had always been her favorite. Rosemary for remembrance—but there was nothing to remember.

Still, they'd been happy in those early years, she and Robert. She was a lively and accomplished hostess, and he'd been so proud of her. Then there'd been all those wonderful holidays—Australia, Thailand, South Africa—places they couldn't have afforded to visit if they'd had a family to educate.

During this musing the car had emerged onto a wider road, and, realizing she'd no idea where she was, Sybil pulled over to study the map, tracing the route she'd come with one finger. If she stayed on this road, in a few miles she'd come to a small town. She decided to continue; it was, after all, too early to turn round and go home.

In tossing the map on the backseat, she inadvertently knocked the mirror, and lifted a hand to straighten it. Then, abruptly, she paused, really looking at her reflection for the first time in weeks. And experienced a shock.

Her graying hair hung limply round a colorless face—she'd not bothered with makeup lately—what was the point? Even her eyes, her best feature, were puffy and webbed by a network of fine lines. She looked twenty years older than she actually was. Oh Robert, she thought, on a wave of self-pity, look what you've done to me!

Drearily, she restarted the car and edged out on to the road. She had never felt so utterly alone. Perhaps she should get a dog; at least it would be company, and she could take it for long walks on the hills. A black Labrador— she'd always liked them, but Robert was allergic to dogs. Ebony? Sooty? Jet?

She was approaching the outskirts of the town. Yellow brick houses lined the road, each with a smooth lawn, double-glazed windows, and an air of smug complacency, seen through a relentless curtain of rain.

Outside the school a group of mothers huddled under umbrellas, some of them with younger children encased like chrysalises in their buggies under a clear screen of plastic. Soon they'd return to their yellow houses, close their doors on the wet afternoon, and prepare tea for the family. Sybil envied them with every fiber of her being.

On her left a service road gave on to a parade of shops, and quite suddenly the need to speak to another human being—anyone—overpowered her. She turned off the main road and parked outside the supermarket. Only then did she realize she had no umbrella. Not that it mattered; nothing mattered.

Turning up the collar of her jacket, she left the car and hurried across the gleaming pavement into the store, almost colliding in the entrance with someone trying to disentangle a trolley.

The woman looked up ruefully. "These things have a mind of their own. They cling together, and when you do finally manage to detach one, it refuses to go in the direction you want."

Sybil smiled uncertainly. "I'll hold on to the next one while you pull," she volunteered, and between them the trolley was freed. The woman offered to return the favor, but Sybil declined. "I've only a few things to get—a basket will do."

In fact, there was nothing she needed. She was hardly eating, and there was only herself to cater for. She walked aimlessly down the aisles, looking at the brightly colored packaging and tempting displays.

Rounding a corner, she found herself in the pet-food section, stretching halfway down the aisle, and her eye was instantly caught by a brand of dog food that had on its label a picture of a black Labrador. Jet! she thought, and reached out for one. There, she'd committed herself to buying a dog!

She smiled at the fancy, and one of the assistants, restocking the shelves across the aisle, said brightly, "Nice to see a happy face on a day like this!"

Sybil felt cheered beyond reason. On the strength of the girl's smile she selected a packet of digestive biscuits and added them to the can in her basket. This impulsive shopping trip was lifting her spirits; when she'd finished here, she'd go on to the other shops in the parade. There'd be people to talk to there, as well.

But though the baker's smelled enticingly of fresh bread, the assistant was too busy to indulge in small talk, and Sybil, her burgeoning confidence wilting again, left the shop with her modest purchase and nothing more.

Out on the pavement she hesitated, reluctant to return to the car and its solitary confinement. The next window belonged to a hairdressing salon, and displayed placards of attractive young women with artfully wind-tossed curls. Sybil moved idly along, noting the price list for the various treatments. As she reached the door a young woman emerged and, thinking Sybil was about to go in, smilingly held it open for her. Almost without thought, Sybil walked inside and, though she didn't realize it, into a new life.

The salon was warm after the chill rain, softly lit and decorated in pink and gray. There was a long counter down one side, where several women sat in front of mirrors, in various stages of refurbishment. On the right, comfortably ensconced with books and cups of tea, another set were seated under purring driers. Sybil felt the relaxed and friendly atmosphere reach out for her, wrapping around her like a warm towel.

The girl at the desk was asking, "Have you an appointment, madam?" and she came quickly back to earth.

"No, no, I—"

"It doesn't matter, Beverley can fit you in if you'd like to sit down for a minute." She indicated a sofa in front of the window. "Shampoo and set, is it?"

Sybil, suddenly emboldened, took the plunge. "I'd like a new style, if she has time."

"I think we can manage that. Could I have your name?"

She never knew why she lied. Perhaps it was simply an unwillingness to let her real life intrude in these pleasant surroundings. Glancing at the biscuits in her carrier-bag, she said impulsively, "McVitie. Mrs. McVitie."

Which set the stage for what was to follow. On that first visit, though, she was content merely to relax and have her scalp massaged with soothing, sweet-smelling lather, to watch, mesmerized, as Beverley's clever fingers fashioned a style out of her limp, unkempt locks.

"Pity to let it go gray when it's such a lovely color," the girl said, snipping away, and Sybil, surprised, saw that the conditioner had brought out the chestnut lights of her youth.

"Why not let me touch it up for you?" Beverley added, and before she realized it, Sybil had agreed to a tint the following week.

She'd be coming back, then. The thought filled her with pleasure—it would be something to look forward to, another pampered session in this perfumed place.

At the position next to hers, an animated conversation was going on between client and assistant, involving grandchildren, Masonic dances, holidays. Sybil listened avidly, envying the woman her full and interesting life, and a feeling of excitement began to stir. Here, miles from home, she was totally anonymous—even her name wasn't real. She was just one of a row of ladies whiling away a Friday afternoon. And it dawned on her that she was free to shape a whole new life for herself, to speak casually about Charles and Rosemary, and no one would raise an eyebrow.

And her husband? Not Robert; certainly not someone who'd let her down so badly. But in view of "McVitie," a Scottish name was called for. Angus, then—that had a ring to it. And, like Robert, he could travel extensively on business and be fluent in several languages.

By the time that, swathed in a silken net, she was led to the drier, anticipation had her in its grip. She could come here *every week!* Like everyone else, no doubt. And every week, in this alternative world she'd discovered, she could talk as the other women did, about her dream family, her full and fascinating life. And speaking about it openly would make it all seem real.

The die was finally cast when, propping her carrier-bag against the desk to make next week's appointment, it slipped sideways and tipped the tin of dog food onto the floor. One of the girls retrieved it for her and Sybil, sleekly coiffeured, smiled her thanks. "I'd be in trouble with Jet if I arrived home without that!" she said.

Ron Wilkes settled himself more comfortably on the sofa and Bev snuggled against him, her spiky hair tickling his chin. The film they'd been watching had ended and neither was interested in the news.

"So, how are things at work, then?" Ron asked casually.

"Fine." Beverley's pleased tone showed she was flattered by his interest. Little did she know! "That new lady I told you about has become a regular. I done her a lovely tint and she was over the moon with it. Gave me a good tip, and all. Mind you, she could afford it."

Ron blew smoke rings at the ceiling. "What makes you think that, doll?"

"Well, the way she talks. Her husband has some fancy job—always going abroad and that—and they're having ever such a big wedding for her daughter. No expense spared. Know what they're giving her as a wedding present? Only a house!"

When he remained silent, she turned around to peer into his face. "What do you think of that, then?"

"All right for some, innit? Where does she hang out, this Mrs. Rockerfeller of yours?"

"Dunno. Her name's McVitie," Bev added naively.

Ron made no comment, his mind busy. Bev's chatter about her clients had provided some nice pickings over the months since he'd met her, and the beauty was there was nothing to connect them to him. This old bird might be worth investigating.

On his way home that evening, he called in at a pub and, going over to the pay-phone, thumbed through the directory. To his frustration, no McVities were listed; the number must be ex-directory. It figured, if her husband was a big shot. So the only way to discover where she lived was to follow her home from the salon.

He ordered a pint, drank it thoughtfully, and went on his way, well satisfied with the evening's outcome.

Having checked with Bev, Ron positioned himself outside the supermarket the following Friday in time for his quarry's two-thirty appointment. He'd chosen his place with care, close enough to see who went into the salon, but not near enough to be noticed.

What he hadn't expected was that no fewer than three ladies arrived at the same time, and he was forced to move forward until, keeping out of Bev's line of vision, he could peer through the window and see which of them had gone to her table.

Gotcha! he thought in triumph, as a tall woman with reddish brown hair sat down and Bev began fussing over her. Right, he'd be back in an hour to follow her home.

"We've had quite a few problems with the dress," Sybil was saying happily, watching in the mirror as Beverley's deft fingers wound the strands of hair round a roller. "Rosemary's lost weight since the last fitting—wedding nerves, I suppose."

"What does her young man do?" Bev queried, engrossed in her task.

"He's in computers." It sounded convincing, Sybil thought, pleased. Most young people seemed to be in computers these days. "He's doing very well," she added, feeling she owed her imaginary daughter a successful husband.

Beverley was asking about the wedding reception and Sybil enthusiastically replied. This alternative world was becoming more and more real to her. Nowadays, when she left the salon, it took some time to revert to her normal self, so reluctant had she become to give up Mrs. McVitie, with her clever and successful family. Perhaps if she could really convince herself it was true, she'd be able to slip permanently into that other life, never have to return to the lonely house she'd come to dread.

Ron, following her in his shabby Metro, was surprised how far they were traveling. All his previous targets, whose details he'd gleaned from Bev, were within a two-mile radius of the salon. Why the hell did this one trail all the way to Scissors to have her hair done? Must be plenty of places nearer. Come to that, with all her money it was a wonder she didn't go to the really fancy places in town. Still, he mustn't grumble, not if it turned out to his advantage.

He continued to follow her at a discreet distance cross-country to the outskirts of the next town, where she surprised him again by turning into an ordinary-looking driveway. Reasonable enough house, he supposed—detached, with a fair-sized garden—but from the way Bev had gone on, he'd expected a mansion. He drove slowly past, noting the address, and by the time he reached the corner was already making his plans.

During the week that followed, Ron spent several hours observing the house on Oakwood Drive, to the detriment of his job at the garage. Every day, at varying times, the old bird came out, got into her car, and drove off, but as far as he could see, no one else either emerged from or entered the house.

Ron was puzzled. Where was this wealthy husband of hers, then? Away on business? And the daughter who, Bev said, was getting married next month? Shacked up with her boyfriend, no doubt, he thought with an inward grin. But at least his stakeout had been productive: when the old girl set out for the hairdresser's next Friday, he was pretty confident there'd be no one else at home.

By the time Friday came he was on edge, as always before a job. He was also nervous about his car; it was on the shabby side for this neighborhood. Suppose she'd noticed it, even though he'd parked in different places and at different times? Still, even if she had, she'd only think it belonged to a workman at one of the other houses.

And now here she came, driving out of the gateway and straight off, without a glance in his direction. He waited for ten heart-stopping minutes, in case she'd gone off without her purse or something and came back for it. Then he got out of the car, looked swiftly up and down the road, and slipped at last into the overgrown driveway. The house, solid and uncommunicative, stood waiting for him.

A quick glance at the front windows ruled them out for forced entry. They looked secure, but, more importantly, though trees shielded the house from neighbors on either side, he'd have been in full view of anyone passing the entrance who happened to glance inside. A flimsy wooden gate barred the way around the back, but this was no deterrent. Ron reached over the top, located the bolt, and was able, by contorting his fingers, to draw it back. In one movement he was through, with the gate closed behind him.

So far, so good. He followed the wall of the house along the narrow passage until the back garden opened up in front of him—long grass, rampant shrubbery, overblown roses.

Again, he was surprised. If the absent husband wasn't interested in gardening, why didn't he pay someone else to do it?

The back door was secure, as was the window next to it, but to one side a flat-roofed single story extension had been added and, standing back to look up, Ron had his first piece of luck. Immediately above the flat roof was a frosted glass window—presumably the bathroom—and it was open half an inch at the top. Bingo! he thought exultantly, and, gripping the drainpipe as to the manner born, he shinned swiftly up it.

In the house directly opposite, the three watchers had seen it all—his stealthy approach, his fumbling over the side gate to release the bolt, his quick disappearance. PC Tom Parsons said to the woman beside him, "That the man, madam?"

"Yes—yes, that's him. He's been hanging around all week." She paused, looking expectantly from one officer to the other. "Well, aren't you going after him? We know there's no one home."

"We'll give him a minute or two to gain entry. Better if we catch him red-handed. You say the owners are a Mr. and Mrs. Price?"

"That's right."

"Are they aware their house was being watched?"

"It wasn't, not specifically. He obviously saw Mrs. Price go out, and seized his opportunity. But he's been parked at various places up and down the road—this could have happened to any of us. At first I thought he must be a decorator or something, but when the people whose houses he'd parked by denied all knowledge of him, I became concerned. I decided that if he came back again today, I'd call you."

"Seems odd he should have waited till now. The Prices—and the rest of you—must have been in and out several times, if he's been hanging around all week."

"She has, certainly, but I haven't seen him for a while. Probably away on business."

"Know where he works?"

"I'm afraid not."

"Right, well, come along then, Jenkins. Let's see what Chummie is up to."

Ron had managed to get in through the window, though he'd landed awkwardly and wrenched his ankle in the process. He rubbed it, swearing softly, before moving out onto the landing, where he stood listening. A sudden whirring brought his heart to his mouth, then he realized it came from the old clock at the foot of the staircase.

He ran lightly down and, by means of a piece of wire, turned the lock in the front door. His first action on a job was always to ensure a quick getaway; he didn't fancy climbing out of the bathroom window with his loot.

But as he went systematically from room to room, he grew more and more frustrated. There was little here to interest him. Some silver, certainly, but it was heavy and could probably be traced, and though the furniture was good, it was solid and old-fashioned and too cumbersome to nick. Might as well cut his losses down here and go for money and jewelry, which would probably be in the bedrooms.

He went back up the steps two at a time, and at the top paused and looked about him. There was a strange, sweet smell up here that he'd been faintly aware of as he came out of the bathroom. Decaying apples? Perhaps they stored windfalls in a spare bedroom. But wasn't it too early in the year?

Shrugging, he turned into the first room, which was obviously in use. A nightdress lay on one of the pillows and some clothes were folded over a chair. No pajamas on the other pillow, but then there wouldn't be, if hubby was still away on that business trip.

Ron opened a dressing-table drawer, and, sure enough,

there was a leather jewelry box inside. Quickly he opened it. This was more like it. Pearls—looked real, but he couldn't be sure—a couple of diamond rings, some gold bracelets. He stuffed them quickly into his pockets. There were a couple of handbags in the wardrobe, and he found a five-pound note in one of them, but that was all. Bit of a letdown all around; a week's reconnoitering, and all for a handful of baubles. He'd raise a few bucks on them, but they wouldn't knock over any houses.

Might as well check the other rooms, in case the daughter had left some trinkets lying around. He hurried across the landing and paused, his hand on the doorknob. The sweet smell was stronger here, and for no reason he could explain he felt his gorge rise. Quickly, because time was running out, he flung open the door. Then staggered back, holding his nose against the stench that hit him, and slammed the door shut again.

Groping blindly, he stumbled into the bathroom and bent, retching, over the lavatory bowl. It was there that Constable Parsons found him.

It was half an hour later. During that time, the house had filled with grim figures, white-coated and masked, who had entered the dread room above and closed the door behind them. There were policemen on the gate, a doctor and a pathologist conferring in the kitchen. A shotgun had been found, pushed to the back of the wardrobe in the front bedroom, and there seemed little doubt this was the murder weapon.

Ron Wilkes, white and shivering, was sitting in one of the police cars in the drive. For as long as he lived, he thought bleakly, he would never get that smell out of his nostrils, never forget that one, horrified glimpse of the blood-soaked sheets, the spattered wall behind, and the naked, decaying bodies on the bed.

PC Parsons was saying, "You mean you targeted this house deliberately? Why?"

Ron shuddered. Why, indeed? He had never regretted anything more. "'Cos I heard the woman that lived here was loaded."

"Mrs. Price?"

"Nah—McVitie's the name."

Parsons shook his head. "The owners of the house are a Mr. and Mrs. Price," he said. Though it seemed likely that Mr. Price had relinquished his claim some six weeks previously.

Ron looked up, frowning. Were they telling him, after all he'd been through, that he'd picked the wrong bleeding house? But he *couldn't* have. He'd seen her going in and out all week.

"McVitie," he repeated stubbornly. "My girlfriend does her hair. She goes every Friday—that's where she is now."

Parsons turned sharply. "You know where Mrs. Price is?"

"Mrs. *McVitie*'s having her hair done." Ron glanced at his watch. "Should be back any minute now."

Parsons reached for his phone, spoke quickly into it. "Tell the inspector the suspect's due back any minute. Better move the cars out of sight—we don't want to frighten her off."

Sybil was smiling happily to herself. Only another month to the wedding, then she and Angus would fly to South America for six weeks. It would be lovely to relax, after all the strain and stress. She must buy herself some new clothes for the trip.

She turned into Oakwood Drive. There seemed to be a lot of cars about. Vaguely, she wondered whose they were. Then, as she drew up at the familiar gate, two policemen emerged from the shrubbery and one of them bent to open the car door. She smiled questioningly up at him.

"Mrs. Price?"

"No, Constable, my name is McVitie. Is something wrong?"

Over the roof of the car, the two policemen exchanged puzzled glances. That name again. The one who had spoken fell back on a well-tried formula as he firmly helped her from the car.

"We'd like a word, ma'am," he said.

Anthea Fraser illustrates the perils of living in a daydream in this story. Fraser, author of nearly 30 mystery novels, including the recent *The Gospel Makers* (1996), was secretary of the British Crime Writers Association from 1986 until 1996.

Come Sable Night
(A Phryne Fisher Mystery)

Kerry Greenwood

"But in her heart a cold December . . ."
—Thomas Morley, *April Is In My Mistress' Face*

Nineteen twenty-eight was a good year for madrigals.

The Honorable Miss Phryne Fisher surveyed the crowd of singers, drawn from the Glee Club and the Women's Choir, as they moved through patches of sunlight in her sea-green parlor, shoes clicking on the polished bare boards. It was a summer's day, still cool enough to make the sunshine welcome, and they were worth looking at. So was Phryne, in a rose-red afternoon dress embroidered with golden bees, her Dutch-doll hair as shiny as embroidery floss. She had invited the Madrigal Choir to her bijou residence for their rehearsal. She provided the refreshments and they provided the music—and the scandal. Phryne had taken the day off. She was not detecting anything at the moment.

Phryne Fisher watched the distribution of champagne cup and listened to the low voice of the large economy-size bass who stood behind her. Claude Greenhill—engaging, calm and the best-informed gossip in the Western world—

was providing a situation report. Phryne's neat, black head came up to his first waistcoat button.

"Lawrence has done something outrageous," commented Claude dispassionately. Phryne watched the tall, blond, athletic scion of the Newhouse-Gore fortune as he divided his attention between two adoring young women.

"Lawrence is always outrageous," she replied. "He treats the Women's Choir as a harem, always has—and his success, I have to say, is remarkable. I don't know how Diane stands him."

"She doesn't have to endure him anymore," whispered Claude.

"Oh? Come to her senses, has she? I wouldn't have thought it—she seemed quite besotted with him. He does have a clean-cut, Captain of the Boats charm, you have to admit."

Diane Hart was sitting by the window. The light set her long red hair aflame and bronzed her grass-green dress. A bunch of red roses lay on her lap, and she was staring at Lawrence with an expression that Phryne could not read.

"I admit the charm, but this is going too far," said Claude, taking a gulp of champagne cup. "He's dumped Diane and taken up with Violet."

"Oh, dear," said Phryne lamely. Violet was Diane's younger sister, mouse to her bright scarlet. "How do you know?"

"Diane spent most of last night telling me about it." Claude made a gesture that mimed wringing out the shoulder of his white shirt. "I suppose that they can transfer the wedding plans to the sister. The funeral baked meats, that sort of thing."

"The dress won't fit," said Phryne. "Lord, lord. Any more gossip, Claude?"

"Oh, yes. Poor Alexandra is devastated. She's always been Button B in that ménage, and now she's pipped at the post. Violet looks sweet enough, but she's got a will of adamant. Our Lawrence won't be dropping in to Alexandra's house for tea and sympathy anymore. And she really did love him."

Phryne noticed Alexandra. She had plaited her long black hair into a punitive braid and was on her third cocktail. Her dark eyes were shadowed with grief.

"Damn Lawrence, why *will* he do it?" said Phryne suddenly. "He's rich enough to buy all the companionship he needs. Must he reap the Women's Choir like wheat?"

"He's not as bad as Victor," said Claude.

"This is true. Victor is a rake-hell, a Casanova, a totally unreliable, cold, hungry bastard," agreed Phryne. "But he lays all his marked cards on the table. No young woman, however self-deluded, could think that Victor really liked her or appreciated her."

"There's one who does," said Claude, angling his chin to indicate a drooping figure leafing through a photograph album: Jane, who had been a fiery proponent of Free Love, with all her fire gone and a suspicious bulge at her waist. Victor caught Phryne looking at her and advanced with a plate of cheese straws, expostulating.

"Miss Fisher, you shouldn't believe all you hear."

"Oh?" Phryne disliked Victor's practiced smile even more than usual. He was slim and dark and moved like a dancer. His eyes were blue and knowing. "Why shouldn't I?"

"You know Causeless Claude—gossips like an old woman."

Phryne grinned. "I know Claude, Victor, and I know you." His smile faded. Claude leaned over her and collected a handful of cheese straws. He was opening his mouth to speak when Lawrence clapped his hands and bellowed, "I've got an announcement to make."

Silence fell. He was the center of attention, always where he felt he ought to be. He took the hand of the girl standing next to him and said, "Violet has agreed to be my wife. Congratulate me."

There was some scattered applause. Violet looked up at

the blond Adonis with such an expression of perfect trust that Phryne's mouth dried. He patted her shoulder.

"Champagne," said Victor. He produced an opened bottle of Moet and two glasses.

"To the bride and groom!" he said, and watched as Lawrence and Violet, laughing, drank. "You're all invited to sing at the wedding," said Lawrence, grinning. The assembled choristers toasted them. Talk broke out in an excited babble. Alexandra looked crushed and bit the end of her plait. Diane, sitting by the fireplace, came up to the happy couple and thrust her bouquet of red roses into Lawrence's hands.

"I hope you'll be very happy," she murmured.

"That's good of you, old girl. No hard feelings?" Phryne heard Lawrence ask, in a condescending tone, as she and Claude came up to add their congratulations.

"None," said Diane in a tight voice. Phryne marveled that Lawrence seemed to instantly accept her statement. After all, it had only been six months since the same man had announced that Diane was going to marry him, and with the same panache as he showed now. Lawrence's fingers closed on the stems as he leant to kiss his fianceé's sister on the cheek.

"Ouch," he said, shaking his hand. "These roses have thorns!" he told Phryne, insulted that they should dare to prick him.

Phryne took the flowers and handed them to a waitress, saying "Put these in water, will you?"

"Time to start singing." Arthur Dauphin, the chorus master, decided to intervene before anyone said anything he might later regret. "It's only two weeks to the concert. Claude's got the music. This is the order in which we will sing the madrigals. Don't shuffle them. Nothing worse than a choir that rustles. All right, come along, please, ladies and gentlemen."

Phryne sat down out of the way and watched the inchoate gathering resolve itself into groups of sopranos, altos, tenors, and basses. Sleek Arthur raised his hands and they began to sing warm-up exercises. Collaring a glass of champagne, Phryne surveyed the choir. They were very young, mostly good-looking, and although they were shaken and excited by Lawrence's announcement, they were relatively disciplined and professional. Even Alexandra had shelved her broken heart. Diane, among the sopranos, drew in a deep breath. Claude, among the basses, was concentrating on low notes, while Lawrence was mopping his brow, possibly in relief at having escaped a scene. Victor, among the tenors, was ogling an alto on whom he had his eye. She was blushing.

They opened their music and began. *"Now is the month of Maying, when merry lads are playing . . ."*

"Tenors, you are flat. That's a major third," said Arthur, slicking back his hair dubiously. "Sopranos, pay attention to the timing. Timing is of the essence in madrigals. All right. Now, the next song. *Fyer, fyer.* Crisply, now."

They completed the song with only minimal grumbling from the conductor.

"Ay me, ay me, I sit and cry me, and call for help alas! But none comes nigh me."

"Sopranos, that was an interesting interpretation, but I prefer Thomas Morley's version. Let's get on. Page four, please."

"Come, sable night," they sang, so sadly that Phryne was moved. *"Put on thy mourning stole . . . and only Amyntas wastes his heart in wailing. In wailing,"* The carefully pitched voices rose in exquisite harmony. *"In wailing . . ."* Arthur's hand flicked at the basses. Their voices rose. *"In wail . . ."*

With excellent timing, Lawrence Newhouse-Gore's voice hit the top note, stuck, and failed. In failing, he fell, sprawled among the surprised choir. A stockingless medical student called Anne bent over the prone figure, felt for a pulse, and shot a look at Phryne.

"He's dead," she told her hostess, quietly.

"Lawrence!" screamed Alexandra. She clawed for the

body and was held back in the firm embrace of three sympathetic friends. Diane did not move a muscle. Victor, into the sudden silence, laughed. Claude raised both eyebrows. Everyone else stood astonished, at a loss for a response.

Arthur's was possibly uncharitable.

"Damn, the concert's in two weeks."

This was the signal for the choir to start reacting. Phryne watched them with interest. Those who usually screamed and cried, duly screamed and cried and were comforted by those who usually comforted. Claude had wrapped his arms around an alto half his height who was snuffling into his chest. Violet had retreated from the body, shocked into blankness, and someone had found her a chair and a drink. Her sister Diane did not come to her side. In fact, she did not even turn to look at the fallen man.

Phryne took charge. "Well, we'd better call a doctor—no offense, Anne dear. Claude, Jack, can you lift him?" Claude and Jack, another large bass, disengaged their petitioners and bent to heave up the long form of Lawrence Newhouse-Gore and lay him on the couch. Phryne and Anne inspected him.

The face was dusky with blood, swollen, and the lips were blue. He was definitely dead. Phryne untied her golden scarf and covered his face.

"Arthur, I think you should move the choir into the drawing room," said Phryne. "There's nothing to be done for you now, Lawrence," she said to the impassive death mask. "I think we'd better keep singing."

"Take your music, everyone," ordered Arthur, gathering up the reins. "Come along. We musn't give way," he added, ushering the last soprano out of the room. Phryne, sitting by the body, heard them begin the next madrigal, raggedly and out of tune—*"Oyez, has any found a lad? Take him quick before he flieth."*—but by the time they came to the next song they had recovered most of their skill. *"Sleep fleshly birth . . . thy doleful obit keeping."*

Summoned away from his Sunday dinner, a cross local

doctor was announced. Dr. McAdam had been looking forward to roast lamb and minted peas and had promised his wife he would not be called away, just for a couple of hours. He was elderly and displeased. But he examined the dead man expertly and quickly.

"Anaphylactic shock," he said crisply. "He was allergic to something. Very allergic. What did he have to eat or drink?"

"Er . . . well. Some egg and mustard cress sandwiches, some caviar, a glass or two of champagne, I don't really know," Phryne replied.

"Strawberries?" snapped the doctor.

"Yes, there were strawberries."

"Well, that's it then. I'll certify death." He scribbled busily. "These are the undertakers I use, though doubtless his people will make their own arrangements. Coroner will have to sit on him, of course. Pity, really. He's very young. Good afternoon, Miss Fisher."

He bustled off to his interrupted lunch and Phryne was again alone with the dead young man. Anne came in and sat down with her.

"The doctor said he died of anaphylactic shock. What's that?"

"Oh, was that it?" asked the young woman. "Yes, that explains the cyanosis. No one knows how it works, but some people are so sensitive to some foods—strawberries are one of them, mustard, but it can be anything—that their whole body reacts. Their throat swells up, their lungs fill with fluid, and they suffocate."

"But Lawrence must have known that he was allergic—he wouldn't have eaten whatever it was," protested Phryne.

"It can sneak up on you. Like bee stings. One bee sting just creates a swelling, the next makes you really ill, and the third can kill. What are you going to do about the body?"

"I've had his parents called. They told me to order an undertaker, so I've done that. And I thought it was going to be such a relaxing day. You're very cool, Anne."

"If I started to get worried about every corpse I saw, I'd be a wreck. It's not as though I liked Lawrence. Sorry, old chum," said the medical student, laying the scarf over the puffed and horrible face.

Next door, the choir was singing *"Weep, weep mine eyes, a thousand deaths I die."* Phryne asked, "Could someone have given him the substance—ground up, so that he wouldn't recognize it?"

"Could have. What are you thinking of?"

"Can you go and cut Victor out of the crowd for me, Anne? And Claude."

"All right." Anne seemed not much interested. Phryne wondered if this callousness was real or affected. Anne had been mentioned as one of Lawrence's many conquests.

Phryne contemplated death. Here was a beautiful young man, who had every reason to assume that the world would continue to conform to his desires, through a suitable marriage and the production of pattern children to an honorable career until a replete old age. And he was dead, faster than she could snap her fingers. Snatched out of the world. Phryne lifted the cooling hand and laid it on the immaculate breast.

Victor and Claude came out of the drawing room, closing the door on *"Death do thy worst, I care not."*

"I say, Phryne," Victor began excitedly "is old Lawrence really dead?"

"He's really dead, and I'm wondering if you really killed him," replied Miss Fisher.

Victor went as pale as his screen-idol's tan would allow. "What do you mean?" he demanded.

"He died of a violent allergy to some substance," said Phryne firmly. "That bottle of wine, Victor. Where did you open it?"

"Just outside the room. I wanted it to be ready and I didn't want the pop to be heard before he made his announcement."

"Unconvincing," said Phryne, pulling the palpitating tenor down to sit between her and Claude. The bass nodded. "Very unconvincing."

"What did you put in that otherwise unexceptional wine,

Victor?" she demanded. Victor looked into green eyes as cold as jade and faltered.

"Nothing, nothing, I swear."

"Why don't I believe you? How well did you know Lawrence?"

"We were old friends, used to go out together, you know that." Victor was sweating.

"Used to go out together? Or stay in together?"

"I don't know what you're suggesting," bridled Victor.

Claude shook his head sadly. "Yes, you do. Not a new suggestion, either. Not that we mind. Some of Miss Fisher's best friends are practitioners of the love that dare not speak its name. Come on, Vic, this is serious. Was Lawrence your lover?"

"How dare you!" Victor blustered. Both pairs of eyes considered him, gray and green. He collapsed. "Yes, yes, once or twice. He didn't really like me, you know. How did you know?"

"I always suspect young men who make such a show of their manliness. You protest too much, Victor. Now, about that bottle of wine. Did you know that Lawrence was allergic to some food? What was it?"

"I never knew, he ate what he liked, always." Victor squirmed, then said, "He was allergic to bee stings, though. He must have been stung, that's it, no one killed him, it's an accident. I'm glad he's dead. He had a letter of mine. He wanted me . . . he wanted me to . . ."

"Tell us," said Phryne, grasping the shaking hands.

Victor gasped, "He wanted me to marry Diane. Take her off his hands, make her a good husband. She likes me well enough, but I couldn't—I couldn't . . ."

He burst into tears, leaning his forehead into Phryne's bosom. She held him for a moment, then pushed him gently away. Not even for pity could she really bear Victor this close. He stank of California Poppy and fear.

"There, there, now blow your nose and sit up. Go and wash your face, Victor. The bathroom's through there."

"Do you think he did it?" asked the bass, seriously.

"I don't know. We'll know if he comes back. He's scared enough to bolt. That's why I am giving him the chance."

"He might be faking. And we still don't know why he opened the bottle outside the room."

"Bee stings? Can you be that allergic to a bee sting?" asked Phryne. The large bass shrugged.

The choir began on the next madrigal, *"Adieu Sweet Amaryllis for since to part your will is"* as Victor returned, mopped-up and red-eyed.

"There's something I want you to do, Victor."

"Yes, anything," Victor was eager to please this woman, who was in possession of knowledge that could ruin him.

"Jane. She's in a bad way. I want you to resolve her future, Victor. Settle quite a lot of money on her. I'm not asking you to marry her," said Phryne, gently but inexorably. "But you must take care of her. And abandon all this philandering. You don't like women, you know. Go and find someone you can love."

Victor straightened. For a moment his customary sneer visited his lips. Then it fled, and he said brokenly, "As you wish, Miss Fisher."

Claude lit Miss Fisher's cigarette and his own. Phryne sent Victor into the rehearsal to find Violet and Alexandra.

They came out together, holding hands. Alexandra was half-embracing Violet, who looked exquisitely uncomfortable. Phryne asked, "Did you know that Lawrence was allergic to something?"

Both heads, dark and mouse, shook. They looked at her solemnly, like two good children unfairly battered by fate. The fact of Lawrence's death had not sunk in. They were still shocked and numb. Phryne wanted to talk to them before they woke to a world without Lawrence in it and recognized their loss. She had never had much patience with hysterics.

"He would have told me, he told me everything," said Violet blankly.

"I thought the same," said Alexandra. "When he was with me, he talked, sometimes we talked all night."

"Diane might know," said Violet. "She's—she's not happy about all this, about him and me. I don't know how much she loved him, you know. She never said. But Lawrie said . . . She wanted to go to the Sorbonne, he said she could go to Paris, she's always wanted to go there, it's her dream. Ever since we were children. She's so clever. She ought to have been a man. Mother said—oh, God, I have to tell Mother, we have to cancel the wedding, all the arrangements . . . oh, Lawrence . . ."

Alexandra bore up Violet's drooping weight and said, "We neither of us know anything, Phryne. I'd better take Violet home."

"Not yet. Go back into the rehearsal, you needn't sing. Sit down on the couch with this cognac and have a drink or three. You're doing well, Alexandra. I'm proud of you." Phryne smiled into the tear-wet eyes. Alexandra murmured something, hoisted Violet, and went back into the drawing room, where the choir was beginning on the penultimate madrigal, *"Hark All Ye Lovely Saints Above."* Phryne listened. *"Diana hath agreed with love, his fiery weapon to remove."*

"Well, it doesn't look like they knew about it," commented Claude Greenhill, butting out his cigarette.

"No, Claude dear, but you did," said Phryne, suddenly enlightened. She seized Claude by the earlobe and led him, protesting, into the alcove where a view of the assembled choristers could be had.

"Phryne, what's this all about?" he said, doing "outraged innocence" quite well.

"You're the librarian, aren't you?" she demanded, dragging his face down to hers. His gray eyes were watering with pain and he smelt of wine and tobacco smoke, musky and attractive.

"Ouch, yes!"

"So you arranged the music in the order in which it would be sung," she continued, keeping hold of the offending lobe.

"Dammit, Miss Fisher," he protested, then grunted, "I did."

"Stay still unless you want to go through life in a monaural state. So you were responsible for *'Now Is the Month of Maying,' 'Fyer, Fyer,' 'Come Sable Night,' 'Oyez,' 'Sleep Fleshly Birth,' 'Weep weep mine eyes,' 'Adieu Sweet Amaryllis'* and *'Hark All Ye Lovely.'* "

"Well, actually, Morley, Ward, Tomkins, Ramsey, Wilbey and Weelkes were, but . . . ouch! . . . I put them in that order, yes."

"To spell out a message to the hearer. One particular hearer, I suspect."

She released him and he sat up, rubbing his ear.

"What message?" he bluffed.

"The one that identified the murderer. You knew this was going to happen, Claude. Why didn't you prevent it?"

"No, I didn't *know.*" He was offended. "I didn't think that she'd do it. She's been breathing fire and brimstone about it, screaming that she'd kill him. So I . . . challenged her, perhaps. Any of the choir who were paying attention could have noticed it. I thought I'd shock her out of it."

"But you didn't."

"No, it appears not."

"*'Merry lads are playing. And call for help. Put on thy mourning stole. Oyez has any found a lad; Take him quick before he flieth. Thy doleful obit keeping. A thousand deaths I die. Death do thy worst I care not. Adieu sweet Amaryllis'* and *'Diana hath agreed with love his fiery weapon to remove.'* She must have known he was allergic to bee stings. She pressed a bunch of roses into his hand. One of the thorns pricked him. You can see it here—the whole hand has swelled." Phryne put down the damaged hand onto the silent chest. "She was furious at being jilted and . . . oh, Lord, I wonder if he left her any money?"

The large bass was pale. "Yes, he changed his will when he was going to marry her. He's worth a fortune."

"Wills made in expectation of marriage are vitiated if the marriage does not take place," said Phryne.

"Yes, but does *she* know that? He borrowed her Sorbonne money, you know. Short on his allowance—he always was. But she never got it back."

"You know, I'm beginning to feel that he had it coming to him," sighed Phryne. "All she had to do was to smear that rose thorn with bee venom—only requires one to dissect a bee—and it's pretty, Claude, a really pretty plan. The problem with most poisons is making sure that the right person gets the bit of cake or whatever. In this case, if that thorn had pricked anyone else, they wouldn't have been killed."

"What are we going to do?"

"We haven't any proof. The bee venom, if it was there, would have been washed off when the roses were put in the vase." She lifted the bunch and scrutinized the stems. They seemed quite clean. "Nice roses. She must have bought them specially."

Phryne looked through the little window at the choir. Diane Hart was standing among the sopranos, pitching her voice carefully and without strain, to judge by her expression. A faint smile lingered around her mouth.

"It's a good idea, generally, not to offend women with that shade of Titian hair," mused Phryne. 'What do you think of your part in all of this, Claude?"

"I . . . rather wish I hadn't done it," admitted the bass.

"Hmm." Phryne leaned back against Claude. He was superlatively comfortable to lean against, and Phryne could understand the popularity of his shoulder among the distraught. Equally, there was a sharp mind and a sense of moral outrage that made Claude a dangerous enemy. There was more behind the arrangement of songs than just an attempt to shock Diane Hart.

"We can't prove any of this, Claude. In fact, I almost wish that you hadn't known about it. I'm no good at ethics. Lawrence made a complete blackguard of himself and to some extent invited revenge—you might almost feel that someone had to get him, sometime. But I wish it hadn't been here, in my house. Gosh, I sound like Lady Macbeth.

Well, if Diane killed him, I fear that she is going to go free. I expect she'll get her Sorbonne money back out of the estate. She's got away with a near-perfect murder."

"We could tell the police," said Claude, distastefully.

"And they'd laugh in our face. Besides, do we want to tell anyone? Dammit, Claude, I hate dilemmas."

"There's nothing to be done," he insisted. "There'll be an inquest, maybe it will come out there."

"Not a chance. Known allergy, and what if no one noticed the bee? It was a hot day and the windows were open. Drat." Phryne lit another cigarette and threw herself back against the bass hard enough to make him sway and grab her.

The choir were concluding *"The Silver Swan."*

"Farewell all joys, oh death come close my eyes. More geese than swans now live, more fools than wise."

"Miss Fisher . . ." gasped Claude. "Phryne, look!"

Phryne turned in his embrace to follow the pointing finger. Her eyes widened comically, then she started to laugh. Claude joined in after a moment, and they reeled, clasped in a close embrace, slipping down onto the Persian rug where they laughed until they cried.

Drunkenly, unsteadily, out of the velvety heart of Diane's red roses, a bee was crawling.

Australian Kerry Greenwood provides another of her mysteries featuring flapper Phryne Fisher in this story of a 1928 murder amidst madrigals. The sensible and glamorous Phryne also appears in *Flying Too High, Cocaine Blues, Murder on the Ballarat Train,* and *Death by Misadventure.*

Murder Mid-Atlantic

Edward Marston

"I've lost my feet!" exclaimed Rhoda Hubble.

"Your feet?" he said.

"Yes, young man. Both of them."

The purser was taken aback. Work on an oceanic liner had given him a whole range of strange experiences, but he had never before had a plump, pink-faced, elderly Englishwoman bursting into his cabin in a state of polite hysteria. As she stood before his desk, she was positively quivering.

"Didn't you hear me?" she said. "I've lost my feet."

He raised himself discreetly from his chair so that he could glance over the desk to take full inventory of her anatomy. Rhoda Hubble's feet appeared to be intact. So, however, did her surging bosom and her bulging midriff. From their owner's point of view, the size-five shoes would be obscured by the intervening landmass.

"They are still there," he assured her.

"My feet have gone!"

"Take my word for it," he said tactfully. "They are both exactly where they should be. Look in any mirror. If you want a direct sighting, I can recommend our Weight Watchers' Program . . ."

Indignation made her strike a dignified pose.

"Not *my* feet, you imbecile!" she said.

"I do beg your pardon."

"My elephant's feet."

The purser gulped. "You have an *elephant?"*

He studied her warily. She was stout, but not inelegant, with a handsome face and short, well-groomed silver hair. She exuded a sense of wealth that was kept decently in check by an even stronger sense of Christian virtue. He was dealing with a First-Class Passenger. Extra caution was needed.

"Would that be a pink elephant?" he said, tentatively.

"No, it would not!" came the vehement denial. "And I will thank you to stop looking at me in that irritating way. I am neither inebriated nor insane. I am Mrs. Rhoda Hubble, and I have come to report a serious crime."

"You believe the elephant's feet have been stolen?"

"Probably."

"Then how is he still standing up?"

"Young man, this is no time for levity. The feet are curios brought back from Africa. They are twenty inches in height and astonishingly lifelike. We used one as an umbrella stand and kept the other solely for decorative purposes. An elephant's foot does not have the remainder of the elephant attached to it."

"I begin to understand," he said apologetically.

"I suspect that *I* do as well." She raised a mistrustful eyebrow and spoke with disdain. "Are you, by any chance, an American?"

"Yes, Mrs. Hubble."

"I thought so!"

"A Bostonian."

"That is even worse."

The purser did not dare to inquire why. His primary concern was for the welfare of the passengers aboard the liner as it cleaved its way across the Atlantic to New York. He chided himself for not being more considerate towards a woman in such obvious distress. He got up and walked around his desk to indicate the armchair.

"Please, sit down," he invited.

"But this is an emergency."

"At least be comfortable while you tell me about it."

Taking her gently by the elbow, he guided her to the chair. Rhoda Hubble consented to be lowered into it. The purser knelt solicitously beside her.

"We seem to have got off on the wrong foot," he said. "I mean," he added quickly, "that I'm sorry for being so slow on the uptake. Perhaps we could take this one step at a time?" He winced as he heard himself. "I hate to keep treading on your toes like this." Another wince. He sought damage limitation. "Just tell me what happened," he gabbled. "In your own words."

"I already have, young man. My feet have gone."

"Front or back feet?"

"Front."

"Where were they kept?"

"In a case, in my cabin."

"And the case has vanished?"

"Completely."

"There is no chance that you might simply have mislaid it?"

"None whatsoever."

The purser nodded thoughtfully. Crossing to his desk, he perched on the edge of it and looked down at her.

"Then we must conclude that the feet were stolen."

"Thank you!" she said, partially mollified. "For one hideous moment, I thought you were about to suggest that they had gone for a walk on the First-Class deck."

"No, Mrs. Hubble. Are they valuable?"

"Extremely. The feet are over a hundred and fifty years old. I had to pay duty on the export of antiques."

"And they must have sentimental value as well."

"They have been in my family for generations."

"We will restore them to you as soon as possible," he said

confidently. "I will set an investigation in motion at once. You were right, Mrs. Hubble. This is a serious crime."

"But it is not the only one I came to tell you about."

"There is something else?"

"I lost my feet, but acquired a body."

"A body!"

"A dead one. I wish to report a murder!"

A crisis always brought out the best in the purser. He acted with commendable speed. The captain was the first to be informed. Security was alerted, and the scene of the alleged crimes was immediately cordoned off. A nurse was summoned to treat Rhoda Hubble for shock. The purser, meanwhile, went off to the relevant cabin with the ship's doctor in tow. They let themselves in with a master key, and flinched when they saw the corpse.

The man lay facedown in the middle of the cabin. He was wearing the uniform of a deck steward, but its starched whiteness was ruined by the pool of red blood around the wound between his shoulder blades. No murder weapon was visible. The doctor checked for signs of life, but there were none. His examination disclosed a large bruise on the man's temple.

The victim seemed to be in his twenties. As he gazed down at the body, the purser reflected on the amazing self-possession shown by Mrs. Rhoda Hubble. Confronted with such a grisly spectacle, most women would either have screamed or fainted or done both simultaneously. Mrs. Hubble had the presence of mind to notice that her elephant's feet were also missing, and it was that crime she had burst into the purser's cabin to announce. The blood-covered deck steward was a secondary matter.

"How long has he been dead?" asked the purser.

"No more than a couple of hours, at a guess," said the doctor, standing up again. "Well, I can't do anything for him. Out of reach of my medical knowledge. He's all yours."

"Let's find out who he is."

Crouching beside the body, the purser conducted his own examination, then searched the man's pockets. They were empty. He found no clue to the identity of the corpse.

"That bruise on his temple," he noted. "Does it suggest to you that he was knocked out before he was stabbed?"

The doctor shrugged. "Possibly."

"Where would the assailant have been standing in order to strike him on the side of the head?"

"Search me. I'm no Sherlock Holmes."

"What about Doctor Watson?"

"Not even that. You're on your own, chum."

Leaving the cabin guarded, the purser went to give a full account to the captain. Details were then telephoned to the police in New York. The luxury liner, however, was still in mid-Atlantic, and there would be a long delay before a murder inquiry could be instituted by homicide detectives. The captain wanted more immediate action. Murder was bad for passenger morale.

"Find him!" he snapped, peremptorily. "I will not have a killer loose on my ship. Find him. Soon!"

It was a tall order, but the purser obeyed, returning to his cabin to begin his investigation by questioning Rhoda Hubble more closely. As he came through the door, she was talking airily to the nurse about the mating habits of African elephants. She broke off mid-sentence and turned to face him.

"Well?" she said. "Do you believe me now?"

"Yes, Mrs. Hubble."

"Let that be a lesson to you, young man."

The nurse was amused to hear someone twice her age being referred to as a "young man" but all things were relative. Rhoda Hubble's advanced age meant that she viewed the nurse as no more than a mere child.

The purser reached for a notepad and pen.

"When—precisely—did you discover the body?" he said.

"When I returned from the hairdressing salon."

"And what time would that be, Mrs. Hubble?"

"Eleven-thirty this morning."

"What did you do?"

"I came straight to you, of course."

"Leaving it all exactly as you found it?"

"Yes."

"You didn't . . . disturb anything?"

"Only myself," she said angrily. "I looked for my feet and they were gone. Robbed! It was heartbreaking!"

The purser traded a glance of disbelief with the nurse.

"Did you tell anyone else about the feet?" he wondered.

"I may have mentioned them in passing."

"To whom?"

"My new friends," she explained. "Mr. Faraday and the Draycotts. The four of us played bridge last night. In the Draycotts' cabin. Cecil—er, Mr. Faraday—was my partner. I believe that my feet may have come up in conversation."

While she rambled on, the purser made copious notes on his pad, feeding her with fresh questions whenever she paused for breath. A tap on the door interrupted them. The Head of Security came in, whispered to the purser, then left.

"Doesn't he know that it is bad manners to whisper in company?" said Mrs. Hubble. "Another American, I suppose."

"He's as English as you are," corrected the purser. "He has been trying to identify the murder victim."

"And?"

"He failed."

"Is the whole ship staffed by incompetents?"

"Bear with us, please. We are not trained detectives. Some progress has been made. The murder victim was not a deck steward, nor was he a passenger. He seems to have had no legitimate reason to be aboard."

"What are you telling me, young man?"

"He was a stowaway."

* * *

Gail Higham was a slim, lithe, attractive woman of thirty with a soft voice and a pleasant manner. When the purser called at the hairdressing salon, she was bidding farewell to one customer and welcoming another. The purser took her aside.

"Do you remember a Mrs. Rhoda Hubble?"

"Extremely well," she said.

"I understand that she was in here this morning?"

"And last night," volunteered Gail helpfully. "Mrs. Hubble came to me on both occasions."

"What time did she leave this morning?"

"Eleven-thirty."

"Are you sure?"

"Completely. As you can see, we're very busy in here. We have to keep strictly to appointment times." Her face puckered with anxiety. "What's the problem? Has Mrs. Hubble complained about me? She told me she was pleased with what I did. Am I in trouble?"

"No, no," he soothed. "Far from it. Her hair looks great. Terrific advert for you." Gail Higham relaxed. "She came in yesterday as well, you say?"

"Only for a manicure."

"What did she talk about?"

"That's a private matter," said the other, stiffening. "I couldn't possibly tell you. It would be breaking a confidence."

"It's vitally important," he assured her. "Don't pass this around, but a man was murdered in Mrs. Hubble's cabin this morning. Certain items were stolen."

The hairdresser stepped back in alarm. She took time to absorb the news. He could see the fear in her eyes.

"Ask me anything you like," she offered.

"Did Mrs. Hubble talk about her feet?"

"She came in for a manicure—not a pedicure."

"Her *elephant's* feet."

"Oh, yes," recalled Gail, "I believe that she did. Mrs. Hubble said that she was taking them to America to give to her sister. She was very sad that they were going abroad. Especially to New York. I don't think she likes Americans."

"Is that all she told you?"

"About the feet, yes. But she said plenty of other things. Mrs. Hubble loves to rattle on. I just nod and throw in the odd reaction." A memory nudged. "But she must have told someone else about the elephant's feet because *she* talked about them as well."

"'She'?"

"My first customer of the day. We open at eight, and she was sitting down in my chair on the dot. She was rather sarcastic about those feet. Seemed to know a lot about them."

"Who did?"

"Mrs. Draycott."

He found them in their cabin. Eileen Draycott was a rather forbidding creature, with double chins and watery eyes, but her husband, a retired investment banker, was a much more affable character. He invited the purser in. Hugh Draycott's bonhomie vanished when he was told about the murder. He was shocked, and the grim news sent his wife's double chins into orbit. The purser waited until the husband stopped shaking and the chins returned to base.

"You played bridge with Mrs. Hubble, I hear?" he said.

"That's right," agreed Hugh. "They beat the pants off us. Rhoda and Cecil. That's Cecil Faraday, her partner. She and Cecil really hit it off."

"They had a run of luck, that's all," said Eileen. "Any other night, we would have won every game. We have a system, you see. It's impregnable. Well, almost."

"Did she refer to her elephant's feet?" asked the purser.

"Several times," said Hugh. "Rhoda was proud of them."

"Couldn't stop boasting about them," added Eileen testily. "I blame Mr. Faraday. He egged her on relentlessly."

"He was *interested,* darling," reminded her husband.

"When I play bridge, I do not wish to talk about feet."

"Professional curiosity on Cecil's part."

"In what way?" asked the purser.

"He's an art dealer," replied Hugh. "He was fascinated by the elephant's feet. To be quite candid, he was also fascinated by Rhoda Hubble."

"Hugh!" reproved his wife.

"It's true, Eileen. And she took a shine to Cecil."

"What a dreadful expression!"

"He went back to her cabin with her."

"Only to see the feet."

"Which ones? Hers or the elephant's?"

"Don't be disgusting! He's younger than she is."

"I'm younger than you, Eileen. Or had you forgotten?"

While she blustered, the purser learned all the detail he needed from Hugh Draycott. A lifetime in investment banking had sharpened his intuition and honed his judgment of his fellow mortals. If he sensed an incipient romance between Rhoda Hubble and Cecil Faraday, then that is what was in the wind. Only one question remained.

"Would you *trust* Mr. Faraday?" asked the purser.

"Good Lord, no!" returned Hugh. "I'd never trust any art dealer. Especially if he trounced me at the card table."

Cecil Faraday was promenading along the deck when the purser finally tracked him down. The art dealer was a tall, stately individual in his fifties with a bald head and cadaverous face that added ten years to his age. His manner was at once urbane and slightly sinister. When the purser gave him the bad tidings, the passenger's first thought was for Rhoda Hubble.

"I must go to her at once!" he said. "She needs me."

"All in good time, Mr. Faraday."

"But Rhoda will be in a terrible state."

"Mrs. Hubble is holding up remarkably well."

"A man murdered in her cabin. Her precious feet stolen. She must be in a blind panic. My place is beside her."

"Answer a few questions first."

"Rhoda's wants are paramount."

"What she really wants is for these crimes to be solved as soon as possible. And I believe that you can help me to do that, Mr. Faraday. Will you, please?" He smiled disarmingly. "For Mrs. Hubble's sake?"

"Well, if you put it like that . . ."

"I do."

The purser led him across to two empty deck chairs and they sat down. Cecil Faraday mastered his concern. He turned an obliging face towards his interrogator.

"I'll do anything in my power to assist Rhoda."

"How long have you known her?"

"Long enough," he said wistfully. "Long enough."

"And how long would that be?"

"Twenty-four hours."

"I see."

"I know what you're thinking," continued the other. "And you could not be more mistaken. At first glance, Rhoda can seem a little intimidating. But when one is fortunate enough to explore below the surface . . ." His eye kindled. "A splendid creature! That silken sheen. That beautiful hair. Those generous proportions. I've always been a Rubens man where women are concerned."

The purser did not recognize this description of the elderly lady who had charged into his cabin, but he made due allowance for artistic license.

"I understand that you saw the elephant's feet?"

"It was a privilege," said Cecil. "They were an exquisite pair. Rhoda knew that I would appreciate them."

"They were in her cabin?"

"Yes. In a special case."

"And they were still there when you left?"

"Naturally."

"At what time would that be?"

"Midnight at the latest." He shook his head. "Poor Rhoda! To suffer such a double blow. Murder *and* theft."

"The two crimes were closely linked, Mr. Faraday."

"How?"

"That is what I am struggling to find out." He changed his tack. "How did you get on with the Draycotts?"

"Tolerably well."

"He seemed like an amiable guy."

"He is," said Cecil. "A most agreeable companion."

"What about his wife?"

"She cheats at cards."

"Indeed?"

"She took her beating with ill grace and tried to get her revenge by underhand methods. Rhoda and I were not to be outsmarted by Eileen Draycott. We annihilated her."

"How did the Draycotts take defeat?"

"Hugh laughed and reached for the whiskey bottle. His wife seethed in silence. Until Rhoda rhapsodized about her elephant's feet, that is. Eileen was quite spiteful then."

"How spiteful?"

"Spiteful enough to steal them, if that's what you're asking. She'd have no qualms about taking those feet in order to get back at the pair of us."

"But would she commit murder in the process?"

"Only if *I* was the victim."

"Why do you think that?"

Cecil Faraday talked at greater length about the four personalities around the card table. The purser was intrigued. It had been less a game of bridge than a battle for power between two single-minded ladies. The art dealer gripped his arm.

"May I go to Rhoda now?"

"I need to speak with her alone first. Come to my cabin in thirty minutes. Mrs. Hubble will be delighted to see you."

Rhoda Hubble was alone. Having dismissed the nurse, she was pacing the cabin restlessly. When the purser entered, she came to a sudden halt, her head framed by the porthole. He scrutinized her properly for the first time. Cecil Faraday was right. She was a striking woman. Rhoda Hubble did have a certain adipose charm.

"Where are my feet?" she asked urgently.

"I am getting closer to them all the time."

"Who stole them?"

"You must tell me that, Mrs. Hubble."

"But I have no idea."

"You do," he insisted. "Unbeknownst to you, the name of the thief—and, therefore, the murderer—is locked away in a corner of your brain. All we have to do is to root it out."

"I have told you all I can."

"That's not true. You said that you may have mentioned the elephant's feet in passing to your bridge partners. According to the Draycotts, you gave them one helluva buildup. Mr. Faraday was so inspired by your description of them that he went to your cabin to view the feet."

She was almost girlish. "You've talked with Cecil?"

"He was most cooperative."

"Such a cultured human being."

"He spoke very warmly of you." She gave a winsome laugh. "But he confirmed that you discussed the feet at exhaustive length over cards and—earlier—over the dinner table. You also told your beautician about them. And several other ears must have picked up the tale. One of those people robbed you. Now, I know that you have a low opinion of my countrymen . . ."

"Only because my sister married a New Yorker."

"We need to work together, Mrs. Hubble. Anglo-American solidarity. It's the only way we will ever get those feet back where they belong. Are you with me?"

"Yes, young man!"

"Then tell me what you've done, when, and with whom, since you stepped aboard this ship."

Summoning up full concentration, she described her voyage thus far, throwing up a number of new names for his list. The purser listened attentively and wrote constantly on his pad. When it was all over, she sat down with a gasp of relief.

"There! You know everything now!"

"Not quite, Mrs. Hubble. One detail was overlooked."

"Detail?"

"Your whereabouts last night."

"I was sleeping in my cabin."

"Were you?" he said gently. "I hate to pry into your personal affairs, but it is imperative if we are to establish the exact time when the crimes were committed."

"During the two hours when I was in the salon. I told you. I got back to discover the outrage at eleven-thirty."

"Only if you spent the night in your own cabin. If, for the sake of argument, you were elsewhere. And if, this morning, you went directly from that other place to your appointment at the salon, your cabin would have been empty for the best part of twelve hours. That would give the thief plenty of leeway. He might not have stolen your feet and committed a murder at one and the same time." He gave her a persuasive smile. "Where were you, Mrs. Hubble?"

She tried to look defiant, but her heart betrayed her.

"I have been widowed for fifteen years," she said with a sigh. "Loneliness is a daily battle. That is why I was so thrilled to meet . . . a kindred spirit. He sensed my needs and he responded to them. Magnificently." She lowered her head. "Mr. Faraday invited me to his cabin to look at some Rubens prints. We did not realize how fast the time slipped by."

"So your cabin remained unoccupied all night?"

"He had a very large number of prints."

"That is all I wished to know."

"I have great difficulty sleeping. I take pills. Last night, they were not necessary." She clutched at his sleeve. "I hope I can rely on your discretion, young man."

"Totally. I'm a Bostonian, remember."

"Tell nobody about this."

"Not even Mrs. Draycott?"

A smile of triumph spread slowly over her whole face.

"Oh, yes! Tell *her*. She'll be livid!"

"I'm sure," said the purser with a grin. He moved to the door. "Wait a few minutes, and Mr. Faraday will join you."

"Where are you going?"
"To have a haircut."

The salon was busier than ever. It was late afternoon before Gail Higham was able to take her break. As she strolled back to her cabin, she wondered why the purser had turned up. His hair was immaculate, and yet he had asked one of her colleagues to fit him in on short notice. It was puzzling. A solution soon presented itself in the most disturbing way.

"Come on in, Gail!"

"What are *you* doing in here?" she gasped.

"Waiting for you."

The purser was sitting on the solitary chair in her cabin. Side-by-side on his lap were matching elephant's feet. She was startled at first, but recovered her poise at once.

"How dare you barge in here!" she protested.

"Yes," he said seriously. "Illegal entry into someone else's cabin is an appalling thing. That's what I came to talk over with you." He lifted the feet. "And with these."

"How on earth did they get in here?"

"I found them under your bunk with the other items you stole. Quite a haul. You've been very assiduous. How many Mrs. Hubbles did you rob?"

Gail Higham realized that the game was up and tried to make a dash for it, but a bulky security guard was blocking the door. She turned back to the purser and glared at him.

"It had to be you," he explained. "That's why I came to the salon this afternoon. To watch you in action. I saw you in the mirror. Listening and planning. Finding your next target." He stood up. "Mrs. Hubble was too garrulous for her own good. She told her life story. And boasted about these." He tapped the elephant's feet together. "You knew that she'd be sound asleep at night because she took pills. You could steal the case without any danger of waking her. But Mrs. Hubble was not in her cabin last night. You were, Gail."

"You can't prove that!" she challenged.

"These feet are proof enough. Unless you're going to tell me that they danced a hornpipe all the way to your cabin." He touched her shoulder. "Why, Gail?"

"I hate them," she hissed. "I hate them all!"

"Rich ladies in First Class?"

"Some of them treat me like dirt. They deserve to be robbed. I spend twelve hours a day on my feet in that salon. It's a treadmill. I have to find some way to make it worth my while."

"How did you get into their cabins?"

"With a master key. On my last voyage, I tricked it out of one of the stewards."

"Did you trick a uniform out of him as well?"

She feigned surprise. "What are you on about?"

"Your accomplice. The one you killed."

"I'm a thief—not a murderer."

"Who was he, Gail?"

"I have no idea."

"Don't think you can fool me," he warned. "I spend my whole life going in and out of cabins. You've thrown his gear away, I daresay, but he was here. I can feel it. Two people shared that bunk." He fixed her with an accusatory stare. "Who *was* he?"

He knew too much. Further evasion was pointless. After a token show of spirit, she capitulated. Gail Higham sank down on the chair with her head in her hands.

"I smuggled him aboard," she confessed. "Hid him in here. Told him which cabins were empty while their passengers were in the salon. Worked like a charm at first." Her face hardened. "Then Tony got greedy. Stole things for himself and not for us. Also—and this was the worst part—he lost interest in me. You can't share a tiny cabin like this with someone who's gone off you. It's unbearable."

"So you killed him?"

"It was an accident," she bleated. "When I told him about the elephant's feet, he couldn't wait to get his hands on them. So I beat him to it. Stole them last night and hid the case in the salon." She gave a hollow laugh. "All the time Mrs. Hubble was crowing about them, they were hidden in a cupboard right in front of her. Those feet were only feet away."

"Tell me about Tony."

"He went to Mrs. Hubble's cabin at eleven," she said. "I left her under the dryer and slipped along there myself. Just to gloat when he couldn't find the case. Tony went berserk. Demanded to know where they were. When I wouldn't tell him, he tried to strangle me. It was him or me. In the struggle, I grabbed this onyx ashtray and hit him with it. Stunned him."

"Then what?"

"I'm not sure. I suppose I was in a bit of a rage by this time. And I had these scissors in my pocket . . ."

"So you stabbed him?"

"He betrayed me. Tony ruined *everything.*"

"No, Gail," he said quietly. "You did that."

Rhoda Hubble and Cecil Faraday were among the last to leave the ship when it docked. She was beaming happily and he was carrying the case containing the elephant's feet. A shipboard romance would clearly continue on dry land. The purser was waiting for them at the top of the gangway. Warm handshakes were exchanged.

"Good-bye, Mrs. Hubble," he said.

"I can't thank you enough, young man."

"I hope this revises your opinion of Americans."

"Oh, it does," she affirmed. "I had no idea we could combine so effectively. What a splendid team we were! A shining example of hands across the sea."

"Yes," said the purser. "Hands across the sea—and feet across the ocean!"

The hunt for a missing pachyderm's foot is the offbeat premise for this shipboard tale from Edward Marston.

Marston is the author of two mystery series featuring the Domesday Book *(The Wolves of Savernake, The Ravens of Blackwater, The Dragons of Archenfield)* and Elizabethan theater company manager Nicholas Bracewell *(The Queen's Head, The Silent Woman, The Nine Giants, The Mad Courtesan, The Roaring Boy)*. He was nominated for an Edgar in 1996 for *The Roaring Boy.*

City Boy

Susan Moody

Everybody's heard of love at first sight. The lucky ones will even have experienced it. They'll know all about that instant pounding in the blood. The trembling knees. Eyes meeting across a crowded room in what ethologists call the copulatory gaze. Pheromone calling unto pheromone.

What Eve Cook felt that afternoon as she opened the front door in response to a knock was certainly immediate. As her eyes met those of the man on her doorstep, her blood recognizably pounded. He was the color of a piece of underdone toast: gingery eyebrows over rust-brown eyes, mustache like bran flakes, thin, sandy hair combed across a shiny scalp. His stocky body was crammed into loose trousers of indeterminate cut and fit and a short-sleeved shirt. She could, although she had no wish to, see his nipples through the pilled locknit cotton. A shabby bag rested on the step, beside feet covered with nylon socks and sandals. Was it possible to feel so much emotion within the first second of meeting someone? At first sight?

"Eve?" he said uncertainly. "Evelyn Howe?"

"Yes."

"I'm Jim. Your cousin Jim. From South Africa." He held out his hand and, reflexively, she took it and then dropped it. Sweaty. Disgusting. She wanted to wipe her hand on her skirt.

"Oh." From South Africa? "Aunt Rose's son?"

"You got it," he said. He picked up his bag and began to move forward, over the threshold, subtly pushing her back. "All right if I come in?" Whatever answer she might have given to the question, it was too late. He was already inside the house and closing the door behind him.

"Well," he said, following her into the kitchen, his foxy gaze moving possessively around the room. "This is very nice."

"Yes." Automatically she filled the kettle and put it on the stove. "Tea?"

"Coffee, please. I don't mind instant." He pulled a chair out from the wooden table and sat down. "So when would a place like this have been built, then?"

"It's late eighteenth century."

"That old?" He whistled softly. "Must be worth a bob or two. Mind you . . ." He laughed, showing rows of creamy teeth. ". . . doesn't look like it's been decorated since then. If you like, I could slap some paint on the walls for you while I'm here."

"While you're . . ." She was alarmed. "How long are you . . .?"

"You've got room for a visitor, haven't you?" he said easily. He got up and went over to the long garden-facing window above the old-fashioned stone sink. "Nice bit of land you've got out there. Needs tidying up a bit. I could give you a hand with that, too."

"I don't want it tidied up." She could feel a stress headache beginning. It was to avoid stress that she lived out here in the country, by herself. After the years with Ned, the demands, this having no one to think about but herself was a constant delight. Waking in the morning in the uncluttered bedroom, seeing the light through the uncurtained windows, knowing she could lie there all day, if she wanted, or go straight outside in her nightclothes, eat breakfast at lunchtime, supper at midnight, the freedom to do as she pleased, never failed to flood her with well-being. It was the kind of satisfaction that she had once only been able to obtain from devouring cream buns, french pastries, chocolates, biscuits, supermarket cakes: an immediate gratification that went a little, temporary way towards blocking out Ned's voice, Ned's needs. Ned's demands.

When she first arrived here, she had feared that loneliness would crowd in on her too much. She wondered how she would structure her days so as to disguise how little there was to fill them with. How to build a framework on which to rest the dragging hours. It had never been like that. First there had been the organizing of the house, the simplification. It had astonished her to discover how little she needed in the way of possessions. Tables, a bed, chairs, a comfortable armchair, a radio, and a television. Kitchen utensils, pots and pans, crockery, cutlery. She had sold most of her life's clutter when she moved, and enjoyed gathering slowly around her an entirely new set of objects that reflected her newly singular status: pretty cracked plates from junk shops, mismatched cups and saucers, pieces of glass, jugs, bits and pieces that caught her fancy and that she displayed on the big built-in dresser that took up most of one wall of her kitchen.

And when she had sorted out the house, there was the garden to enjoy. To acquaint herself with. The unkempt wildness of it. The encroachment of nature, grass rioting, fruit tumbling, flowers springing out of the earth without the slightest help or encouragement. In summer, the garden was bounded by luxurious hedges of elder, tangled with dog rose and bramble, leaning lilacs, banks of cow parsley. In spring it brimmed with blossom from apple and pear, which by autumn had turned to fruits of luscious green-gold or yellow-streaked crimson. In winter, there was holly and yew, bramble and mountain ash. The constant abundance of root and leaf and berry, self-sustaining, requiring nothing of her but the freedom to be what it was, seemed a generosity she did not deserve.

Until she remembered Ned. Then she knew that this was her reward. For the years of submission. For having the courage—finally—to end them.

Pushing through a tangle of blackberry bushes and elder trees during her first summer, she discovered an overgrown patch where someone had once planted soft fruit: raspberry canes, strawberries, gooseberries, currants that hung jewel-like among the leaves, white and ruby and black. Over the years, she had tended them, weeding, feeding, holding back the rest of the interloping garden. One summer, almost apologetically, she planted lettuce and runner beans, fearing that she trespassed; hitherto, the garden had been allowed to grow as it pleased, and she was reluctant to alienate it by interfering. But in fact, as though approved of, the beans had thrived, the lettuce had sprouted as enthusiastically as though grown under professional glass. Since then, she had tentatively added parsley, radishes, kale, purple sprouting broccoli, all of which had flourished.

The garden had been responsible for her new occupation. Her blossoming career. For years she had attended art classes, despite Ned's sneers, despite the cups of tea spilled over her sketch books accidentally-on-purpose, the confiscation of her materials, despite his weekly attempts to prevent her going. Now, freed from him, and with time to spare, she began to transfer to paper some of the profusion around her. And then, greatly daring, to send them to an agency. And then, scarcely believing her luck, to take commissions for illustrations: birthday cards, post cards, calendars, even, finally, books. She earned enough to live more luxuriously than she did. She always had more work than she needed. She was happy.

The summer that Jim arrived, the soft fruit had plumped and ripened as though on steroids, heavy and abundant, more than she could possibly consume herself, or even deal with by putting up in preserving jars, turning into jam, freezing in the big cabinet in the tumbledown shed. Other plants had flourished, too, that lavish summer, especially the wild growths that crowded the edges of the garden: blackberries, sloes, wild plums, crab apples, even the plumes of fennel, the spreading dock and hawkweed, elder and plantain, nightshade and comfrey, abundant as the heavy-headed grasses.

After he had sucked down his coffee, she took him out into the garden. The sight of so much luxuriance seemed to oppress him. Standing knee-deep in the grasses, he looked around him. "Bit of a mess, isn't it?" he said uneasily.

"I like it like this."

"Who'd ever have thought it," he said.

"Thought what?"

"That someone from the backstreets of Liverpool would settle in a place like this. If anyone had asked me, I'd have said you'd fade away if there wasn't a chippie down the road or a dance hall across the way. That's the sort of girl you used to be when we were kids."

"It was a long time ago. I've changed."

"I haven't. I'm a city boy, and proud of it. I like pavement under my feet. People on the other side of the party wall. Place like this'd give me the willies. Not a neighbor for miles. Not even a proper road."

"That's exactly what makes it so perfect."

"Perfect?" He made an unlovely sound in his nose. "But, like I say, sort it out and it'd be worth a small fortune." He waved his arms around so that the sun glinted on the ginger hairs. "Mow the grass, trim the hedges, tie back some of the plants and root out all those weeds. Show what it could be like." He looked at her with affectionate contempt. "Don't know much about gardens, do you?"

"How do you mean?"

"I'm a townie born and bred, but even *I* know those're weeds over there. That lacy stuff. And there." He pointed again. "Cow parsley. It'll take over if you're not careful. But once you've got the place bang to rights, the sky's the limit."

"In what sense?"

"Planning permission," he said. "Shouldn't be too difficult. Grease a palm or two, if they try to make it difficult for you."

"I don't know what you mean." Sitting down at the table outside the back door, she began to shell peas picked earlier from the vegetable patch. There was a reddish haze about him, as though his foxy color was leaching into the air.

"Valuable site, I should imagine, especially with that view." he said. "You could get five or six nice little places onto this much land and still give them the feeling of being in the country. Two bedrooms, sitting room, integral garage. Starter homes, we call them."

"Starter homes? What on earth are you talking about?"

"Money, Evie. That's what I'm talking about. And by the look of the place, you could do with some. The kitchen, for instance—it's straight out of the dark ages. Rusty old stove thing—"

"It's an Aga, and it's not—"

"—paint falling off the walls. Black mold in the khazi."

The years with Ned had inured her to acceptance. She listened to him, hatred heaving in her heart, but said nothing. Such discourtesy. Such lack of even basic politeness. "In that case," she said quietly, "you'll want to find somewhere more comfortable to stay. I'll give you lunch and then you can get off again on your travels."

"Evie," he said, drawing the word out into geniality. He came over to her and she smelled him, rank and sweaty. Beads of moisture glistened on his forehead. "Evie, old girl. Don't you go taking offense. I speak as I find. Always have. Of course I'm not going to go off and leave you so soon. We're cousins, after all."

"We haven't met for more than forty years."

"All the more reason to be friends now, right? I'm on my own, and so are you. Never had any children, did you? And no husband anymore. We should stick together." With some difficulty he bent his fat haunches and squatted down beside her chair. "And whatever I may have said, I do like your house. It's . . . quaint."

"No," she said. "You're right. It needs fixing up. It's not really geared to guests. I'm used to it myself, but I'm sure you'd prefer somewhere more comfortable. A hotel or guest house—"

"You wouldn't be trying to kick me out, would you? Just when we've met up again after all these years? All I meant was that it must get pretty brass monkeyish in the winter. But then, I've got used to South African weather. I don't suppose it would be too difficult to install central heating. If you can afford it?" His forehead wrinkled with inquiry.

"I can afford it."

"Got a bit of a nest egg, have you? Something stashed away for a rainy day?"

"I'm doing all right, thank you."

Despite her hints, he stayed that night. And the next. One morning she awoke and realized he had already been there a week. As she padded downstairs to put the kettle on, panic filled her. Was he going to be there forever? How could she get rid of him? He seemed impervious to any suggestions she dropped about his departure, and she was reluctant to force him out through open confrontation. There had been too much of that with Ned. Besides, Aunt Rose had always been kind; some kind of debt was owed. Even if it had to be repaid via her obnoxious son.

His presence was constant. It was impossible to get away from him. If she went up to her bedroom, he came and knocked on the door. If she said she was going for a walk, he came, too. All day he followed her about the house, talking. Perspiring. The smell of him made her gag. It filled the house. It was more than sweat. Damp clothes. Unwashedness. Feet. And his voice. Those flat, misshapen vowels made her face twist with dislike. When she went to her studio in the shed, he stood behind her, breathing. Commenting on her work.

"Should bring in a nice little sum," he would say, as though that was the only reason she painted. The garden seemed less bright when he was in it. Where he pushed through them, the grasses wilted.

Once she found him rooting through her files. "They seem to like your work," he said, unabashed. "I had no idea you earned so much."

"How dare you go through my papers," she said.

"No, seriously, Eve. If they're prepared to fork out that much without quibbling for a few drawings of grass and berries, maybe you're not getting as much as you deserve."

"Don't touch my things," she said. She suspected that he had already searched her desk. Had examined her bank statements, her building society book.

"I'm your cousin," he said. "Your only living relative. Surely you've nothing to hide from me. Especially when—" He broke off, assuming an expression of injured goodwill.

"When what?"

"I dropped in on the lawyer's in town the other day. Got him to draw up a new will. I haven't got much, Evie, but what there is, well, I want you to have it."

He waited. Almost certainly in the hope that she would not only express her gratitude but offer to do the same for him. With all my worldly goods I'll go down to my solicitor and thee endow. As though the two of them were locked into some hideous marriage. Since she suspected that he was lying, and that even if he were not, he had nothing whatsoever to leave, she said nothing. After a while, he switched on the TV and watched a football match, filling the house with raucous sound.

She longed to be alone again. The house was no longer hers. Her peace was tainted.

He seemed to think that she had nothing to do all day but look after his needs: cook, clean, serve meals, clear them away. He did nothing. His appetite was prodigious, his greed immense. He helped himself to her drink supply; he made long phone calls without offering any contribution toward the expenses. He came shopping with her and filled her basket with things he himself wanted. He did not offer to pay.

Once, as they drove back from the village, he said: "Since we happened to be on the spot, I popped in to the council offices and asked about planning permission."

"What for?"

"That land behind your cottage. Remember me saying that I thought it wouldn't be too difficult? Well, I was right. One of the previous owners was granted it. Sets a precedent, you see? They'd have a hard time refusing it to you."

"But why should I want it?"

He rubbed stubby fingers against his thumb. "Dosh, Evie. Boodle. Don't tell me you'd turn it down. And that garden's much too big for you to cope with on your own. Look at the state it's in."

"I *like* it like that."

"Now, maybe. But what's going to happen five, ten years down the line?"

"Listen, Jim," she said quietly. "I don't want planning permission. I don't want horrible little houses in my back garden. I don't want people round me. I don't want you."

He laughed. Ginger stubble poked through the thick skin of his jaw. "Now, now," he said. "You know you don't mean that."

"I do."

"But I'm your cousin."

"That doesn't make any difference."

"There's only the two of us left. We have to stick together."

"I want you to go."

He was silent for a while. Then he said: "Tell you what. When we get home, you put your feet up, and I'll make you a nice cup of tea, right?

The week became two. Obsession gripped her. At night, she lay awake, thinking about him, fantasizing. When she slept, his image stalked her dreams. Even when he was not present, he was always on her mind. She had been like this when she met Ned. Unable to think of anything but him. Love at first sight. How similar love and hate could be.

Her work grew coarser. Instead of field mice swinging from eared stems of corn, she drew weasel faces sly among rank undergrowths of fleshy stems. Instead of the flimsy petals of poppy or corn cockle, she painted cuckoo pint and wood spurge. Fungi sprouted in the backgrounds of her pictures, decadent, menacing, where once there would have been a tapestry of leaf and grass stems. Instead of juicy blackberries, she surrounded her paintings with borders of nightshade and wormwood. She sought out the plants with the ugliest names: fleabane, hemlock, dead-nettle, woundwort.

Christine, her editor, telephoned. "What's going on, Eve?" she demanded without preamble.

"What do you mean?"

"I just got the stuff you sent by special delivery."

"And?"

"I don't have to be a professional psychiatrist to see that something's wrong. What is it—a man?" Eve heard Christine pull in on her cigarette and blow the smoke out into the receiver.

With a heartiness she was far from feeling, Eve said, "Man? After Ned, I wouldn't have one in the house."

"Then it's something else. Whatever it is, get rid of it. The country calendar people aren't going to take what you've sent me. I don't even have to submit it to know that."

Jim was coming down the stairs. Eve followed the sound of his heavy tread into the kitchen, heard the door of the fridge open, the clatter of a spoon against crockery. She didn't have to be in the room to know that he'd be helping himself to whatever was in there, sucking in the food like some vast suntanned pig as he ate directly from the bowl or the plate.

"What are you saying, Christine?" With an effort she restrained herself from screaming out her hatred of him, her passionate wish that he would leave, the intensity of her desire to return to the solitude she had so loved.

"I'm saying that if you don't buck your ideas up, we'll both be out of a job."

"That bad?"

"Have you looked at your work recently?"

"Well . . ."

"Those drawings you sent for the kiddy nature book—forget it. The idea is to give the darlings some idea—however misguided—of the idyllic joys of living in the country. What you've just sent me is more likely to give them nightmares."

Eve did not reply. It was his fault. If he didn't go soon, he'd destroy everything she'd worked so hard to build.

Softening her voice, Christine said: "Why don't you come up next week and have lunch with me? We can talk it over."

"All right. What day?"

"I have to go up to London tomorrow," Eve said.

"I'll come, too." His scalp was shiny with sweat, beads of it clinging to the sparse hair.

"No." She was firm. "It's business."

"Maybe I can help." He gave her a judicious look. "Might help if they know that you're not alone now, there's a man watching out for your interests."

"No," she said again.

"All right. I'll have a nice quiet day on my own," he said. "What about lunch?"

"I'll make something tonight and leave it ready before I go. I'll pick some of the soft fruit, too. You can have it with cream."

"Very nice." He looked at her fondly. "You're very good to me, Evie. More so than I deserve."

"I know."

He laughed, as though she had said something amusing.

She was up early the next day. The casserole she had made the night before would only need heating up. She went outside. The garden welcomed her as she pushed through the dew-dripping grasses to the raspberry cages. Cow parsley caressed her skirt. There was still plenty of fruit among the leaves: she picked a bowlful, adding a few leaves of mint. In the kitchen, she shook plenty of castor sugar over it and put it in the fridge. He'd polish that off without any problem, along with the casserole and the piece of Stilton she'd left temptingly in the cheese dish on the dresser.

He was dead when she got home. She had deliberately lingered after her lunch with Christine, visiting an exhibition at the Royal Academy, buying a ticket for something with Maggie Smith in it that had received rave reviews. She wanted him to have as much time to die in as was necessary.

She called the police.

It took them nearly an hour and a half to get there. Waiting for them, she replaced the telephone that she had removed from its jack and hidden before leaving that morning, so that help could not be summoned. She spiked the note she had written earlier on one of the cuphooks on the dresser. She poured herself a brandy and stood out in the garden. He'd vomited copiously. And before dying, his bowels had loosened. Added to his personal odor, the atmosphere in the house was noxious. He'd broken one of the bentwood chairs, collapsing onto it, she would guess.

"I left him a note," she explained, when the pathologist had examined the body, and pronounced the ginger carcass a probable victim of failure of the respiratory system. From his preliminary examination, the most likely cause was poisoning, almost certainly from the ingestion of some toxic berry from the garden. "It's there on the dresser, where I put it this morning. I left early, you see, and I didn't want to disturb him."

"There's a casserole for your lunch in the fridge." One of the officers read aloud. *"It only needs heating up. And there's still plenty of fruit. Pick as much as you like. I'll be back around 11 this evening. Hope you have a nice day. Evie."*

"It's my fault," Eve said. "I should have remembered."

"Remembered what?"

"That he didn't know about country things. Plants and so on. He was always saying that he was a city boy. I ought to have realized, I ought to have picked the fruit for him myself. He must have gone out there at lunchtime and filled the bowl with any berries he could find, not knowing."

"Don't distress yourself, Mrs. Cook."

"But it was such an ugly, painful death. Or it looks like it, anyway. And he died all alone, too."

"It wasn't your fault."

"I did my best for him," she said, weeping. "Looked after him, and glad to do it. He was my cousin, after all. And it was lovely to have someone in the house again, after so long. A companion. We hadn't seen each other for forty years or more, but we got on like a house on fire. Never had a cross word. I'm really going to miss him."

"You mustn't upset yourself. You weren't to know he'd think the nightshade was edible."

"It's hard to see how he could have done—those berries always look so poisonous, don't they?" she agreed. Unless, of course, they are covered with a thick coating of sugar. And mixed in with raspberries, strawberries, red currants. And mint leaves to offset the taste.

"Nobody's going to blame you," soothed the policeman. "It was a tragic accident."

Ned's death had been accidental, too. More or less. A fall from a cliff while they were out walking. Ned had been keen on walking, though she had never enjoyed it.

She looked up at the police. "I don't know what I'm going to do without Jim," she said sadly. "Now he's gone, I'm going to be all on my own again."

Susan Moody illustrates the grim results when the sanctuary of this story's protagonist is invaded. Moody is the author of the Cassandra Swann Bridge series *(King of*

Hearts, Grand Slam, and *Death Takes a Hand),* and the series featuring photographer Penny Wanawake *(Penny Saving, Penny Pinching, Penny Royal, Penny Post, Penny Dreadful, Penny Black, Penny Wise).* Moody lives outside of London.

One in Every Family

Betty Nathan

"What's wrong with Aunt Emily?"

Jan pronounced the name as if savoring it, very delicately. She made a dainty pussycat face, mouth pursed, two little vertical lines holding up the perfect arches of her dark, tapered eyebrows. The lines deepened. Apparently she had found the taste unpalatable.

"You tell her, Mom," said Tom. "If I do, you'll ream me out for using bad language."

Tom is my oldest. He's a senior at State and an honor student in biochemistry, but when he's home, it's hard for either of us to remember that he has grown up. So I explained to Jan.

"Emily is my aunt, my mother's sister. She visits us every couple of years, but this is the first time she's come for Christmas. Tom wants me to tell you that she can be a bit trying at times. We all have to be patient and forbearing."

"Mom is saying, in her gentle way, that Emily is the relative from hell, Jan. Now, Mom, you know you agree with me. Can't you tell her to come another time? This is Jan's first visit to our family, and if I subject her to Aunt Emily, she's likely to break off our engagement."

"You know very well I can't put Aunt Emily off. ("No one could," Tom muttered.) And it would be very unkind. Both Henry and Norman are going away for the holidays with their families this year ("Wish we'd thought of that," from Tom), so she has no one to spend Christmas with but us. I'll really need you all to help, and be kind and generous. It'll be good for your karma, I'm sure. And I'm afraid I'll have to ask a special favor of you two. We'll need the guest room for Emily. She's used to it when she visits here, and she says she can only sleep in a double bed. You two will have to make do in Tom's room on his bunk."

"Oh, Mom! I'm bigger than Emily just by myself . . ."

"Well, the only alternative is for Jan to take your bed and for you to sleep on the living room sofa. Or we may be able to rent another bed if they aren't all already taken for the holidays."

That silenced Tom, but I did feel sorry for him. He deserved better when he brought his girl home to introduce to us, but what could I do? We tend to run large in our family. Tom and his dad are well over six feet. The girls and I are all at least five foot eight. And Emily is a big woman, heavy-framed, almost six feet tall and substantial. I could understand her insistence on a comfortable amount of sleeping space. Jan, on the other hand, was only a little bit of a thing, and considering the way she and Tom clung to each other in public, it seemed to me they'd manage just fine in Tom's bachelor bunk.

Emily was due the day before Christmas. Ed picked her up at the airport and drove her home in one of the heaviest downpours we've had in years.

"Delilah!" she trumpeted in greeting and offered her cheek. "It is perfectly frightful outside. I told Edgar we should wait out the worst of it, but he insisted on driving through! He's very stubborn, isn't he?" She was clearly implying that I must have a lot to put up with. Ed made a face at me over her shoulder. She knows he hates to be called Edgar and I hate to be called Delilah. I'm sure she does it just to annoy us, although she claims to disapprove of nicknames.

After I had unpacked her bags—she always directs me in putting her things away and fetching unlikely necessities for her comfort, like Tums and bedsocks—she emerged from the guest room to take stock. I had briefed her on the Tom-Jan engagement, but I didn't tell her that the girl's full name was Janice Sue. I thought it was the least I could do for Jan.

Emily's ice-blue eyes surveyed the household. Large and round behind her gold-rimmed spectacles, they expressed neither humor nor guile. With Emily, what she thought was what one got.

"When will Anne and Elizabeth be here? Surely they should be home on Christmas Eve. Delilah, you look peaky. You need to get more rest. And who is this? Speak up, Thomas. Oh yes, this is Jan, your fiancée. Aren't you both a bit young for marriage? What do you do, Jan?"

Jan murmured that she was a senior at State, like Tom.

Emily knows how to say "Humph!" better than anyone.

"Well, don't get married until at least one of you is earning a living. Otherwise the rest of the family will have to sacrifice to support you. I don't approve of all this welfare nonsense for young people. Much healthier for you to stand on your own feet."

Her own sturdy walkers were planted firmly on my kitchen floor, and I wanted everyone out so I could get on with my cooking. I suggested she might like to go sit down in the living room and catch the six o'clock news on TV.

From the next room her deep alto carried clearly to me.

"You've got some new furniture. That black chair looks like a dentist chair for Martians. Why do they make such ugly things?"

"Well, actually, Aunt Emily, Del gave me that chair for my birthday. It's a special ergonomic design, tailored to fit me. I've developed a bad back, and the chair really helps. So we don't worry about what it looks like. You know what they say, if it does the job, it's handsome."

"Oh, that's what they say, is it? Let me try it. Mmph. Not bad. Most chairs hit one's back in the wrong place if you're tall, don't they? And it's at a good angle for watching the TV, too."

Ed meandered into the kitchen.

"I heard that. Here, have a beer."

"Better make it a scotch. Double. I suppose that's the last I'll see of my chair until she leaves. Not that it's not worth it if it keeps her quiet."

Ed was right about Emily's usurpation of his chair, though the rest of us, at one time or another in the days to come, explained to her that he was still in trouble with his back and that the chair was wonderfully therapeutic in easing his pain. She didn't pretend not to hear, as she sometimes did, but merely remarked that she, too, found it remarkably comfortable.

Nancy and Liz, our daughters, came home from their last-minute Christmas shopping just as I put dinner on the table. It was our traditional Christmas Eve dish, a family favorite.

"Beans?" said Emily, eyebrows raised, no doubt assessing our budget or my lack of *savoir faire.*

"Cassoulet," young Liz told her firmly. "It's a French regional dish that's got sixteen trillion ingredients. It takes Mom hours to prepare."

"Oh," said Emily, "Of course. How nice. But you shouldn't exaggerate, Elizabeth."

She quizzed the girls about their schoolwork and boyfriends, and warned them not to follow their brother's example and get tied down too young. *"My* boys didn't get engaged until they had professional jobs, and they didn't get married until they were earning enough to support a family. And they didn't have *babies* until their careers were quite settled."

I was aware of Tom's foot, on my right, carrying on a complicitous conversation under the table with Jan's. I frowned at him, and the jiggling stopped. But of course, I was just as tempted to disgrace myself as were the girls, who were choking back their laughter with difficulty. Emily's two sons were notorious in our family for the pallor of their personalities and the crashing dullness of their lives. Poor crushed snails, Ed had once called them, and it did seem miraculous that they had survived childhood under Emily's jackboot. Even more amazing that they had been willing to risk marriage.

Our Christmas Eve ritual took Ed and the children into the living room to decorate the tree, leaving me at peace in the kitchen to do my traditional special things with cranberries and dressing and vegetables. I'd already baked the pies and steamed the plum pudding. Tomorrow the kids would help with appetizers and the table setting, and leave me to concentrate on the goose and last-minute sauces. Ed took Emily along to help them with the tree. She watched and made suggestions from the embrace of Ed's chair, calmly observing that he had plenty of hands to help him. After a bit, I heard her clarion voice again.

"Jan, my dear, I would like you to give me a hand. I need you to wrap the little presents I brought for the family. I have nothing for you, of course, since I didn't know you'd be here, so you're the best person to help. I'm no good at wrapping. I've always been all thumbs, I'm afraid. Oh, and do ask Delilah for some of her gift paper and ribbons. I couldn't carry all that."

I moved to the door. Jan was smiling that uptilted little feline smile, her eyes blue and innocent as an infant's under the dark fringe of her luxurious eyelashes. I didn't feel that she and I had made real contact yet, or that I had any idea what made her tick (what every woman wants to be sure she knows about a prospective daughter-in-law), but I certainly appreciated the skill with which she employed her battery of charms.

"I'm so sorry, Aunt Emily. I may call you Aunt, mayn't I? I'm afraid I'm just all thumbs, too. I'd make such a mess of the wrapping. You'd better ask someone else to help you."

Score one for Jan. Clearly there was something more

there than just the little bit of fluff she looked. I wondered if Tom knew what he'd taken on. I wondered if he could handle it.

I gave Nancy a significant look and a little nod. She had worked one summer as a gift-wrapper in a department store and knows all the tricks. She sighed resignedly.

"I'll do it, Aunt Emily. I don't mind seeing my present in advance if you don't mind."

Things went pretty smoothly on Christmas Day. I could count on Emily not to offer to help in the kitchen. Tom escaped with Jan for a walk around town before dinner in exchange for promising to do the dishes afterwards, so Ed and the girls and I managed very efficiently. My dinner was much enjoyed and the goose was a great success, though Emily said *she* always served ham for Christmas.

Only when cleanup was complete and we could all relax did we settle down to opening presents. I had bought two gifts for the whole family, including Jan, to give to Emily—an electric tea kettle and a bed jacket—and she was quite pleased. She called each of us to her where she sat in state in Ed's chair so that she could give us each a thank-you peck on the cheek. Taking our cue, each of us in turn kissed her when we opened the presents she had brought and Nancy had spectacularly wrapped—a ballpoint pen for Tom, a small bottle of toilet water each for the girls and me, a tie clip for Ed, who only wears bow ties. But perhaps she'd forgotten. Judging from that little smile of Jan's that I was coming to know well, it was perhaps just as well that she had no gift for which to kiss Emily.

We didn't run into any trouble until late that night. Our house is one of those open plan, slab-floored ranch styles, where only the living room is separate from the other living areas. The kitchen, dining room and family room are all part of one space, and there really isn't a family room because I use that area as my study, where I write cook-books. The house was plenty big enough when we first bought it and the kids were small. Even now, most of the time, especially with Tom away at college, it's still big enough, but Emily's presence used up the margin of livability.

I was at my desk when Tom came in to me to complain, about ten o'clock.

"Mom, I invited the guys over ages ago to meet Jan, and we all want to watch that sci-fi special tonight and drink a little beer. But Emily wants to watch choir boys singing more Christmas carols, for God's sake, and she's bound to sound off on the evils of alcohol. I can't budge her. Do something, please."

"I'll see what I can do, dear. Maybe I can persuade Dad to put our TV set in Emily's room. I hate to ask him to give up his hockey game, but I will if I can't move Emily any other way."

But when I entered the living room, Jan had the situation well in hand.

"We're going to change the channel now, Aunt Emily," she was saying, "but Tom has a wonderful little portable radio. I've put it in your room and you can lie down comfortably and listen to the singing. They said it was simulcast, so you won't miss a thing."

Emily's mouth opened, then closed without a word. She made a great show of struggling out of Ed's chair, a great ceremony of saying good night, and sailed out with great dignity. But she went.

I saw very little of any of the children that vacation. Liz and Nancy spent most of their time at friends' houses. Tom and Jan were out a lot, too, and when they were home, closeted themselves in Tom's room, from whence came giggles and loud music.

In the coming days, Aunt Emily frequently remarked that I seemed nervous and tired. Of course she was quite right. Every night, Ed gripped the bar of Cashmere Bouquet soap and slashed a white mark on the corner of the bathroom mirror as if he were wielding a sword.

"Aha, another day survived. Just a few more to go, and we'll have chased the Minotaur!" he'd growl. It made me laugh, which was the general idea.

By the twenty-ninth, I'd pretty well run out of forbearance. Emily decided, after indulging along with the rest of us on Christmas Day, that she must go on a no-fat, no-cholesterol, no-salt diet, so I had a choice of giving up all the lovely menus I'd planned with the kids' favorite, admittedly rich, foods, or preparing separate meals for Emily. Of course I opted for cooking separate meals. What made the extra work particularly irksome was that, when no one was looking, Emily helped herself to snacks from our sinful leftovers.

"Why don't you just buy some low-cal TV dinners for her? That's probably what she eats at home, anyway."

"Just pride, I guess. And what if word got out that the author of *Cooking the Right Way* and *Classical Cuisine* served her aunt TV dinners? Sales would plummet. I'd lose all my credibility. No, I'll survive. At least it gives me an excuse to try out some ideas I've been gestating for a collection of healthy-heart dishes."

That was true. I had been thinking of putting together a book on dieting without tears. Now I thought that I should dedicate it to Emily and call it *The Gourmet Grump.* Ed was worried about me. I'm the sort that tries to be perfect, puts up with things, and then snaps when the cord pulls too thin. Ed has learned over the years to monitor my mood. He had been casting anxious glances at me all day. Now he suggested to the kids that they might like to stay home and play a few games with us. (Translation: Give us a hand keeping the old woman company. Your mother has had it.) Like Charades. Or Murder.

"Great," muttered Tom, *sotto voce,* "Emily could be the victim."

Emily said that the only game she ever played was Scrabble, and that she would be happy to oblige Tom and Jan and one of the girls with a game. Looking at me sheepishly, Tom said they'd all promised to go ice-skating with friends.

"I'm sorry, Mom," he told me next day, "but we couldn't take it. I played with her once when I was young, and she kept making up new rules so she could win. She didn't care what I said. She'd just go, 'It's in *my* rule book at home,' or, 'That's the way my friends and I *always* play.' She wouldn't let me use 'the' for a word, but she got to use 'an.' Heck, I was only about twelve, but she was more childish than I've ever been. And that was ten years ago! She'll have refined the torture by now."

"I know," I said bitterly. "Your father and I got stuck with Scrabble à la Emily last night while you were out partying. I figured the only thing to do was to play to lose as quickly as possible and get it over with."

Perhaps Ed told the kids I needed a respite, or perhaps they had noticed that I was on the thin edge, or perhaps they just took pity on their defenseless parents. The next night, Ed invited me to a movie, and before Emily could offer to come along, Nancy said brightly that there was a great film on TV, and she was sure Emily would like it, too.

"You go with Dad, Mom. We'll keep each other company."

The movies in town were all holiday fare, geared to children. We had a choice of several particularly saccharine Walt Disney films, or a couple of reruns. We chose Shaw's *Caesar and Cleopatra* with Claude Raines and Vivien Leigh, although we'd seen it twice before, years ago. I found it still very enjoyable, particularly after the penny dropped.

"Who does Vivien Leigh remind you of?" I asked Ed on our drive home.

"Gosh, I don't know. I hate guessing games."

"How about Jan?"

"I hadn't noticed, but you're right. Both sex-kittens, I guess. And something about the smile . . ."

"Yes, it's those sharp little teeth, and the look of knowing a secret. Like a cat. Are you happy about having her as our daughter-in-law?"

"Nothing I could do about it even if I weren't. Tom is smitten, and she certainly seems keen on him, too. That's what's important, after all. Don't you like her, Del?"

"I don't think *like* is the operative word. There's nothing to disapprove of or not to like. It's just that I think maybe she's a bit manipulative. . . ."

"Well, aren't all women?"

"No, that's not what I mean. It's not just a question of feminine wiles. Considering her age, she seems very sure of herself. You know, like the world's very much her oyster, and she knows exactly how to serve it up. I don't know that I'm expressing myself very well. I just hope Tom doesn't get hurt."

Ed turned the car into our street. Halfway down the block there was an array of vehicles, all flashing red lights as if they, too, were decorated for Christmas, but the effect was far from jolly. Ed slowed down and parked across from our house, which was blocked by the ambulance and two police cars, and some curious neighbors.

First, of course, I thought of the children. One always does. Before my foot was even out the car door, I had had a vision of every conceivable kind of household disaster—fire, electrocution, a fall (where could one fall from or to in our single-story house?), poison, drugs. Drugs? Surely not my children.

I raced for the house, outpacing Ed. It wasn't until my foot was actually over the threshold that Aunt Emily came to mind. And then, of course, I knew that's who it had to be. She was well over seventy, sedentary, and given to overeating. Her heart, I thought, and immediately felt guilty. Why had I been so cynical about her need for the special diet?

We found everyone in the dining/family room. What caught the eye first was our silly holiday tablecloth with its jaunty pattern of red and green holly sprigs. It had been removed from the table and was spread over a large shape on the floor. Two feet in Dr. Scholl walkers protruded at one end. Large, lumpy, utterly human, utterly familiar. The essence of Emily's mortality seemed captured in those pathetic, ugly shoes.

Nancy and Liz were in tears. A stricken Tom had his head in his hands. Jan stood behind him, stroking his back. I gathered that one of the ambulance attendants had just given up on his efforts to resuscitate Emily. He was rolling up bits of tubing, a plastic mask, all his failed gear. His partner was talking quietly on the phone. Two of the policemen left. The other two stood by and watched us.

"She's dead? Was it her heart?"

The ambulance man shook his head. "I'm afraid she was gone by the time we got here. The kids were doing what they could, but it was no good. Seems to have strangled on some food. Happens sometimes, you know, when it goes down the windpipe by mistake. Usually gets coughed up, but this time it jammed in solid."

Liz was sobbing. "Oh, Mom, I'm so sorry. I should have known what to do. They showed us the Heimlich maneuver in Girl Scouts last year, but I was so scared I forgot all about it till too late."

The ambulance man consoled Liz. "I don't think it would have made any difference, honey. That food was really *lodged.* Even Heimlich doesn't always work."

Ed wrapped her in his arms. "Hush, sweetie. Not your fault."

I steeled myself for what I knew I had to do. I knelt by the tablecloth at the end opposite to those pathetic feet, and drew the cloth away from her face. Suffused, mottled red and bluish, almost the color of the marble eyes, open and glaring still, as if she was letting death know she disapproved.

Bit by bit the story emerged.

Emily didn't like the TV movie and wanted to play Scrabble again. Tom had nobly volunteered to play with her, and Jan had joined them in the dining room, leaving the girls to watch TV. At Emily's request, Jan had brought out a plate of leftovers from the family's dinner, a few skewers of shaslik threaded with beef, potatoes, and peppers. She'd removed the skewers, and both Tom and Emily had helped themselves generously to the chunks of food. Apparently Emily had swallowed the wrong way. She'd sputtered, tried to cough, clutched her throat, tried to dislodge the food with her finger. Tom had patted her back vigorously, then gone to get her a drink of water. By this time, Emily was sitting on the floor, down in Jan's range. Jan also tried to dislodge the morsel. She thought it might have been a piece of meat because she could feel it and it seemed unyielding. She was unable to get a purchase on it, or hook it out, even with her small fingers. ("I'm all thumbs," I remembered her saying). Emily couldn't drink the water, and it wouldn't have helped anyway, of course.

At this point, they called to the girls to phone for an ambulance, and Liz came in and remembered after a bit about Heimlich, but before she could get her arms around her, Emily'd passed out and collapsed on the floor. So Liz had done mouth-to-mouth instead. Then the police came, and the ambulance, and the kids were chased into the other room, and about ten minutes later, one of the ambulance men came out and asked them when she'd started choking and all about it. Then they'd told the kids Emily was dead, and let them come see her. Somebody had covered her with the tablecloth.

"We'd have taken her to Emergency if there'd been a prayer of reviving her, ma'am, but it was too late."

A doctor came, too, and examined poor Emily.

"Funny," he said, "I wonder why she has bruises around her mouth."

"Wouldn't that have been from the oxygen mask?"

"I shouldn't think so. Doesn't usually have that effect. Besides, she was probably dead before they put the mask on her."

"Maybe it was me," said Jan. "I tried to get the food out of her throat. My hands are a lot smaller than hers. I may have been kind of rough, though, feeling around. I didn't even think I might be hurting her mouth. I mean, it was an emergency, wasn't it?"

Tom nodded. "Yeah, Jan was great. God, what a crazy accident." He started to cry then, my big boy. "She was such a pest, poor old Aunt Emily, but it's awful she died like that." I hugged him. I wept, too.

"I know. Poor old dear. She was difficult, but she was

really fond of us, in her own way, and she meant well. Every family needs one strong character, and she certainly was ours. I believe I'm going to miss her."

"Well," said Ed, irreverent as usual, "I just hope they've got a double bed for her in Heaven."

What seemed hours later, the doctor packed his bag, Emily was taken away and the policemen left. Ed packed up the Scrabble set and threw it in the trash. It wasn't likely any of us would want to play that game again.

I went to the kitchen and began to prepare hot cocoa and cookies for us all. The girls set the table. Jan came into the kitchen area and gave me a hand. She was quick and deft. I'd noticed that before. (All thumbs?) And she always seemed to know the next thing that needed doing. As I handed her the plate of cookies, I looked at her closely. There was something I wanted to know.

"Were you ever in the Girl Scouts?" I asked her. Those velvety lashes dropped so that I couldn't see the expression in her eyes as she nodded. Her shapely mouth was pursed as she turned away with the plate.

"Indeed," I thought, and involuntarily I shivered. "Every family has to have one strong character. But one's enough. With two, you could start a chemical reaction. There'd be a battle for domination. Maybe a catastrophe."

Jan hadn't waited for me, but had started pouring the cocoa. She brought me a cup. Then she looked sideways at me. And then she smiled at me. And I swear she winked.

In this story, Betty Nathan examines a relative burden in sensible shoes. Nathan, an American who divides her time between Australia and the United States, writes mysteries set in both places. Her recent book featuring ex-professor and rookie farmer Will McHugh is *Top Paddock.*

The Two Ladies of Rose Cottage

Peter Robinson

In our village, they were always known as the "Two Ladies of Rose Cottage": Miss Eunice, with the white hair, and Miss Teresa with the gray. Nobody really knew where they came from, or exactly how old they were, but the consensus held that they had met in India, America, or South Africa, and decided to return to the homeland to live out their days together. And, in 1939, they were generally believed to be in or approaching their nineties.

Imagine our surprise, then, one fine day in September, when the police car pulled up outside Rose Cottage, and when, in a matter of hours, rumors began to spread throughout the village: rumors of human bones dug up in a distant garden; rumors of mutilation and dismemberment; rumors of murder.

Lyndgarth is the name of our village. It is situated in one of the most remote Yorkshire dales, about twenty miles from Eastvale, the nearest large town. The village is no more than a group of limestone houses with slate roofs, clustered around a bumpy, slanted green that always reminded me of a handkerchief flapping in the breeze. We have the usual amenities—grocer's shop, butcher's, newsagent's, post office, school, two churches, three public houses—and proximity to some of the most beautiful countryside in the world.

I was fifteen in 1939, and Miss Eunice and Miss Teresa had been living in the village for twenty years, yet still they remained strangers to us. It is often said that you have to "winter out" at least two years before being accepted into village life, and in the case of a remote place like Lyndgarth, in those days, it was more like ten.

As far as the locals were concerned then, the two ladies had served their apprenticeship and were more than fit to be accepted as fully paid-up members of the community, yet there was about them a certain detached quality that kept them ever at arm's length.

They did all their shopping in the village and were always polite to people they met in the street; they regularly attended church services at St. Oswald's and helped with charity events; and they never set foot in any of the public houses. But still there was that sense of distance, of not quite being—or not *wanting* to be—a part of things.

The summer of 1939 had been unusually beautiful despite the political tensions. Or am I indulging in nostalgia for childhood? Our dale can be one of the most grim and desolate landscapes on the face of the earth, even in August, but I remember the summers of my youth as days of dazzling sunshine and blue skies. In 1939, every day was a new symphony of color—golden buttercups, pink clover, mauve crane's-bill—ever-changing and recombining in fresh palettes. While the tense negotiations went on in Europe, while Ribbentrop and Molotov signed the Nazi-Soviet pact, and while there was talk of conscription and rationing at home, very little changed in Lyndgarth.

Summer in the dale was always a season for odd jobs—peat-cutting, wall-mending, sheep-clipping—and for entertainments, such as the dialect plays, the circus, fairs, and brass bands. Even after war was declared on the third of

September, we still found ourselves rather guiltily having fun, scratching our heads, shifting from foot to foot, and wondering when something really warlike was going to happen.

Of course, we had our gas masks in their cardboard boxes, which we had to carry everywhere; streetlighting was banned, and motor cars were not allowed to use their headlights. This latter rule was the cause of numerous accidents in the dale, usually involving wandering sheep on the unfenced roads.

Some evacuees also arrived from the cities. Uncouth urchins for the most part, often verminous and ill-equipped for country life, they seemed like an alien race to us. Most of them didn't seem to have any warm clothing or Wellington boots, as if they had never seen mud in the city. Looking back, I realize they were far from home, separated from their parents, and they must have been scared to death. I am ashamed to admit, though, that at the time I didn't go out of my way to give them a warm welcome.

This is partly because I was always lost in my own world. I was a bookish child, and had recently discovered the stories of Thomas Hardy, who seemed to understand and sympathize with a lonely village lad and his dreams of becoming a writer. I also remember how much he thrilled and scared me with some of the stories. After "The Withered Arm," I wouldn't let anyone touch me for a week, and I didn't dare go to sleep after "Barbara of the House of Grebe" for fear that there was a horribly disfigured statue in the wardrobe, that the door would slowly creak open and . . .

I think I was reading *Far from the Madding Crowd* that hot July day, and, as was my wont, I read as I walked across the village green, not looking where I was going. It was Miss Teresa I bumped into, and I remember thinking that she seemed remarkably resilient for such an old lady.

"Do mind where you're going, young man!" she admonished me, though when she heard my effusive apologies, she softened her tone somewhat. She asked me what I was reading, and when I showed her the book, she closed her eyes for a moment, and a strange expression crossed her wrinkled features.

"Ah, Mr. Hardy," she said after a short silence. "I knew him once, you know, in his youth. I grew up in Dorset."

I could hardly hold back my enthusiasm. Someone who actually *knew* Hardy! I told her that he was my favorite writer of all time, even better than Shakespeare, and that when I grew up I wanted to be a writer, just like him.

Miss Teresa smiled indulgently. "Do calm down," she said, then she paused. "I suppose," she continued, with a glance toward Miss Eunice, "that if you are really interested in Mr. Hardy, perhaps you might like to come to tea someday?"

When I assured her I would be delighted, we made an arrangement that I was to call at Rose Cottage the following Tuesday at four o'clock, after securing my mother's permission, of course.

That Tuesday visit was the first of many. Inside, Rose Cottage belied its name. It seemed dark and gloomy, unlike ours, which was always full of sunlight and bright flowers. The furnishings were antique, even a little shabby. I recollect no family photographs of the kind that embellished most mantelpieces, but there was a huge gilt-framed painting of a young girl working alone in a field hanging on one wall. If the place sometimes smelled a little musty and neglected, the aroma of Miss Teresa's fresh-baked scones more often than not made up for it.

"Mr. Hardy was full of contradictions," Miss Teresa told me on one occasion. "He was a dreamer, of course, and never happier than when wandering the countryside, alone with his thoughts. But he was also a fine musician. He played the fiddle on many social occasions, such as dances and weddings, and he was often far more gregarious and cheerful than many of his critics would have imagined. He was also a scholar, head forever buried in a book, always studying Latin or Greek. I was no dullard, either, you know, and I like to think I held my own in our conversations, though I had little Latin and less Greek." She chuckled, then turned serious again. "Anyway, one never felt one really *knew* him. One was always looking at a mask. Do you understand me, young man?"

I nodded. "I think so, Miss Teresa."

"Yes, well," she said, staring into space as she sometimes did while speaking of Hardy. "At least that was *my* impression. Though he was a good ten years older than me, I like to believe I got glimpses of the man behind the mask. But because the other villagers thought him a bit odd, and because he was difficult to know, he also attracted a lot of idle gossip. I remember there was talk about him and that Sparks girl from Puddletown. What was her first name, Eunice?"

"Tryphena."

"That's right." She curled her lip and seemed to spit out the name. "Tryphena Sparks. A singularly dull girl, I always thought. We were about the same age, you know, she and I. Anyway, there was talk of a child. Utter rubbish, of course." She gazed out of the window at the green, where a group of children were playing a makeshift game of cricket. Her eyes seemed to film over. "Many's the time I used to walk through the woodland past the house, and I would see him sitting there at his upstairs window seat, writing or gazing out on the garden. Sometimes he would wave and come down to talk." Suddenly she stopped, then her eyes glittered, and she went on. "He used to go and watch hangings in Dorchester. Did you know that?"

I had to confess that I didn't, my acquaintance with Hardy being recent and restricted only to his published works of fiction, but it never occurred to me to doubt Miss Teresa's word.

"Of course, executions were public back then." Again she paused, and I thought I saw, or rather *sensed* a little shiver run through her. Then she said that was enough for today, that it was time for scones and tea.

I think she enjoyed shocking me like that at the end of her little narratives, as if we needed to be brought back to reality with a jolt. I remember on another occasion she looked me in the eye and said, "Of course, the doctor tossed him aside as dead at birth, you know. If it hadn't been for the nurse, he would never have survived. That must do something to a man, don't you think?"

We talked of many other aspects of Hardy and his work, and, for the most part, Miss Eunice remained silent, nodding from time to time. Occasionally, when Miss Teresa's memory seemed to fail her on some point, such as a name or what novel Hardy might have been writing in a certain year, she would supply the information.

I remember one visit particularly vividly. Miss Teresa stood up rather more quickly than I thought her able to, and left the room for a few moments. I sat politely, sipping my tea, aware of Miss Eunice's silence and the ticking of the grandfather clock out in the hall. When Miss Teresa returned, she was carrying an old book, or rather two books, which she handed to me.

It was a two-volume edition of *Far from the Madding Crowd,* and, though I didn't know it at the time, it was the first edition, from 1874, and was probably worth a small fortune. But what fascinated me even more than Helen Paterson's illustrations was the brief inscription on the flyleaf: *To Tess, With Affection, Tom.*

I knew that Tess was a diminutive of Teresa, because I had an Aunt Teresa in Harrogate, and it never occurred to me to question that the "Tess" in the inscription was the person sitting opposite me, or that the "Tom" was any other than Thomas Hardy himself.

"He called you Tess," I remember saying. "Perhaps he had you in mind when he wrote *Tess of the d'Urbervilles?"*

Miss Teresa's face drained of color so quickly I feared for her life, and it seemed that a palpable chill entered the room. "Don't be absurd, boy," she whispered. "Tess Durbeyfield was hanged for murder."

* * *

We had been officially at war for about a week, I think, when the police called. There were three men, one in uniform and two in plainclothes. They spent almost two hours in Rose Cottage, then came out alone, got in their car, and drove away. We never saw them again.

The day after the visit, though, I happened to overhear our local constable talking with the vicar in St. Oswald's churchyard. By a great stroke of fortune, several yews stood between us and I was able to remain unseen while I took in every word.

"Murdered, that's what they say," said P.C. Walker. "Bashed his 'ead in with a poker, then chopped 'im up in little pieces and buried 'em in t' garden. Near Dorchester, it were. Village called 'igher Bockhampton. People who lived there were digging an air-raid shelter when they found t' bones. 'Eck of a shock for t' bairns."

Could they possibly mean Miss Teresa? That sweet old lady who made such delightful scones and had known the young Thomas Hardy? Could she really have bashed someone on the head, chopped him up into little pieces, and buried them in the garden? I shivered at the thought, despite the heat.

But nothing more was heard of the murder charge. The police never returned, people found new things to talk about, and after a couple of weeks Miss Eunice and Miss Teresa reappeared in village life much as they had been before. The only difference was that my mother would no longer allow me to visit Rose Cottage. I put up token resistance, but by then my mind was full of Spitfires, secret codes, and aircraft carriers anyway.

Events seemed to move quickly in the days after the police visit, though I cannot be certain of the actual time period involved. Four things, however, conspired to put the murder out of my mind for some time: Miss Teresa died, I think in the November of that same year; Miss Eunice retreated into an even deeper silence than before; the war escalated; and I was called up to military service.

* * *

The next time I gave any thought to the two ladies of Rose Cottage was in Egypt, of all places, in September 1942. I was on night watch with the 8th Army, not far from Alamein. Desert nights have an eerie beauty I have never found anywhere else since. After the heat of the day, the cold surprises one, for a start, as does the sense of endless space, but even more surprising is the desertscape of wrecked tanks, jeeps, and lorries in the cold moonlight, metal wrenched and twisted into impossible patterns like some petrified forest or exposed coral reef.

To spoil our sleep and shatter our nerves, Rommel's Afrika Corps had got into the routine of setting up huge amplified speakers and blaring out "Lili Marleen" over and over all night long. It was on a night such as this, while I was trying to stay warm and awake and trying to shut my ears to the music, that I struck up a conversation with a soldier called Sidney Ferris from one of the Dorset regiments.

When Sid told me he had grown up in Piddlehinton, I suddenly thought of the two ladies of Rose Cottage.

"Did you ever hear any stories of a murder around there?" I asked, offering Sid a cigarette. "A place called Higher Bockhampton?"

"Lots of murder stories going around when I was a lad," he said, lighting up, careful to hide the flame with his cupped hand. "Better than the wireless."

"This would be a wife murdering her husband."

He nodded. "Plenty of that and all. And husbands murdering their wives. Makes you wonder whether it's worth getting married, doesn't it? Higher Bockhampton, you say?"

"Yes. Teresa Morgan, I believe the woman's name was."

He frowned. "Name don't ring no bell," he said, "but I do recall a tale about some woman who was supposed to have killed her husband, cut him up in pieces, and buried them in the garden. A couple of young lads found some bones when they was digging an air-raid shelter a couple of years back. Animal bones, if you ask me."

"But did the villagers believe the tale?"

He shrugged. "Don't know about anyone else, but I can't say as I did. So many stories like that going around, they can't all be true, or damn near all of us would be murderers or corpses. Stands to reason, doesn't it?" And he took a long drag on his cigarette, holding it in his cupped hand, like most soldiers, so the enemy wouldn't see the pinpoint of light.

"Did anyone say what became of the woman?" I asked.

"She went away some years later. There was talk of someone else seen running away from the farmhouse, too, the night they said the murder must have taken place."

"Could it have been him? The husband?"

Sid shook his head. "Too slight a figure. Her husband was a big man, apparently. Anyway, that led to more talk of an illicit lover. There's always a lover, isn't there? Have you noticed? You know what kind of minds these country gossips have."

"Did anyone say who the other person might have been?"

"Nobody knew. Just rumours of a vague shape seen running away. These are old wives' tales we're talking about."

"But perhaps there's some tru—"

But at that point I was relieved of my watch, and the next weeks turned out to be so chaotic that I never even saw Sid again. I heard later that he was killed at the battle of Alamein just over a month after our conversation.

I didn't come across the mystery of Rose Cottage again until the early 1950s. At that time, I was living in Eastvale, in a small flat overlooking the cobbled market square. The town was much smaller and quieter than it is today, though little about the square has changed, from the ancient market cross, the Queen's Arms on the corner, the Norman church, and the Tudor-fronted police station.

I had recently published my first novel and was still basking in that exquisite sensation that comes only once in a writer's career: the day he holds the first bound and printed copy of his very first work. Of course, there was no money in writing, so I worked part-time in a bookshop on North Market Street, and on one of my mornings off, a market day, as I remember, I was absorbed in polishing the third chapter of what was to be my second novel when I heard a faint tap at my door. This was enough to startle me, as I rarely had any visitors.

Puzzled and curious, I left my typewriter and went to open the door. There stood a wizened old lady, hunch-shouldered, white-haired, carrying a stick with a brass lion's head handle and a small package wrapped in brown paper, tied with string.

She must have noticed my confused expression, because, with a faint smile, she said, "Don't you recognize me, Mr. Riley? Dear, dear, have I aged that much?"

Then I knew her, knew the voice.

"Miss Eunice!" I cried, throwing my door open. "Please forgive me. I was lost in my own world. Do come in. And you must call me Christopher."

Once we were settled, with a pot of tea mashing beside us—though, alas, none of Miss Teresa's scones—I noticed the dark circles under Miss Eunice's eyes, the yellow around the pupils, the parchmentlike quality of her skin, and I knew she was seriously ill.

"How did you find me?" I asked.

"It didn't take a Sherlock Holmes. Everyone knows where the famous writer lives in a small town like Eastvale."

"Hardly famous," I demurred. "But thank you anyway. I never knew you took the trouble to follow my fortunes."

"Teresa would have wished it. She was very fond of you, you know. Apart from ourselves and the police, you were the only person in Lyndgarth who ever entered Rose Cottage. Did you know that? You might remember that we kept ourselves very much to ourselves."

"Yes, I remember that," I told her.

"I came to give you this."

She handed me the package and I untied it carefully.

Inside was the Smith, Elder & Co. first edition of *Far from the Madding Crowd,* complete with Hardy's inscription to "Tess."

"But you shouldn't," I said. "This must be very valuable. It's a fir—"

She waved aside my objections. "Please take it. It is what Teresa would have wished. And I wish it, too. Now listen," she went on. "That isn't the only reason I came. I have something very important to tell you, to do with why the police came to visit all those years ago. The thought of going to my grave without telling someone troubles me deeply."

"But why me? And why now?"

"I told you. Teresa was especially fond of you. And you're a writer," she added mysteriously. "You'll understand. Should you wish to make use of the story, please do so. Neither Teresa nor I have any living relatives to offend. All I ask is that you wait a suitable number of years after my death before publishing any account. And that death is expected to occur at some point over the next few months. Does that answer your second question?"

I nodded. "Yes. I'm sorry."

"You needn't be. As you may well be aware, I have long since exceeded my three score and ten, though I can hardly say the extra years have been a blessing. But that is God's will. Do you agree to my terms?"

"Of course. I take it this is about the alleged murder?"

Miss Eunice raised her eyebrows. "So you've heard the rumors?" she said. "Well, there was a murder all right. Teresa Morgan murdered her husband, Jacob, and buried his body in the garden." She held out her tea cup and I poured. I noticed her hand was shaking slightly. Mine was, too. The shouts of the market vendors came in through my open windows.

"When did she do this?" was all I could manage.

Miss Eunice closed her eyes and pursed her cracked lips. "I don't remember the exact year," she said. "But it really doesn't matter. You could look it up, if you wanted. It was the year the Queen was proclaimed Empress of India."

I happened to know that was in 1877. I have always had a good memory for historical dates. If my calculations were correct, Miss Teresa would have been about twenty-seven at the time. "Will you tell me what happened?" I asked.

"That's why I'm here," Miss Eunice said rather sharply. "Teresa's husband was a brute, a bully, and a drunkard. She wouldn't have married him, had *she* had any choice in the matter. But her parents approved the match. He had his own small farm, you see, and they were only tenants. Teresa was a very intelligent girl, but that counted for nothing in those days. In fact, it was a positive disadvantage. As was her wilfulness. Anyway, he used to beat her to within an inch of her life—where the bruises wouldn't show, of course. One day she'd had enough of it, so she killed him."

"What did she do?"

"She hit him with the poker from the fireplace and, after darkness had fallen, she buried him deep in the garden. She was afraid that if the matter went to court the authorities wouldn't believe her, and she would be hanged. She had no evidence, you see. And Jacob was a popular man among the other fellows of the village, as is so often the case with drunken brutes. And Teresa was terrified of being publicly hanged."

"But did no one suspect her?"

Miss Eunice shook her head. "Jacob was constantly talking about leaving his wife and heading for the New World. He used to berate her for not bearing him any children—specifically sons—and threatened that one day she would wake up and he would be gone. Gone to another country to find a woman who could give him the children he wanted. He repeated these threats in the ale-house so often that no one in the entire county of Dorset could fail to know about them."

"So when he disappeared, everyone assumed he had followed through on his threats to leave her?"

"Exactly. Oh, there were rumors that his wife had murdered him, of course. There always are when such mysteries occur."

Yes, I thought, remembering my conversation with Sid Ferris one cold desert night ten years ago: rumors and fancies, the stuff of fiction. And something about a third person seen fleeing from the scene. Well, that could wait.

"Teresa stayed on at the farm for another ten years," Miss Eunice went on. "Then she sold up and went to America. It was a brave move, but Teresa no more lacked for courage than she did for beauty. She was in her late thirties then, and even after a hard life, she could still turn heads. In New York, she landed on her feet and eventually married a financier. Sam Cotter. A good man. She also took a companion."

"You?" I asked.

Miss Eunice nodded. "Yes. Some years later, Sam died of a stroke. We stayed on in New York for a while, but we grew increasingly homesick. We came back finally in 1919, just after the Great War. For obvious reasons, Teresa didn't want to live anywhere near Dorset, so we settled in Yorkshire."

"A remarkable tale," I said.

"But that's not all," Miss Eunice went on, pausing only to sip some tea. "There was a child."

"I thought you said—"

She took one hand off her stick and held it up, palm out. "Christopher, please let me tell the story in my own way. Then it will be yours to do with as you wish. You have no idea how difficult this is for me." She paused and stared down at the brass lion's head for so long I feared she had fallen asleep, or died. Outside in the market square a butcher was loudly trying to sell a leg of lamb. Just as I was about to go over to Miss Eunice, she stirred. "There was a child," she repeated. "When Teresa was fifteen, she gave birth to a child. It was a difficult birth. She was never able to bear any other children."

"What happened to this child?"

"Teresa had a sister called Alice, living in Dorchester. Alice was five years older and already married with two children. Just before the pregnancy started to show, both Teresa and Alice went to stay with relatives in Cornwall for a few months, after it had been falsely announced that Alice was with child again. You would be surprised how often such things happened. When they came back, Alice had a fine baby girl."

"Who was the father?"

"Teresa would never say. The one thing she did make clear was that no one had forced unwanted attentions on her, that the child was the result of a love match, an infatuation. It certainly wasn't Jacob Morgan."

"Did she ever see the child again?"

"Oh, certainly. What could be more natural than visiting one's sister and seeing one's niece grow up? When the girl was a little older, she began to pay visits to the farm, too."

Miss Eunice stopped here and frowned so hard I thought her brow would crack like dry paper. "That was when the problems began," she said quietly.

"What problems?"

Miss Eunice put her stick aside and held out her tea cup. I refilled it. Her hands steady now, she held the cup against her scrawny chest as if its heat were the only thing keeping her alive. "This is the most difficult part," she said in a faint voice. "The part I didn't know whether I could ever tell anyone."

"If you don't wish—"

She waved my objection aside. "It's all right, Christopher. I didn't know how much I could tell you before I came here, but I know now. I've come this far. I can't go back now. Just give me a few moments to collect myself."

Outside, the market was in full swing, and during the ensuing silence I could hear the clamor of voices selling and buying, arguing over prices.

"Did I ever tell you that Teresa was an extremely beautiful young girl?" Miss Eunice asked after a while.

"I believe you mentioned it, yes."

She nodded. "Well, she was. And so was her daughter. When she began coming by herself to the house, she was about twelve or thirteen years of age. Jacob didn't fail to notice her, how well she was 'filling out' as he used to say. One day, Teresa had gone into the village for firewood and the child arrived in her absence. Jacob, just home from the ale-house, was there alone to greet her. Need I say more, Mr. Riley?"

I shook my head. "I don't mean to excuse him in any way, but I'm assuming he didn't know the girl was his step-daughter?"

"That is correct. He never knew. Nor did *she* know Teresa was her mother. Not until much later."

"What happened next?"

"Teresa came in before her husband could have his way with the struggling, half-naked child. Everything else was as I said. She picked up the poker and hit him on the head. Not once, but six times. Then they cleaned up and waited until after dark and buried him deep in the garden. She sent her daughter back to her sister's and carried on as if her husband had simply left her, just as he had threatened to do."

So the daughter was the mysterious third person seen leaving the farm in Sid Ferris's account. "What became of the poor child?" I asked.

Miss Eunice paused again and seemed to struggle for breath. She turned terribly pale. I got up and moved toward her, but she stretched out her hand. "No, no. I'm all right, Christopher. Please sit."

A motor car honked outside and one of the street vendors yelled a curse.

Miss Eunice patted her chest. "That's better. I'm fine now, really I am. Just a minor spasm. But I do feel ashamed. I'm afraid I haven't been entirely truthful with you. It's so difficult. You see, I was, I *am,* that child."

For a moment my mouth just seemed to flap open and shut and I couldn't speak. Finally, I managed to stammer,

"You? *You* are Miss Teresa's daughter? But you can't be. That's not possible."

"I didn't mean to shock you," she went on softly, "but, really, you only have yourself to blame. When people see two old ladies together, all they see is two old ladies. When you first began calling on us at Rose Cottage fifteen years ago, Teresa was ninety and I was seventy-six. I doubt a fifteen-year-old boy could tell the difference. Nor could most people. And Teresa was always remarkably robust and well-preserved."

When I had regained my composure, I asked her to continue.

"There is very little left to say. I helped my mother kill Jacob Morgan and bury him. And we didn't cut him up into little pieces. That part is pure fiction invented by scurrilous gossip-mongers. My foster-parents died within a short time of one another, around the turn of the century, and Teresa wired me the money to come and live with her in New York. I had never married, so I had no ties to break. I think that experience with Jacob Morgan, brief and inconclusive as it was, must have given me a lifelong aversion to marital relations. Anyway, it was in New York where Teresa told me she was really my mother. She couldn't tell Sam, of course, so I remained there as her companion, and we always lived more as friends than as mother and daughter." She smiled. "When we came back to England, we chose to live as two spinsters, the kind of relationship nobody really questions in a village because it would be in bad taste to do so."

"How did the police find you after so long?"

"We never hid our identities. Nor did we hide our whereabouts. We bought Rose Cottage through a local solicitor before we returned from America, so it was listed as our address on all the official papers we filled in." She shrugged. "The police soon recognized that Teresa was far too frail to question, let alone put on trial, so they let the matter drop. And to be quite honest, they didn't really have enough evidence, you know. You didn't know it—and Teresa would never have told you—but she already knew she was dying before the police came. Just as I know I am dying now."

"And did she really die without telling you who your father was?"

Miss Eunice nodded. "I wasn't lying about that. But I always had my suspicions." Her eyes sparkled for a moment, the way a fizzy drink does when you pour it. "You know, Teresa was always unreasonably jealous of that Tryphena Sparks, and Mr. Hardy did have an eye for the young girls."

Forty years have passed since Miss Eunice's death, and I have lived in many towns and villages in many countries of the world. Though I have often thought of the tale she told me, I have never been moved to commit it to paper until today.

Two weeks ago, I moved back to Lyndgarth, and, as I was unpacking, I came across that first edition of *Far from the Madding Crowd.* 1874: the year Hardy married Emma Gifford. As I puzzled again over the inscription, words suddenly began to form themselves effortlessly in front of my eyes, and all I had to do was copy them down.

Now that I have finished, I suddenly feel very tired. It is a hot day, and the heat haze has muted the greens, grays, and browns of the steep hillsides. Looking out of my window, I can see the tourists lounging on the village green. The young men are stripped to the waist, some bearing tattoos of butterflies and angels across their shoulder blades; the girls sit with them, in shorts and T-shirts, laughing, eating sandwiches, drinking from pop or beer bottles.

One young girl notices me watching and waves cheekily, probably thinking I'm an old pervert, and as I wave back I think of another writer—a far, far greater writer than I could ever be—sitting at his window seat, writing. He looks out of the window and sees the beautiful young girl passing through the woods at the bottom of the garden. He waves. She waves back. And she lingers, picking wild flowers, as he puts aside his novel and walks out into the warm summer air to meet her.

A Yorkshire native who now resides in Toronto, Peter Robinson constructs a touching mystery in this story that encompasses an entire lifetime. Robinson is the author of the Inspector Banks series *(Gallows View, A Dedicated Man, A Necessary End, The Hanging Valley, Past Reason Hated, Wednesday's Child, Final Account,* and *Innocent Grave). Past Reason Hated* won the Crime Writers of Canada Award for best novel in 1992, and one of Robinson's short stories, "Innocence" won the CWC Award for best short story in 1991.

Sweet Fruition

David Williams

Henry Trublit was a born loser. I should know, I married him. He was Captain Henry Trublit when I first met him, serving in the regular army, in the infantry. He wasn't in one of the grand British regiments, but my parents were impressed all the same when I brought him home to suburban Ealing the first time. He looked like a soldier, an officer, even when he was in civilian clothes. He was tall, dark, and ramrod upright, with a well-trimmed, bristly mustache, a plummy accent, and a vacant expression that people mistook for thoughtful.

"You can always tell good breeding," I remember my mother saying afterwards. Good breeding was one of her things. She kept spaniels, where bad breeding usually meant ear infections. There was nothing wrong with Henry's ears.

"Comes from a long line of army officers, he told me," my father had put in, narrowing his eyes, and applying the coded inflections they both used to indicate what was socially acceptable and what wasn't.

My father was a clerk in a small, exclusive London bank. Before she married him, my mother had been a hotel receptionist in Park Lane. Both were snobs by inclination, which meant they hadn't been impressed at all by Norman Walsh, who I'd been going out with for the previous two years. Norman was a coach driver—except he owned the coach (or bus, as my parents called it), and intended to own more, in fact, a whole fleet of luxury coaches. At the time though, it was just the one coach, or bus, and that one only partly paid for. My father was never inspired by Norman or his prospects—apart from evidently not trusting him.

It was shortly after I'd split up with Norman that I met Henry. I suppose you could say I was caught on the rebound, because, to be honest, it was Norman who dropped me, not the other way around.

Henry had come for a meeting at the Chancery Lane legal firm where I worked. It was soon after his father's death, and he was seeing my boss, old Mr. Plumley, about the will. He arrived very early, and I'd had the chance to chat with him while he waited for Mr. Plumley to come back from an outside appointment. Mr. Plumley was the partner who had looked after the Trublit family business for donkey's years. He was impressed with Henry, too. "Fine young man," he said when he was giving me dictation, after Henry left. "Credit to his father, the colonel. Should do better than the old man, too. Yes, definite touch of his grandfather in Henry." I made a note to look up grandfather straight away. It turned out he'd been Major General Sir Francis Edmund Trublit, M.C., D.S.O.

That started it, especially since, as he was leaving, Henry had plucked up the courage to ask if I'd join him for the evening. He said he was booked to stay the night in a London hotel, didn't know anybody, and would I like to do a theater and supper. Not wanting to sound too available, I said it just might be possible, but only if I could arrange to cancel another engagement. I promised to leave a message at his hotel by tea time, which I did—saying I'd come, of course. Which was probably the biggest mistake of my life.

It was hard to tell from the papers how much family money the Trublits still had. Henry, and his three married sisters, were getting fifteen thousand pounds each from the will. The rest of their father's estate, total value unspecified at the time, but which included the family house in Wiltshire, was to be held in trust for their mother during her lifetime. The house was to go to Henry on her death.

I was twenty-three then, still living at home, and with marriage definitely in mind, though no prospects offering in that direction after the bust-up with Norman. If I say so myself, I was quite a looker in those days, and had never lacked for boyfriends. It was just that none of them ever had what my father considered bankable prospects.

Henry seemed more than just an eligible bachelor. He was thirty-five, single, good-looking, serious—too serious, but I didn't find that out till later—and a career army officer with good chances of promotion, or so everybody thought, with a house in the country on hold, plus a quarter of whatever else his mother left eventually. There was also the social cachet of the grandfather's knighthood. Even though it was the sort of title that died with the owner, after the engagement my mother bragged to all her friends, and most of her acquaintances, that I was marrying into the aristocracy. After that, everyone seemed to expect I'd end up as Lady Trublit. I didn't do anything to discourage the expectation either, because I knew it would reach Norman Walsh.

Henry had asked me to marry him three months after we met—after a lot of pushing on my part. I can't say that I was ever really in love with him, but he seemed a good catch, and I was getting my own back on Norman and the slut he took up when he dropped me.

There'd been no what my mother called hanky-panky during the courtship—she had always suspected Norman's intentions in that area, and she'd been right, as well. Henry was too much of a gentleman—she insisted—to impose physically on our relationship before he'd made an honest woman of me. Trouble was, he didn't impose much on the relationship in that way afterwards, either.

Henry's mother never really approved of me. At the time, I'd put that down to his being her only son—that no woman would have been good enough for him in her estimation.

One of his uppity sisters told me, years later, that her mother felt he had married me because he was shy of women of his own class, which was hardly a compliment. It was true, though, that he never seemed to have had any girlfriends in the debutante set. Anyway, at the time I figured I wasn't marrying his mother, whose line-up in the snobbery stakes made my parents look like non-starters. For the first twelve years of the marriage Henry was posted abroad most of the time, and I went with him, so we scarcely ever saw his family.

Despite the expectations of Mr. Plumley and my father, Henry's promotion prospects seem to wither with time. He did become Major Trublit at thirty-nine, but he stayed in that rank until the end of the Cold War, when the British Army started to contract in all directions. You could say Henry became a quite early military economy. He was retired at forty-eight, given a puny pension, and about twenty thousand pounds in redundancy money. But what was an ex-infantry officer of his age supposed to do next? He tried financial services, which was another name for selling insurance, but that fell through because he couldn't sell as much as a funeral expenses policy to even his closest friends, a good many of whom, whether army or civilian, had also been made redundant: there was a world recession beginning at the time.

It was by luck, not intention, that we'd never had any children, so at least we didn't have extra mouths to think about. Henry had never been what you might call keen in bed, and we kind of drifted past the time when something might have been done to find out why I'd never become pregnant—not counting Henry's simple neglect of the normal method of going about it, of course. I must admit though that kids have never interested me much. If they had, I suppose the drift wouldn't have been allowed to happen.

Henry's mother died a year after he left the army. She'd made quite a hole in the money her husband had left, so neither he nor his sisters got much out of that. The house turned out to be more of a liability than an asset because of the state it was in. The old lady had avoided spending money on its upkeep for fear of "running down the family capital," as she put it, something she'd still succeeded in doing pretty effectively in other directions. And the place wasn't an historic country mansion, either, which I'd thought it would be when I first learned about it. Built of stone, it was early Victorian, all gables and dilapidated outbuildings, with too much land—about fifteen acres all told, most of it let for grazing. We certainly couldn't afford to live in the place. Henry put it up for sale, but nobody even came to see it—not a single person in a whole year.

It was Henry who was sold the idea that we could make our fortune by turning the place into a "pick-your-own" fruit farm—growing mostly raspberries, with some strawberries and black currants thrown in. That kind of thing was all the rage at the time, and I had to admit we owned the basics needed to set up on our own. Tests showed the soil was right, and the property was close enough to several towns to attract customers. There was also a local growers' cooperative that would take any excess fruit and sell it to the London and other big city markets. The experts Henry consulted said that within two years of making the initial investment we ought to clear over five thousand a year—and that was after deducting living and working expenses.

I still wasn't so certain about it all as Henry, but I was more desperate than he was, and five thousand a year clear seemed promising enough. Remember, this was well after the time when I knew he wasn't ever going to be a general, or even a colonel, even if a major war broke out and he was recalled to the colors. I figured that if we could build the business, and spend a bit on the house, we could probably sell it all as a going concern in about four years, with enough out of the proceeds to buy a small place in Spain, where property and living was cheap, and the weather fabulous. We were renting a small flat near my parents at this point, and I was making more money as a temporary secretary than Henry was as a clerk with the Ealing Council. But I hated the work. It was all so degrading after those high expectations. The notion of breathing clean country air and being our own masters was appealing, too. What tipped the scales for me was seeing adverts for Norman Walsh Coach Tours in the papers—the national papers as well as the local ones. Norman had done well, and, according to my mother's gossip circle, he put it down not just to his own hard work, but to the way Fiona, his tarty wife, had dedicated herself to the business. Fiona Slock, as she was before she married, had been in the same year as me at school, and the only thing she'd been dedicated to was chasing boys; otherwise she'd been as bone-idle as they come. Well I'd show her what dedication meant.

What Henry's fruit farming advisers hadn't stressed enough—although he might not have been listening at the time—was the labor that would need to go into the business, and permanently, not just for the first few years. And the only full-time laborer we could afford besides Henry was me. Every penny we had was soon tied up in making the house habitable, the outhouses usable, in steel netting our boundaries against rabbits and deer, in paying for chemicals for the ground clearance, and the posts and wiring for the raspberries, and for the fruit stock, and the fertilizers, plus the equipment to handle it all. The list was never ending, and there was certainly nothing left for paid employees.

We cut corners where we could, but there weren't many. Henry bought probably the oldest working tractor in the south of England. Only he and I were allowed to use it, not that there was anyone else available in any case. Our machine had been made before tractors were fitted with roll bars. A new law had stipulated since then that only owners, not employees, could use tractors without roll bars. It was because tractors were supposed to be too easy to turn over: we were lucky if we got this one to start. You had to be an expert to get it to do tricks.

It was five years before we saw any of that promised

profit. They'd been five grueling years, too, spent in hard labor out on those fifteen acres during some baking summers and cruel winters, working often from before daybreak and to well after nightfall. Anyone who tells you that soft fruit farming is a three-summer-months doddle has never planted ten thousand raspberry canes in mid-winter, hammered in posts and wire for them, and pruned, trained, fertilized and mulched them in every subsequent year. And that isn't the half of it, nor even the quarter of it. If raspberries make heavy work, strawberries and black currants are even worse. We plowed in our half acre of black currants in the third autumn, wrote off the cost, and replanted with more raspberries.

Work didn't draw Henry and me together, either. I was too tired most of the time for anything but sleep, and we never took holidays. Henry put in even more hours on the farming than I did. I compensated for that by keeping the house, and making our meals. Henry compensated by developing a drinking habit. He insisted rum kept up his strength and his body heat, and helped him to sleep—which was probably all true, but not to the extent he allowed alcohol to take hold of him. Like everything else, I put up with that in the belief that, as with the work we did, and the stress we were both under, the end justified the means—even at the times when drinking made him violent, and there were plenty of such times: he always promised next day it wouldn't happen again.

It was at the end of our fifth fruit farming season that I told Henry after supper one night that I seriously thought the time had come for us to sell.

"Sell? Just because we're in profit at last?" he answered, apparently dumbfounded.

"In profit for the second year," I insisted. "The place is a going concern now. We always said we'd sell when that happened."

"Nonsense, we never agreed on any such thing," he said, pouring himself another rum and Coke—his regular tipple since the time he'd been loaned as a training officer to the Trinidad army. "And anyway, the price of property's still too low for us to think of selling."

"It's lower still in Spain," I countered sharply. He was lying, of course, about what we'd agreed, and I was furious with him—the kind of fury that doesn't go away, that turns into fixation. I'd never have stuck it out for all those years if the final prospect hadn't been clearly set out from the start. I think that was the first time it went through my mind that a dose of paraquat weed killer in what he was drinking would solve my problems nicely. I suppose it wasn't a very serious thought. It was because I was so angry—and paraquat happens to be the color of Coke.

We had a big argument that night. It lasted till we went to bed, and we carried it on the next night. Henry insisted he'd never said we'd sell and move to Spain, and he went on insisting we had a thriving business now that would sustain us for years to come, and allow us to save for our old age.

Old age! I was still only forty-two—but life seemed to be slipping away from me. I wasn't interested in Spain for my dotage. I wanted us to move there while we could still enjoy sunshine all the year round, and live pretty well on our capital gains and Henry's indexed pension. He was immovable though—or nearly. In the end he agreed at least to consider selling in a year's time, provided the profits kept up. Since two could play at that game, I threatened to leave him then and there unless he took on someone to cope with my part of the strenuous work.

We'd been employing a few casual workers during the height of the previous two summers—to weigh out fruit that customers picked themselves, and also to do the picking of produce we sent to market. These helpers were all women. I said I'd put in more time myself on those jobs if we could employ a man full-time. It wasn't a fair swap, and I knew it. One agricultural laborer would cost more than all the seasonal part-timers we'd been using put together, but I still made it an ultimatum—and Henry had to agree to it.

The man we hired was Peter Adler, who we already knew by sight. He was thirty-four, and had been a farm worker all his life. He wasn't married, and had recently come back to live with his widowed, ailing mother in a rented cottage on the outskirts of the village, on the same side as us. It suited us to have him so close. He leaped at the job, because getting to his present work meant cycling eight miles every day. Later the reasons for his staying became centered on me.

Peter was a strapping, blond young man, taller than Henry, strong as an ox, and with arm muscles like steel hawsers. Even so he was a gentle giant. I'll always remember the first time he held me—when he had to lift me down from the tractor. My jeans had got snagged in the seat cover. It had been like floating on air, his grasp around my waist so easy and confident—and so manly. He was quite well-educated, too, with an immense knowledge and wisdom about country things.

The next winter was heavenly—not as heavenly as winter in Andalusia might have been, but for the first time in five years I was treated like a farmer's wife, not his workhorse. Of course, this was mostly because, at last, there was a real man about the place, not just an introverted, semi-drunkard, given to violent outbursts.

Peter and I got on well from the start. He was nearer my age than Henry was. All right, to be exact, he was eight years younger than me, but attitude counts for more than years, I always think, and in those terms he made me feel younger even than he was. He was kind and courteous to me, too, and always around when I really needed his help. They say nearness breeds sexual awareness, and that's what happened in our case. Within six months we were secret lovers. All of a sudden I was reborn as a woman, and it wasn't too late for this to happen—Peter proved that.

Our sixth year of fruit farming was far and away our most profitable, too. At the end of it, I was torn between making Henry honor his promise to sell and move to Spain, and the certainty that this would mean leaving Peter. That was until Henry remarked one night, without any prompting, what fools we'd have been if we'd done what I wanted the year before and sold the place. "It's a little gold mine," he said. "Will be for the rest of our days. Taking on Tarzan was a great investment, too, not a drain on profit." Tarzan was his private name for Peter. "Don't you ever suggest selling again," he went on in a threatening tone. "We're here to stay."

It was his arrogance that upset me most, more even than his ignoring the promise at least to discuss things again. It was only possible to bear because I now had a reason for staying myself, even though Henry didn't know that. Really, I wanted to eat my cake and have it, too—Peter to love, and a new life in a warm country. My problem, of course, was that Henry owned everything. If I left him, divorced him, all I'd get was half his pension and an even smaller share of the farm income—a very small share if the divorce judge knew I was leaving Henry for another man. I got advice on it all from a lawyer in Salisbury, and that's what he said.

And Peter had nothing but his wages.

"Oh, darling, I do so want to live with you. To marry you. If only Henry wasn't in the way," I whispered to him impulsively one evening, when we were in bed together. It was in late November, and Henry was at a growers' cooperative dinner twenty miles away. I remember the occasion vividly because of what came next.

Peter didn't answer straight away, but I'll never forget what he said eventually, quite slowly: "Had an old dog called Henry once. He was in the way as well. Savage sometimes, too. So I put him down. I could do the same with your Henry, that's if you wanted."

My body went cold all over, then warm, fantastically warm again. "You do mean . . . do away with him?"

"Sure. Make it look like an accident. Lot of accidents happen on farms. It's expected. Take that old tractor of yours."

He did away with Henry just after Christmas, when the weather had been wet.

Looking back on it now, it was so simple. It was the time of year when some of the raspberry posts and wiring always needed mending or renewing. Henry regularly carried on with this alone after supper when Peter had gone home. We'd had floodlights put in two years before, so there was no problem with it being dark. Usually Henry had drunk too much by that time to get a lot done, but it made him feel indispensable, or self-fulfilled, or something.

One Friday, Peter left early in the afternoon to see a dentist in the town. But he came back again, quite late, and joined Henry outside, saying he felt he should make up the time lost. Henry was even more fuddled than usual because, as arranged, I'd laced his drinks at supper. He was rewiring the last line of raspberry canes just below the steep, solid escarpment that ran along our northern boundary, and he had the tractor and trailer with him. After a bit, Peter asked him to move the tractor along to where they needed extra posts from the trailer. Henry, a stickler for observing regulations since army days, never let Peter operate the tractor.

As soon as Henry started the tractor engine, Peter unhitched the trailer behind his back, and leaped up behind him. Before Henry knew what was happening, Peter had put his hand over Henry's on the throttle lever, opened the throttle wide, and swung the steering wheel hard left, so that the tractor shot up the steepest part of the escarpment at a crazy angle. Peter leaped off a split second before the huge machine turned itself over and crashed down the bank with Henry under it, killing him outright.

When he'd made sure Henry was dead, Peter went home across the fields, the way he had come. No one had seen him. His now nearly bedridden mother later swore he'd been home all evening. He'd put a pill in her tea on his return from town, so, in truth, she'd been asleep in front of the television since then.

I didn't see Peter kill Henry, but I didn't regret what he did. I believed Henry deserved what happened to him. It was I who had to "find" Henry's body much later when, as I told the ambulance crew, he hadn't come in. I didn't mind that either. Of course, I'd pretended to be hysterical when the ambulance arrived. I'd always been good at theatricals.

The coroner's court returned a verdict of accidental death. The coroner himself added a rider about the tractor being out of date, and Henry taking charge of it while under the influence of alcohol. "A recipe for disaster, I fear," he said. He was right, too.

The police hadn't suspected foul play. Their investigation of the accident scene had been quite thorough, but like the coroner and the pathologist at the hospital, they put what had happened down to Henry being drunk.

Henry's life hadn't been insured, which was a pity, but it had been too late to do anything about that once Peter said he'd kill him—not without risking suspicion later.

Peter and I decided to carry on as usual for the next season, again to avoid suspicion. I played the heartbroken but plucky widow. He was the loyal employee whose devotion to me gradually became more evident as time went on. We married at the end of the following summer. No one in the village was in the least surprised, and that included the vicar who performed the ceremony.

It turned out to be another good year for the farm. Even so, we decided—a bit reluctantly on my part—to give it one more, final year before selling. This was partly because property prices had dipped again, but were predicted to rise in the following spring, and partly because Peter's mother wasn't expected to last the winter. Prices did rise, too, and Peter's mother, who had been moved to a nursing home, died in February.

I have to say that the first careless rapture of life with Peter had worn off before this. The breathtaking, real excitement in our relationship seemed to end after Henry's death, and went altogether after the marriage. We seemed to settle into the same routine of living that I'd had with Henry—except I was working harder again. Peter had been against hiring anyone to replace himself. He said he could easily do his old work and Henry's, which would mean a huge saving. It did as well, except he didn't seem to notice how much extra effort I had to put in, too. Once again, I told myself it was all in a good cause, so I didn't grumble. It was astonishing really—and disappointing—how like the old life the new one became. Peter even took to drinking rum and Coke—not to excess, like Henry, but he was moving in that direction all right. He'd always taken a liter bottle of Coke with him out to where he was working in the warmer weather: it was the rum he added at night that was new—and, for me, uncomfortably reminiscent. And that wasn't to be the only reminder of times past.

It was mid-June when I said to Peter one evening that it was time we put the farm up for sale. He shook his head slowly. "That'd be a daft thing to do, love," he replied. "We're coining it now. What we should be thinking about is buying that extra land. Make a bigger bundle with that, we could, growing more fruit for the market."

There was a ten-acre field for sale next to our western boundary. It was true that while the "pick-your-own" business had more or less leveled-out, we could easily have sold double the amount of fruit we were then sending to the local markets. "But all we want is enough to live on in Spain, after we sell up here. Live simply, I mean," I insisted.

"Who wants a simple life in Spain, doing nothing all day?' he answered. "Not me. Not if we can make a more comfortable living right here. And for as long as we live."

I could hardly believe my ears. He hadn't actually mentioned our old age, but he'd got close. Otherwise he'd used almost the same words as Henry had—and pouring his third rum of the evening while he did it. What's more, we argued the same point for days, and he remained adamant. And this was the man who now owned half my fruit farm. We'd put everything in our joint names when we married. That had been my idea. It seemed only fair at the time. Of course, whichever of us survived, the other inherited everything anyway. We'd taken out a three-year joint life and accident insurance policy at the same time as well. It was our broker who advised that, saying it was prudent, in case one of us came to grief while we were still working the farm—that Henry and I should have done the same thing. I'm glad we accepted his advice, because it did give me some solid consolation later.

Peter's untimely, tragic death occurred during a short heat wave, late in the following spring. That had seemed to me the best time to arrange it.

When the doctor came, I explained through my tears that Peter had always stored a handy amount of concentrated, ready-mixed paraquat in an old liter bottle of Coke in the tractor shed, and that he could have picked it up, by mistake, for a new bottle, early in the morning when it was still fairly dark, and taken it out with him on the tractor. The police inspector agreed later it would have been an easy thing to do, especially after I told him that Peter had kept fresh bottles of Coke in the same shed, only they'd all been used. Peter had been tired, due to overwork, and probably not too aware of his actions: a quite high alcohol level was found in his blood, too, showing he had taken more drink than usual the previous evening. I'd arranged that as well, of course. It had been very hot mid-morning on the day, and, being extra thirsty, Peter had drunk a quarter of what was in the bottle before he realized what it was. All this came out again in the coroner's summing-up at the inquest.

At the time of his death, Peter had been in the new ten-acre field on the far side of the property, and if he'd tried to cry out, there'd been no one close enough to hear him. It was more probable, though, that the poison had instantly paralyzed his throat and vocal chords. He died within a minute. The coroner said how dangerous it was to keep poisonous substances in unlabeled containers—although he accepted Peter had put a label on the bottle that had fallen off. The police found the label later on the shed floor. I hadn't made it too evident, but it wasn't too unobtrusive either.

I hadn't been able to attend the inquest. By then I was in a nursing home, under sedation, and had to stay there for several weeks. They said the shock had been too much for me, and I'd suffered what amounted to a nervous breakdown. Everyone was so sympathetic over my double loss.

I sold the fruit farm for a good price as soon as I "recovered," and bought a pretty little Spanish house, not too far from Seville. It was a year after that when Norman Walsh got in touch again, then came out to stay for a few nights. His business had collapsed in the recession. Fiona left him shortly after—well, she would have, wouldn't she, I thought. He seemed so depressed the day before he left, I said we'd have a whale of a party to cheer him up—just the two of us. We ate and drank till the small hours. Then we made love. I hadn't planned that, but it happened. Afterwards, he told me, in detail, about his terrible life with Fiona, really let his hair down. I was just as frank with him about the awful dance Henry and Peter had led me.

"Till you got rid of them, my clever puss?" he said. He'd always called me that in the old days. "So tell me, how did you do it?" he pressed.

And I told him—the truth, also in detail. Well, it was that kind of night. He was my oldest, trusted friend—oldest lover. We were both high as kites, and I was pleased and cocky about having someone to whom I could tell my story. I'd pretty well decided by then to ask Norman back for a longer stay, probably a permanent one.

A week after Norman left, two British policemen arrived on my doorstep. A month later I was extradited back to Britain, charged with conspiracy to murder my first husband, and with the actual murder of the second one. Norman had put a miniature tape recorder under the pillow. He hadn't been drunk at all, and he'd been paid by Henry's three nasty old sisters to trap me. I was convicted on both charges. Afterwards, the sisters sued me for everything I got for the fruit farm—and they won.

When Norman had been penniless, he'd gone to the sisters, saying he'd never been happy about either of my husbands' deaths, and believed he could make me admit I'd killed them both. If he succeeded, and I was jailed in consequence, he told them they could sue me, and he'd settle for half of whatever they got. It was payment by results, and they had nothing to lose, except his travel expenses.

Would you believe, Norman came to see me after the trial—to make a kind of apology. I asked him why he'd shopped me when, if he'd played his cards right, he could have married me. Cool as could be, he said even if that happened, as my husband the most he'd have been entitled to by law was half my property, and he'd got that anyway, without any hassle—or any of the risks my other husbands had run. What a nerve. *And* he went back to Fiona.

My parents were dead right to say I shouldn't trust Norman.

David Williams illustrates the dangers of marriage, greed, and fruit farming in this short story. Williams lives in Surrey and is the author of 21 mysteries featuring either banker Mark Treasure or Welsh sleuth Merlin Parry. His latest is entitled *Dead in the Market.*

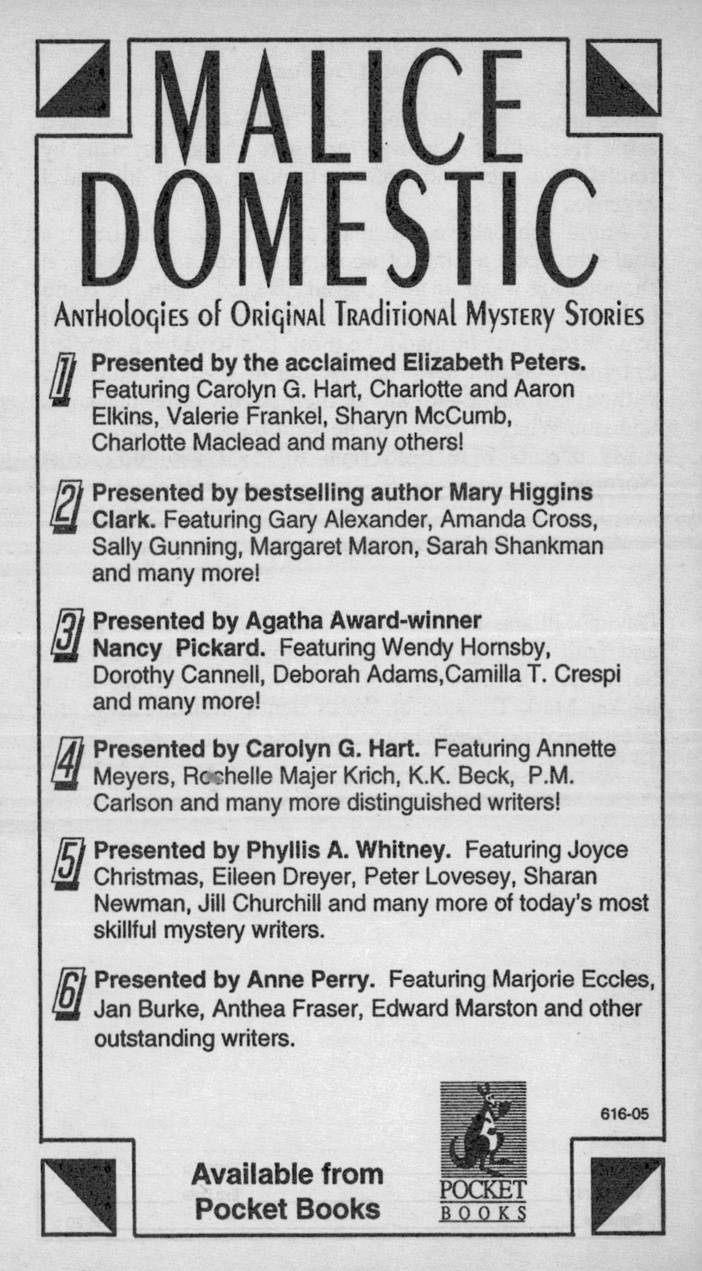
MALICE DOMESTIC
Anthologies of Original Traditional Mystery Stories
1 Presented by the acclaimed Elizabeth Peters. Featuring Carolyn G. Hart, Charlotte and Aaron Elkins, Valerie Frankel, Sharyn McCumb, Charlotte Maclead and many others!
2 Presented by bestselling author Mary Higgins Clark. Featuring Gary Alexander, Amanda Cross, Sally Gunning, Margaret Maron, Sarah Shankman and many more!
3 Presented by Agatha Award-winner Nancy Pickard. Featuring Wendy Hornsby, Dorothy Cannell, Deborah Adams,Camilla T. Crespi and many more!
4 Presented by Carolyn G. Hart. Featuring Annette Meyers, Rochelle Majer Krich, K.K. Beck, P.M. Carlson and many more distinguished writers!
5 Presented by Phyllis A. Whitney. Featuring Joyce Christmas, Eileen Dreyer, Peter Lovesey, Sharan Newman, Jill Churchill and many more of today's most skillful mystery writers.
6 Presented by Anne Perry. Featuring Marjorie Eccles, Jan Burke, Anthea Fraser, Edward Marston and other outstanding writers.
616-05
Available from Pocket Books
POCKET BOOKS